S.J. MARTIN

The Oathbreaker

First published by Moonstorm Books 2024

Copyright © 2024 by S.J. Martin

All rights reserved. No part of this publication may be reproduced, stored or transmitted in any form or by any means, electronic, mechanical, photocopying, recording, scanning, or otherwise without written permission from the publisher. It is illegal to copy this book, post it to a website, or distribute it by any other means without permission.

This novel is entirely a work of fiction. The names, characters and incidents portrayed in it are the work of the author's imagination. Any resemblance to actual persons, living or dead, events or localities is entirely coincidental.

S.J. Martin asserts the moral right to be identified as the author of this work.

First edition

This book was professionally typeset on Reedsy. Find out more at reedsy.com

Contents

Chapter One	1
Chapter Two	9
Chapter Three	21
Chapter Four	29
Chapter Five	42
Chapter Six	54
Chapter Seven	68
Chapter Eight	78
Chapter Nine	88
Chapter Ten	99
Chapter Eleven	109
Chapter Twelve	121
Chapter Thirteen	131
Chapter Fourteen	143
Chapter Fifteen	153
Chapter Sixteen	163
Chapter Seventeen	173
Chapter Eighteen	183
Chapter Nineteen	191
Chapter Twenty	203
Chapter Twenty-One	210
Chapter Twenty-Two	219
Chapter Twenty-Three	229
Chapter Twenty-Four	246

Chapter Twenty-Five	258
Chapter Twenty-six	273
Chapter Twenty-Seven	286
Chapter Twenty-Eight	292
Chapter Twenty-Nine	304
Author Note	309
List of Characters	312
Glossary	314
Maps	317
Also by S.J. Martin	320
About the author	321

Chapter One

June 1101 –West of Rouen

The sun was beginning to set behind them in a blaze of colour, as Conn Fitz Malvais called a halt on a slight rise that looked over the countryside below. A river and several small streams flowed into a picturesque lake, while the top of a stone keep showed through the trees on the far side. Conn had ridden this way several times before, and he now knew exactly where they were.

'That's the small village of Brionne over there. It will only be a three-hour ride from here to Rouen tomorrow morning. We will spend the night here and camp on the far side of the River Risle. Darius, take Gracchus and ride to the village to buy some fresh supplies. Any problems, mention the Malvais name—it's well known here in Normandy.'

Darius nodded, catching a small purse of coins from Georgio who grinned as he watched his squire ride away.

'Darius is astounded by how green it is here—the number of rivers and pastures, lush grass for grazing surrounded by miles of woods. I found him climbing a tree yesterday to look at a ball of mistletoe once I'd explained it wasn't a nest,' he said, shaking his head and smiling.

'The curiosity of the young. Do you remember what we were like when we first experienced the arid plains of Spain in the heat of summer? Our men come from Constantinople, so this landscape differs from what they're used to in Greece and Anatolia. Let us set up camp and light a fire while the horses are fed and watered.'

An hour later, Darius returned with bread, cheese and three chickens dangling from a leather thong.

'Well done! Set up two spits, and we'll quarter and roast them,' ordered Georgio.

'Even better, Gracchus persuaded the steward to part with two sacks of wine. You were right, Sire—the Malvais name worked,' added Darius.

Conn smiled. 'My father, Morvan, was based in Caen for several years. He, and the Horse Warriors he established for King William, rode all of these lands, and this is the main road to Rouen so he'd be well known here.'

Georgio watched the squire's face as he took in every word about the Breton Horse Warriors. Unfortunately, they had only spent nine days at home in Morlaix. Still, Darius had been overwhelmed by their home in Brittany, the castle on the cliffs at Morlaix and meeting Morvan de Malvais. But, when he watched Luc De Malvais on horseback, it had taken his breath away, as although he had watched Conn and Georgio, he had never seen warriors like Conn's father and uncle. Georgio knew this was what Darius aspired to be—he spent hours training with the men. Then there were the horses at Morlaix, where they bred and trained the enormous Destriers; Darius had spent hours at the stables and paddocks, watching the beautiful animals that towered over him.

CHAPTER ONE

Conn walked alone to the lake shore while the chickens turned and sizzled on the quickly constructed spits over the fire. The mention of his father had brought back the bittersweet week spent at his home in Morlaix. It was sweet because his stepmother and Aunt Merewyn had fussed over him and Georgio as if they were fifteen years old again.

It had been sixteen months since his last visit home, but it felt much longer because of the traumatic events of the last year. It was a bittersweet visit because his family asked him to recall those tragic events and tell them what happened at the villa in Aggio. In the end, he found he could not tell them, and he shook his head and indicated that Georgio should recount their pursuit of the Sheikh and the brutal ending. As Georgio described the murder of the people they loved, Conn had felt his father's eyes on his face.

He wasn't surprised when Morvan suggested they go for a ride the next morning. It was a beautiful, early Breton summer morning, with the dew still on the grass, but with a brisk breeze coming off the Atlantic as they rode along the coast. They had stopped on the cliffs for a while and watched, in silence, the waves crashing onto the rocks below.

Finally, Morvan began speaking of his close friendship with Finian Ui Neill, the famous Irish warrior who was murdered in front of Conn by Sheikh Ishmael's men. Before he knew it, Conn realised that tears were streaming down his face, and he was telling his father what happened. He recounted how Finian had died and how he had been powerless and unable to stop it. He had spoken of his love for Marietta, how he had finally decided that he wanted her to be his wife, and the guilt he felt almost every day that he could not save her—that she had died in front of him. Morvan had moved his horse closer and, without saying a word, had gripped his son's forearm in understanding. As they turned and rode back, Conn felt lighter for telling his father of his feelings of loss and guilt, for he rarely, if ever, spoke of them.

Conn sat on a large boulder on the lake shore and stared out across the still waters. There was hardly a breeze in this sheltered valley, and the soft dusk light of the sunset reflected on the water. It was beautiful and peaceful. However, he was pleased they were riding to war and glad it would bring different challenges. Accepting this mission would pay off his debt to Piers De Chatillon once and for all. He didn't doubt that it would be perilous at times, no doubt entailing secrecy, stealth and murder. All he knew so far was that he was to go to England and inveigle himself into the English court to spy on King Henry and his advisors. King Henry—a man with whom he had ridden, hunted and drank, and called a comrade not long ago. Now, he would infiltrate his inner circle again, no doubt placing himself and Georgio in danger if he wasn't careful.

His last conversation with his father at Morlaix now came to him as he sat watching the water lapping near his feet and considering what lay ahead.

"You will be fighting for the enemy, probably against knights on Duke Robert's side whom you have called friends. I have been in your position, for I became a traitor to King William, who was my sworn liege lord, when I fell in love with your mother. I went to fight for Duke Robert, and it was one of the most difficult decisions of my life, betraying everything I believed in and becoming estranged from my family. Fortunately, we won and were then pardoned by the King, but by a cat's whisker—it could have gone the other way.

CHAPTER ONE

It was Piers De Chatillon who persuaded me to betray everything and fight for Robert Curthose. Today, I call Chatillon a dear friend, but he often has his own agenda, so take care and be awake to every move he makes. If in doubt, flee, for there is always a sanctuary for you and Georgio here at Morlaix."

Conn knew in his heart that this assignment was what he wanted. He not only had a debt to pay, but he had signed up with no reservations or regrets to be Piers De Chatillon's protégé, with all the risk and danger that entailed.

He'd sat there for longer than he realised. When he raised his eyes from the lapping water, the sun had gone, and as he stood and turned, he could see the light from the two campfires and hear the laughter of his men. Six of his Horse Warriors and Darius had decided to come with him to Europe. He was pleased and flattered, and he had happily arranged and paid for their release from the Emperor's service. More surprising was that one of them was Gracchus, his serjeant, a man who had resented the younger Breton Horse Warrior at first. They had fought, and Gracchus reluctantly accepted and recognised Conn as the better fighter. Now, after riding and fighting at his side in Byzantium, he was ready to follow Conn Fitz Malvais anywhere.

As he walked through the trees and into the camp, the tantalising smell of roasting chicken assailed his nostrils, and he realised how hungry he was. He was just in time to hear their squire, Darius, asking Georgio who this man in Rouen was who had the authority to order them back to Europe. Conn gratefully accepted a cup of wine from Gracchus and leaned against a tree to hear Georgio's reply. He noticed the interest on his men's faces and smiled; they always liked to know who was paying their wages and whether he deserved their respect.

'Piers De Chatillon is a wealthy French lord with a large estate outside of Paris and houses all over Europe. More importantly, he's the Senior Papal Envoy of the Holy See and was an advisor to several previous popes. He's also a diplomat for the Pope and wields power in several European courts,' explained Georgio as Conn gave a shout of laughter before stepping forward into the light.

'I hardly recognise the man you describe, Georgio—you make him sound so tame! They'll imagine an elderly statesman. Are you afraid of frightening them with the truth?' he asked, crouching down with them near the fire and elaborating.

'Piers De Chatillon is one of the most dangerous men in Europe, who often works in the shadows. Yes, he's an arch-manipulator of kings and princes and directs the Pope in foreign affairs, but he is also probably one of the most lethal swordsmen I've ever seen. He's in a similar league to my uncle, Luc De Malvais, but has a different style, more craft than ferocity—he taught me the tricks that allowed me to disarm you easily back in Constantinople, Gracchus. He has immense charm, but don't be taken in by that, for he has no empathy or sympathy for anyone outside of his immediate family and friends. He is a cold-blooded killer. The assassin who comes in the night, who you never see or hear, and who never regrets a death; he only regrets the ones he should have killed. This may sound odd, but at the same time, I would trust him with my life and the lives of all here, for he does value true friendship and loyalty. However, he's never sentimental about either.'

CHAPTER ONE

He finished and, smiling at the expression on their faces, took a long draught of wine.

'He is a priest then; does this career as an assassin not sit at odds with his values and vows of Christianity?' Darius asked, perplexed.

This time, both Conn and Georgio laughed.

'You obviously have no knowledge of the snake pit at the heart of the Holy See. Christian values are trampled beneath the feet of those scrabbling for position and power in the Lateran Palace. No, Chatillon is not a priest; he's one of the few lay people with the ear of the Pope and influences the political policy of the Holy See. He never interferes or shows interest in the dogma or policy of the Church. He is also married to one of the most beautiful young women in Genoa, and they have two sons, which does not stop him from having at least a dozen mistresses whom he uses as informers. He has the most extensive information network in Europe. Now let us eat the chickens,' said Conn, wielding his dagger with a grin. Georgio, however, noticed the worried frown on his squire's face.

'Do you regret asking now, Darius?' he whispered.

The young Greek shook his head. 'No, Conn is right to give us the bare truth, for then we know what we are dealing with. Chatillon sounds a man to be wary of, but one who would be there in your hour of need.'

Georgio nodded and again thought how lucky he was to find this young man on the streets of Constantinople. He had a wise head on his shoulders, and being quick and resourceful, he would no doubt adapt to the danger and intrigue of the courts of Europe as he had been forced to do in Nicomedia. He just hoped that he could learn to adapt in the same way.

He tended to take people at face value at first, while people like Chatillon and Conn could see their different sides.

Chapter Two

June 1101 – Rouen

Normandy's capital city sat on the banks of the River Seine, and Rouen's streets were crowded as they rode towards the large, bustling inn in the heart of the town, conveniently close to the castle. Conn had sent a man ahead, so he was not surprised to see Edvard waiting for them as they rode through the archway into the busy cobbled courtyard. Chatillon had stayed there dozens of times before; his name and generous purse had influence despite the city being packed with hundreds of knights flocking to the raised banners of Duke Robert. Conn dismounted, and Edvard stepped forward, pulling him, and then Georgio, into a bear-like hug.

'It has been far too long, but you both look well, fit and tanned by the harsh sun of the East. As you can imagine, the castle and bailey are packed to the rafters, so I've found you a room here, but you and Georgio will have to share while your men can have the large room above the stables. The innkeeper owns a meadow just outside the walls, and the grooms will take your horses there.'

'Will they be safe there?' asked Darius, in a concerned voice.

He was now the proud owner of a young Morlaix horse, given to him by Conn, and he was reluctant to leave it in a field, knowing its value.

Edvard looked this young squire up and down and laughed.

'You are not in Constantinople now; you are in Duke Robert's well-guarded demesne lands. I assure you the horses will be safe. I see you still have that black beast you broke and tamed against your father's advice, Conn. Diablo, isn't it?'

Conn nodded. 'Yes, he survived the arrows of the Seljuk bowmen in Anatolia and has, despite everyone's doubt, become the war horse I envisaged.'

On cue, Diablo gave a shrill scream and snapped his teeth inches from the groom's face as he tried to remove the saddle. They laughed while Darius ran to help the boy.

'Come, let us find your room, and I'll bring you up to date. Chatillon is pleased and highly relieved you are here, as things appear to be moving on apace, and none of us has stopped since dawn.'

A bowing innkeeper conducted them to a large chamber overlooking the courtyard. There were signs of a recent hurried exit by the previous occupants, and Georgio smiled as he laid his saddlebags down on one of the beds, knowing that someone would have been evicted.

'We'll need a truckle bed or palliasse for our squire in here as well,' ordered Georgio.

The obsequious innkeeper nodded and bowed his way out while promising to send up wine and food. Edvard sank gratefully into one of the chairs near the window, and Darius slid in to sit quietly in the corner.

'So, Edvard, do we meet with Chatillon, or have you orders for us?' asked Conn, taking the other chair and crossing one dusty booted leg over the other.

'Hundreds of knights have answered Duke Robert's summons, and he has a fleet of several hundred ships almost ready to sail. They're up the coast at Le Treport. There's no doubt that Robert will sail for England this time and take back the crown that is rightfully his. Chatillon spends nearly all his time in the court at Robert's side or sitting in the Council of War, especially since Ranulf Flambard arrived in Rouen.'

'Flambard! What is he doing here?' exclaimed Conn, his face reflecting his shock at this turn of events.

'Ranulf Flambard was imprisoned in the Tower of London as soon as Henry was crowned king. As you know, Flambard was in charge of the Treasury for King William Rufus, responsible for extorting every last penny from rich and poor alike. He was accused by various senior nobles and the Archbishop of Canterbury of misappropriation of funds, and rumour had it that he was to be executed. However, with help, he escaped and took ship for Normandy, throwing himself on the Duke's mercy. He was imprisoned for several months, but Chatillon saw he could be useful, as he had immense knowledge of the finances of England and the Anglo-Norman lords. He also knows the defensive measures that Henry will use, as *he* put them in place. So now he sits in the same room with the Council.'

Conn still shook his head in disbelief at this.

'The man's a dangerous snake,' he protested.

'Yes. Chatillon knows that, but this snake knows the darkest secrets of these noble families—information that Piers can use for bribes or threats if needed.

'Now I must go. Have some food and present yourselves at court for the afternoon audience. Chatillon will be waiting for you.'

With that, he clasped arms with them and was gone.

'So it begins, the intrigue and the plotting, the murder and mayhem,' said Georgio, rubbing his hands in anticipation as Conn rolled his eyes at the melodrama.

'Who was that?' asked Darius, who had stayed quiet, slightly in awe of the big enigmatic man.

Conn smiled. He had forgotten that this was a whole new world to the young Greek warrior, while the people he would meet had always been in their lives.

'The Irish warrior, Finian Ui Neill, once told me that Edvard was a monk originally, repeatedly defrocked for drunkenness and debauchery. Chatillon found him in trouble in the back streets of Paris when they were both in their early twenties. He rescued him, and Edvard has served Chatillon ever since. He is Chatillon's right-hand man—over here, we call that a vavasseur. He takes care of everything and, like his master, he kills as easily as breathing. He was part of the group that came to rescue us as children from the warrior monks, and he came running down into that crypt like a huge avenging angel, roaring with rage and whirling his staff around his head as he took two or three of them out. It's a sight I'll never forget!' exclaimed Conn.

Georgio nodded. 'He terrified me then, not knowing who he was, and he still does at times.'

A few hours later, dressed in their best tunics, and with Darius following them, they presented themselves at the castle door. They were expected, and the steward led them into the impressive Great Hall, full of people—nobles, knights and some of their retinues, gathered around in knots and groups, waiting for an audience with the Duke. There was a loud buzz of conversation, shouts and laughter, and Darius looked around with interest. It may not have had the glittering gold and silver of the Emperor's palace in Constantinople, but it was an impressive chamber, hung with colourful tapestries, and with the walls above lined with flags and banners. The chairs on the dais were empty, so Conn scanned the hall for Edvard while various young knights and cadet sons came to clasp arms with him in greeting. Most of them knew him from his sojourn in the French court, or his months in England the previous summer.

At that moment, the noise quietened as a tall, darkly handsome man descended the stone staircase into the hall. The crowd parted before him, many bowing their heads in respect as he approached Conn and Georgio. Darius immediately realised who this was as he wore a rich, deep purple tunic emblazoned with the gold papal insignia. Darius was surprised as he finally reached them, for he looked much younger than he'd expected from their description. His stare met Chatillon's gaze for a few seconds, and then he dropped his eyes, for the Papal Envoy had piercing, almost black eyes that swept over him but seemed to take in everything at a glance. He certainly had a presence; the younger nobles stepped back to give him more space, some watching him with a wary eye.

Conn and Georgio swept into low bows, but Chatillon smiled, and the dark, intelligent, saturnine face changed when he smiled. It was full of pleasure as he grasped arms with both of them.

'Well met! I'd almost given up on you, but you are now here, and despite fighting in one of the most dangerous places in the world, you survived and returned. But only just, I believe.

You can recount your exploits later over good food and wine. Having spent time in Constantinople and the East, I know Robert will be keen to hear them.'

Suddenly, there was a stir as the Duke and Duchess descended the staircase into the crowded hall. Cheers broke out, and they both smiled and nodded their thanks as they moved to take their seats. Darius felt a hand on his arm, and Edvard was there waving him forward to follow him to a position near the pillar at the front. From here, they could view proceedings and hear what was said but remain out of direct vision.

Chatillon led Conn and Georgio to the front.

'Sire, I ask your leave to present two newly arrived knights to the court; Horse Warriors who successfully fought with El Cid in the Reconquista wars. They have recently returned from the employment of the Emperor Alexios in Byzantium, where they fought against the Seljuk Turks.'

A buzz of surprise and then acclamation at such deeds swept around the hall as Chatillon introduced Sir Georgio di Milan and Sir Conn Fitz Malvais. An even louder hum of conversation broke out at that last name, and Duke Robert sat forward in his seat, waving Conn closer.

'Your father must be Luc De Malvais—you are like him. I know him well, but I call your uncle, Morvan de Malvais, a dear friend; we fought beside each other for many years. How is he?'

'We were with them for a short time at Morlaix last week, Sire, and he sends his best wishes and prayers for the success of your venture.'

'There is room at my side with his Horse Warriors if he wishes to join us, although I hear he's still riding to protect the borders with Maine and Anjou. However, I hope you have come to join us; such warriors as you two will inspire my younger knights.'

Before Conn could answer, another voice broke in on them.

'It's almost as if you were looking in a mirror with those eyes, Sire. Fitz Malvais is, of course, the child that the warrior monks stole on the orders of Cardinal Dauferio,' said Robert de Belleme, limping out from the shadows.

The silence in the hall was deafening as the Duchess sent a questioning look at her husband. Robert frowned at Belleme, who was renowned for his biting but often telling remarks. The buzz of conversation started again as many of the older nobles remembered the story of the stolen children, and it was known that one of them was the bastard son of Luc De Malvais. Now, he was standing here in the hall, and they were curious. It certainly held Flambard's attention, and that of Agnes de Ribemont, Duke Robert's long-term mistress who, despite being cold-shouldered by him, was still in the court in Rouen. She glanced at Flambard's face, wondering what he knew, for he was a master at holding and unearthing secrets.

Piers De Chatillon did not move a muscle in his face at the jibe, or show that he had even heard it—he would not give Belleme that satisfaction as he removed a piece of imaginary fluff from the sleeve of his velvet tunic. But, he did send a significant rueful glance to Edvard that spoke volumes. Edvard had wanted to punish Robert de Belleme several times and Piers had always prevented him from doing so; now, he regretted that decision. As the silence lengthened, Conn took it upon himself to reply.

'Sire, that is ancient history. We were lucky that my family searched for and found us with Lord Chatillon's help. We are now Horse Warriors, knights in our own right, and having recently experienced the harsh climate of Anatolia, we stand back in admiration of what you achieved by taking the great cities of Antioch and Jerusalem.'

Applause and cheers broke out at this speech, and Chatillon quietly smiled at the quick-thinking diplomacy of Conn to deflect attention from what had been said. Belleme was indeed right, for Conn had the bright blue eyes of his mother, Constance of Normandy, Duke Robert's sister. Somehow, Belleme had discovered the truth of Conn's birth, or perhaps he only had suspicions. The Duke bowed his head and smiled in recognition of the compliment, and Chatillon quickly ushered the Horse Warriors back into the crowd as others now clamoured for the Duke's attention.

Edvard led them to a small chamber where Flambard had originally been held as a prisoner. It was well-furnished, and Edvard knew no one would disturb them there. He was the first to speak as the door closed behind him.

'You should have let me silence him, Piers. Belleme is stirring the pot, hoping something nasty will rise to the surface.'

'He is far too wealthy and important for us to remove; Robert needs Belleme for this invasion. The best thing to do is not to rise to his taunts as if there is no substance to them. I presume you can do that, Conn?' asked Chatillon.

'Of course. But I saw the Duke's face as he looked at me, scanning my features carefully as he heard Belleme's comments. He is good at planting seeds of doubt, Chatillon.'

'Everyone heard them, for, as usual, he waited for a complete pause in the conversation to drip his poison into the gap,' growled Edvard.

CHAPTER TWO

'I don't understand. Why is this so dangerous?' asked Darius, perched on a chest against the wall.

Chatillon looked at him in surprise and then gave him a stare that froze his blood, and Darius began to mumble an apology.

Conn, however, laughed at his discomfort. 'Meet Darius, our very resourceful squire, who in his short time with us has rescued Georgio and me from dire situations. He even saved my life in Constantinople. Because of his Spartan blood, he seems to think he can voice his questions and opinions even in exalted company.'

Darius flushed to the roots of his hair while Chatillon regarded the young man and then turned back to Conn.

'Do you trust him?' he asked.

Conn glanced at Georgio, who nodded. 'Yes, Sire, I believe we do.'

Darius now found himself being scrutinised more closely by those piercing dark eyes, and he shifted uncomfortably, drawing his knees up and wrapping his arms around them to make himself as inconspicuous as possible.

'I've always found that it helps to have one very discrete loyal servant who knows where the bodies are buried. Not necessarily all of them, you understand, for some bodies must remain a secret for eternity. I suggest that you tell him the truth about your paternity so he can deflect the curious.'

Darius found it somewhat unnerving to have them talk about him as if he were not there, but it gave him a warm feeling to know he was trusted.

'Luc De Malvais is not my father—I am lucky to resemble him so closely. My father, Morvan de Malvais, fell in love with my mother, Constance of Normandy, Duke Robert's and King

Henry's sister. This information must never be mentioned again, for it makes me the grandson of King William I and a possible threat to the throne if they have no offspring,' explained Conn.

Darius felt his mouth fall open as he listened, and he was overwhelmed that Malvais would share this with him.

'So you're truly royalty!' he exclaimed.

Conn smiled ruefully. 'Yes, but born on the wrong side of the blanket.'

Darius swung his legs to the ground. 'Yes, but that means nothing if you truly want to seize power; our Greek history is full of such warriors and kings. Your grandfather, King William, was known as William the Bastard—the monks taught us that.'

'That is enough, young man. I'm dismissing you now because I intend to speak of things it's better you do not know,' replied Chatillon.

Darius bowed deeply and left to wait outside and lean against the wall. His head spun with what he had just heard as he realised that Georgio was right—they were indeed wrapped up in intrigue and plotting, which could be highly dangerous.

Inside the room, Chatillon waved them to sit.

'Robert's fleet will sail next month, and we know Henry is preparing to repulse the invasion. I need you both in England by next week. You are sell-swords and are offering your services to the highest bidder, who happens to be King Henry, the friend you hunted with whilst in France and England. I give you free rein to describe what you've seen here. You can even exaggerate the numbers as Henry already has several informers planted here. Edvard removed two of them yesterday, and their bodies are now floating back to

England. I believe Robert will win this war. Most powerful Anglo-Norman nobility are in his camp, but your first task will be to kill the Duke of Chester, who may become a key player in England. I'll explain why later.'

In the corridor, Darius was aware of footsteps approaching, echoing on the stone flagstones, so he positioned himself in front of the door, standing to attention. A richly dressed man came into view, a handsome man with an air of authority and intelligence who stopped and regarded the squire with suspicious eyes.

'Are you waiting for me?' he asked.

'No, Sire. My masters are within, and I'm waiting for them to finish,' he replied, bowing.

'They are in my room?' he asked in surprise.

'I think that my Lord Chatillon was under the impression the room was no longer in use,' replied Darius diplomatically, noticing that the man's face changed at the mention of the Papal Envoy's name.

Just then, the door opened, and the four men emerged. Darius noticed that Chatillon was unperturbed at seeing Flambard standing outside, but Edvard narrowed his eyes, and assumed an expression of dislike.

'Ah Ranulf, you remember my friend Malvais, of course, but I don't think you've had the pleasure of meeting this brave young warrior, Georgio di Milan.'

Both men bowed, and Flambard, making a quick recovery, complimented them on their achievements. Excusing himself, he hurriedly moved into the room they had left whilst muttering about papers left in a chest. However, once inside, he leaned against the closed door. Whilst looking at Malvais in the corridor, he had begun to wonder how much truth there was in Robert de Belleme's comment. He determined to visit the Earl at the earliest opportunity and see if he could prise any more information out of him. Then he remembered Agnes de Ribemont. She had been Duke Robert's mistress for over twenty-five years. She would have been around Robert and his friends, the Malvais brothers, when Conn Fitz Malvais was born. She may well know something and not realise that she did, as was often the case. If the young Horse Warrior was related to Robert somehow, he intended to find out how and see if he could use it.

Chapter Three

Chatillon was not surprised when Duke Robert summoned him early that evening to the solar, for the Duke's young wife Sibylla rarely missed anything, and he had noticed her face when Belleme commented on the family resemblance. He noticed immediately that she dismissed all the servants and ladies as he entered the room and bowed to the couple.

'Can I be of service, Sire?' he asked, having been waved to a seat.

'I have now decided on where my fleet will land in England. I'm sharing this information with only a handful of trusted people, and you're the first of those, Piers.'

'I'm honoured, Sire. I'm sure you have given this much thought, having discussed tides, weather and the likely position of Henry's troops over the last few weeks with us. We did examine various locations.'

'Portsmouth! We will land at Portsmouth. The large, sheltered harbour there will contain the whole fleet,' Robert announced, with enthusiasm, as he left his seat and paced around the solar.

'A good choice, Sire, for they'll expect you to land on the east or southeast coast near Count Mortain's castle at Pevensey or Hythe.'

'Exactly, Chatillon, and it means only a day or two's march north to seize the Treasury at Winchester,' he continued in a satisfied tone.

'A very strategic move, Sire. Can I be bold enough to ask who else you will share this information with so I can keep a watchful eye on them and their servants,' he suggested, lowering his voice.

Robert laughed aloud while Sibylla watched them; she knew how much Robert valued this man's opinion.

'You trust no one, do you, Piers?'

'Experience has taught me that, Sire, as sometimes we're sorely disappointed in those we have trusted,' he murmured.

At that, Robert exchanged a meaningful glance with his wife.

'This brings me to my next problem. Belleme, the Earl of Shrewsbury, has been a loyal supporter and friend for most of my life, and for all his vicious nature and poisonous tongue, I do trust him. Am I right to do so, Piers?' he asked, sitting back beside his wife.

Chatillon sighed and decided that honesty was the best bet, although he knew it would shock the young duchess.

'Only yesterday, Edvard remarked that we should have slit Belleme's throat some time ago, for as you know, he enjoys stirring up trouble that sometimes gets out of hand and causes much bigger problems.'

Sibylla paled, but Robert laughed again. 'I agree, for at times, he is infuriating and a trouble-maker. However, he's also the wealthiest and most powerful of my supporters, and I need him, so do not let the blade flash yet, Chatillon.'

Chatillon smiled. 'I think you can trust him, Robert; I believe him to be truly loyal to you. However, if he betrays you, I'll have him removed. The same applies to Flambard. At the moment, he's detailing all of Henry's defences in England so we can circumvent them, but I'm not sure how useful he'll be after that.'

Robert, serious-faced now, nodded in agreement while Sibylla's hands were clasped so tightly her knuckles were white, as she found Piers De Chatillon's casual talk of murder quite chilling. However, it didn't stop her from asking the next question.

'What of Belleme's comment yesterday? Is this Conn Fitz Malvais, in fact, one of my husband's bastards?'

It was Chatillon's turn to laugh while shaking his head.

'I know you have heard of the famous Horse Warrior, Luc De Malvais, but I believe you have never met him. Conn is his son, and as your husband knows, Conn is the image of him, almost his double. Robert de Belleme dislikes the Malvais family and has a vendetta against them because of Luc's younger brother, Morvan, whom he hates. Belleme once tried to rape Morvan's future wife, Minette de la Ferte, at Duke Robert's camp in Scotland, before the battle at Falkirk. Robert will remember the incident because Minette stabbed Belleme with a long dagger so hard through his thigh, that he was pinned to the ground until his cries brought help. Infection set into the wound, and it took him a year to recover. The leg was permanently damaged; he's often in pain, and that is why he limps today. He dares not challenge them openly, as he fears the ferocity of the Malvais brothers, so he does as much damage as he can by dripping poison about them.'

She seemed to accept that, and he could see the relief on her face; Robert had several illegitimate children, and she, no doubt, did not want another one appearing.

The Great Hall was packed that evening. Chatillon, as usual, sat at the top table with the prominent nobles, while Conn and Georgio sat close by at a side table. The food and wine were excellent, and a group of strolling players provided the entertainment—acrobats, jugglers, musicians—and many guests were singing and dancing. One of the pretty young players sat on Georgio's lap while she sang a love song, and everyone cheered when he soundly kissed her. At the end of the performance, the players stood in a line and sang a rousing ditty they had written about Duke Robert defeating his enemies. The hall erupted in cheers while the Duke threw a purse of coins to their leader.

Soon, it settled into a quiet hum as more platters piled high with meat were carried in, and people applied themselves to their food and drink. Belleme chose this moment to comment, again ensuring his voice carried across the hall.

'My contacts and informers tell me that there are rumours of fratricide freely circling in England. They are saying that the usurper who styles himself as King Henry was actually behind the murder of your brother, William Rufus,' he announced. The conversation in the hall died, and those nearby stopped chewing as their eyes travelled to the Duke's face and back to Belleme, who sat a few seats away at the top table.

However, Robert shrugged it off.

'My brother may be a lot of things, Belleme—yes, he is a conniving, treacherous usurper of my crown—but I would call him more of an opportunist than a murderer. I cannot believe that he has it in him to murder our brother.'

'Yet, Walter Tirrel, who apparently fired the fateful arrow, fled the country, but, for some reason, was never pursued. I'm told that he now sits happily on his estate in the Norman

Vexin,' commented Flambard from the side table opposite the one Conn and Georgio were sitting at.

Chatillon wiped his mouth and waved a servant over for more wine while looking across and meeting Edvard's eyes, who was sitting at a lower table. He gave a thin smile, and Edvard nodded, knowing and understanding that look immediately, for this was another man they should have removed. Flambard seemed to think that his new position at Robert's court gave him the right to make bold statements, and Chatillon narrowed his eyes and stared at him. Looking up and seeing this, Flambard immediately dropped his eyes and became interested in what was on his plate.

The hall was still surprisingly quiet as people watched the drama unfolding.

'Young Malvais should be able to tell us, as I remember he was in the forest beside Tirrel when it happened—when your brother was murdered,' suggested Belleme in a louder voice.

Robert turned and looked at Conn in surprise.

'Is this true, Malvais?'

Conn, who was about to spear a piece of venison, put down his dagger and met the Duke's stare.

'Yes, Sire. There was a small group of us, and everything happened so quickly. A huge stag erupted from the bushes in front of us, and several people loosed arrows at the animal, including me, but the King, who was slightly in front of us, made the heart shot. At first, everyone's eyes were on the stag and the dogs as they cheered the King, so no one realised the King had been hit until he slumped forward in the saddle and slid to the ground. People leapt off their horses and ran to him. It was then that several of us realised that it was Tirrel's arrow with the distinctive diamond flights that was embedded in the

King's chest. Tirrel looked as shocked as any of us, Sire; he was as white as a shroud and kept saying it was an accident.'

'But he still fled!' exclaimed Flambard in an accusing tone, and Conn, choosing to stay silent now, just nodded.

The packed hall was silent. The death of any King was grave, but this had been a Norman king, the brother of Duke Robert, and accusations were being made.

'I heard it said that the King bled all the way to Winchester. As far as I know, a dead man does not bleed, but a witness said the blood was dripping from the cart for miles. Does that mean he was still alive and could've been saved? You went with the King's body—tell us, is that true, Malvais?' asked Belleme.

Chatillon could see Conn becoming angry; his face was slightly flushed, but he was trying to contain it. His lips were a thin white line as he glared at Belleme and stood.

'Once they realised the King was dead, there was panic, and they left him on the ground and raced for their horses, whilst ordering a charcoal burner working in the forest to pick him up. Only Chatillon cared enough to ensure that De Clare and I wrapped the body in our cloaks and placed it in the charcoal burner's cart. Yes, we stayed with him and travelled to Winchester, for as the King, that was his due, Belleme—it was the least we could do. Yes, there was blood, because Tirrel leapt forward and savagely twisted his arrow out of the King's chest before he fled, but certainly not the amount you describe. As we wrapped the body and gently placed it in the cart with another cloak under his head, there was no doubt that the King was dead—I assure you of that, Sire.' Conn turned to the Duke with his arms out, palms up in apology that his brother was treated in such a way. He then regained his seat beside

CHAPTER THREE

Georgio, who was worried as he could see the pent-up anger in Conn.

'Thank you for your service to my brother, Malvais,' said the Duke, visibly moved. But Belleme was not finished yet. He could see that he had got under the young Horse Warrior's skin and wanted to make the most of it.

'Death seems to travel at your side, Malvais. I hear that El Cid's son was killed at your side in Spain, then the great Irish warrior, Finian Ui Neill and Chatillon's young ward, Marietta Di Monsi, were killed in front of you while you stood there, sword drawn. I believe you did nothing to save them. Isn't that what you told me, Chatillon? I dread to think what would happen if we took him with us on the invasion fleet. Surely he would be a bad talisman at your side, Sire.'

Conn shot to his feet again, and his hand went to his sword hilt as he glared at Belleme, who was implying that he was a coward. He glanced at Chatillon, waiting for him to come to his defence, but instead, Chatillon took another slow draught of his wine and then nodded, for he suddenly saw an opportunity.

'It was a difficult situation, as we were outnumbered, and there were hostages with knives at their throats. Malvais could have acted, I suppose, as we were all trapped behind him in the doorway. He had the advantage, the only one with a clear run and the element of surprise. If he had attacked immediately, I suppose he could have freed them from the Sheikh's men, and we might have followed him and saved their lives.'

Conn looked at Chatillon in astonishment as pain and then anger chased across his face at the injustice of his comments.

Georgio stood too and began to bluster. 'No! That is not

how….' But Conn gripped his friend's arm and bowed to the Duke and Duchess, who looked stunned by what they had heard.

'With your permission, I will take my leave, Sire,' Conn announced in an icy voice.

Edvard and Darius watched them go as they walked through a silent hall, trestle tables full of knights and their retinues whose eyes followed their exit.

Darius looked up at Edvard, emotion working on his face. 'Why? Why did Chatillon not defend them?' he asked, not quite believing what he had seen—the damage to Conn's reputation that Chatillon could have mitigated. Edvard did not reply at first as a loud buzz of conversation broke out across the hall at what had been said and implied.

'Go after them, Darius. I will see you later,' he said, pushing the young squire towards the door.

Then he stood and stared at Chatillon, who was now deep in conversation with the Duke, while Belleme sat with a satisfied smile that Edvard would have liked to wipe off his face. He knew exactly what Chatillon was doing and why he had done it. He prayed that the Horse Warriors did not run, that although angry at what had occurred, they would stay at the inn tonight. He knew that with the knowledge Conn had about the real events surrounding the death of William Rufus, it could blow up in their faces.

Chapter Four

June 1101 – Westminster

Not long after King Henry held his first Pentecostal Court at Saint Albans, the information from his spies in Normandy arrived. Henry immediately summoned his powerful allies, the Beaumont brothers, and now they were closeted with the King, the Queen, and Archbishop Anselm.

'I am told his fleet is now ready to sail. They estimate at least a hundred and fifty ships. I am the first to admit I am no strategist when it comes to war, so I would welcome your advice, my lords,' said Henry with a worried frown.

'We must use this news to our advantage, Sire—invaders threaten England. Let us notify the people of England themselves and ask for their loyalty and support to defend their land,' suggested the Archbishop of Canterbury.

'I would mention the recent promises you made to them as well, in your Charter of Liberties, my lord husband, to reverse the excesses and crimes of William Rufus and Flambard,' added the Queen.

'A good and clever move. Let a proclamation be read out in every city, town and village. If you compose it, Sire, my brother and I will ensure it is sent to every sheriff and constable, with orders to read it aloud. You are the defender of the people and this land, Sire—remind them of that,' announced Henry Beaumont, the Earl of Warwick.

'More than that, Sire, you need to name him! They should all swear an oath, nobles and villeins alike, to defend England against the attack of Duke Robert of Normandy,' declared Robert Beaumont.

The following day, dozens of riders galloped out in the Beaumont livery to take the proclamation to every part of England, reaffirming the promises made by Henry in his Charter of Liberties and asking for the oath to be sworn.

A week later, the King had placed lookouts on every promontory on England's eastern and southeastern coast. Now, they waited, certain that Robert was coming and could land at any time. They were just not sure where.

The Archbishop of Canterbury was at the King's side daily.

'You need to put your nobles to the test now, my Lord King— you need to summon every one of them to arms. These Anglo-Norman nobles hold land in England only by your leave. Your father may have granted it, but you can certainly threaten to take it away from them if they do not show their loyalty to you.'

Later that night, the summons was sent to all the noble families, and Matilda lay wrapped in her husband's arms. It was a warm June night, and the shutters on the windows were open, allowing a slight breeze to cool them. Henry, as usual, was naked, for only in the deep cold of winter did he deign to wear a gown. Henry had taught Matilda to be bold, and although she was reluctant at first, she now revelled in their lovemaking. She knew he was awake and brooding on

CHAPTER FOUR

the day's events, so she let her hands wander lightly over his body. For months now, he had been at sword practice each day or on horseback, and she could feel the difference in his physique, the muscle in his arms and shoulders. She heard his breathing change as she swept her fingers back and forth over his stomach and then lower still to stroke between his legs. She felt his manhood responding and heard his sharp intake of breath as she grasped it and whispered, 'Make love to me, Henry, but gently. I need to feel your love tonight, and I believe you need me too.'

He gave a low chuckle as he turned towards her, pushing her shoulders down onto the bed.

'You know I'm always ready to oblige you, my lady,' he murmured, as his hands moved under her soft linen gown to cup and then caress her breasts, and his right thigh moved to pin her legs in place. She moaned softly as he pushed the gown further up, and his mouth descended on her nipples. Her body moved and arched in pleasure as he slid his knee between her legs, and his fingers moved down to find the spot that made her gasp aloud. He pushed her legs further apart and guided himself just slightly inside.

'If God wills it, this may make the babe we hope for, my Queen, the heir we need to make our position even more secure.'

There was nothing gentle about the way he thrust into her, but she didn't care—she wanted him as much as he wanted her. She lifted her hips to meet his thrusts, and he slid his hands under her buttocks to hold her, as he plunged into her over and over until, with a cry, he was replete. He fell gently forward, his head between her breasts. She stroked his hair, held him tight and prayed he would be right, and she would bear him a boy, an heir for England.

Several days later, it became clear that many of the nobles would not respond, and those that did showed little enthusiasm, rallying far lower numbers of men than expected. Their excuse was that they were unwilling to take their men from the land with the harvest only a few months away.

'We must have more troops, Sire. I will send messages to all the great ecclesiastical houses and monasteries, as they're often responsible for dozens of villages from which they can raise men. I will summon the fyrd on my own lands and arrange to set up my camp north of Pevensey as soon as possible. If allowed, I'd bet my last groat that he will land at Pevensey,' declared Archbishop Anselm.

Henry nodded his thanks, but the atmosphere was tense in the Great Hall at Westminster as Henry and his supporters waited for news. When it came, it was surprising.

The exhausted messenger, fresh off the boat from Normandy, knelt at the King's feet.

'The great invasion fleet at Treport has not yet sailed, my Lord King, although the Duke has gathered thousands of men, and they're saying the camps fill the fields and meadows for near a league around the port.'

'What is he waiting for?' mused Henry, staring across the crowded hall.

'Sire, this gives us more time. Let us call for our fleet to be assembled and send it out into the channel to attack him as he sails towards Pevensey,' cried the Earl of Warwick.

'Have it done; I place you in charge of our fleet, Warwick.'

'Where is our fleet now, my husband?' whispered Queen Matilda.

The King smiled at her—she had spent much of her life in

the Scottish court or the cloisters of her aunt, the Abbess, and was unaware of how England's fleet was served. However, having heard her question, his loyal friend Robert Fitz Hamon stepped in.

'Many channel ports such as Dover, Hythe, Hastings and Rye were awarded a charter by King Edward the Confessor, my lady. This gives these ports rights and privileges, such as being freemen and the right to free trade. However, it also puts the onus on them in times of war to provide ship service for the King—twenty ships, each to be crewed by twenty-one men, for fifteen days a year. Their task is to protect the coast of England.'

The Queen smiled and thanked him; he was a pleasant and handsome courtier she liked, and a good friend to the King.

By the 24th of June, Henry decided he could wait no longer. The inaction and tension had become too much for him, so he decided to rally and move his forces south.

'Matilda, you are to go to Winchester with sufficient men to guard yourself and the Treasury. You will be safer there. The people of London can be fickle, and the merchants and burghers may come out in support of my brother—Winchester is loyal and more easily defended. Meanwhile, I will join forces with Archbishop Anselm north of Pevensey. It is almost opposite the Norman port of Treport, and Robert will likely take the shortest route.'

Standing, he walked forward, faced the crowded hall and opened his arms wide. 'To arms. To arms, my friends! We ride for Pevensey! Rally your troops to defend the throne of England!'

A huge cheer went up, which echoed around the impressive hall and continued with many resounding huzzahs, stamping of feet and banging of tables. Matilda felt her eyes fill with tears, and she had to stop herself from clinging to her husband's arm. She loved him so much, and never more so than now, as his voice rang out confidently across the Great Hall. She promised to pray at least twice daily in the chapel at Winchester that he would come back alive, and that Robert would not kill him for stealing the crown. She knew Duke Robert's forces would be considerably larger and better trained.

June 1101 – Rouen

Darius was not usually a light sleeper. Georgio often joked that he slept the sleep of the dead, it was so difficult to wake him, but the day's events had unsettled him. He liked things to be clear-cut, with direction, and nothing about Robert's court in Rouen had been comfortable from the moment they arrived. He was sensitive to such things, and he could feel and see the undercurrents and tension after the first comment from Robert de Belleme about Conn's parentage. It was as if he was opening up old wounds whilst stabbing to create new ones for the Malvais family, and he had certainly succeeded in doing damage and triggering whispered questions behind people's hands. Then, at the one moment when he had expected their friend and mentor to step in, he had given an ambiguous answer.

He did not understand that part—this man had saved their lives, summoned them here, but could not say a few words in Conn's defence? He had heard the story several times. The captives had ropes around their necks and knives at their throats—if Conn had attacked, all four of them would probably have died, including Chatillon's wife and son.

He willed sleep to come, but his eyes felt gritty with tiredness. As he tossed and turned, he wondered what would happen to them now. Conn's anger outside the court had been terrifying to see, and both he and Georgio had sunk several jugs of wine on their return to the inn. *Will they still go to England?* he wondered as he finally began to drift off.

He was jerked back to wakefulness by a soft click. He recognised the sound, turned his head towards the door, and saw a tall figure slide into the room. He cursed himself for leaving his dagger on his belt with his clothes on the stool at the end of his palliasse bed. However, the figure stood quietly inside the door until Darius heard the sound of flint striking steel as a candle was lit. All at once, it was knocked from the intruder's hand as Conn leapt from his bed and grabbed the man by the throat. A struggle ensued as a chair and the small, sturdy table went flying. The man gasped, 'Conn, it's me! Edvard.'

Conn reluctantly let him go and dropped to sit back on the bed while Darius relit the candle, and Georgio, who had also sprung to his feet, gave an exasperated snort.

'You, of all people, should know not to creep into our rooms at night.'

Edvard gingerly rubbed his bruised throat and coughed a few times before replying.

'I was unarmed and trying not to wake the whole inn, which we've probably now done,' he said, sweeping a hand towards the overturned furniture, which Darius was righting.

'What are you doing here?' asked Georgio.

'I came to check that the coast was clear for Chatillon—we

can't risk anyone seeing him here. It would be dangerous for you and would imperil the plan.'

'I imagine it'll be dangerous for him to be anywhere near these two after what happened tonight,' muttered Darius to a glare from Edvard.

'That is because you have no understanding of what was afoot and why it was necessary. Now hold your tongue until you are asked to speak, and meanwhile, go and get us some wine, as I'm sure the innkeeper will now be hovering nearby to assess any damage,' he growled at the young squire.

'I have confidence in you both that you understand that Chatillon had no choice but to distance himself from you yesterday. Your leaving Rouen will further reinforce that,' he said while moving to the window and waving the candle back and forth twice, the signal that the coast was clear.

'I had an inkling of that, but could he not have found a better way than by damaging my reputation or apportioning unfair blame?' asked Conn in a cold, unforgiving voice.

'Do not fear. Much later, when the invasion is over, the true circumstances of what happened will be shared widely by me, and you'll be exonerated.'

At that moment, the door opened and the tall, dark figure of Piers De Chatillon entered. Filling the room with his presence, as usual, he smiled as he felt the chilly atmosphere and saw the cold glances directed at him by his young friends. He pulled a chair over and sat on it, sweeping his cloak back and crossing his long, elegantly booted legs. The silence stretched as no one said a word.

'What, no questions? No accusations or righteous rage?' he finally said softly.

'Edvard has explained, but I cannot say that I like your

methods,' replied Conn as Darius returned with the wine.

'I was left with no choice, Conn; I had to do something to remove you from court immediately, and it seemed an opportunity to fracture our relationship, to hide our future liaison in England or at Henry's court. I am unsure how much Belleme knows, but he has triggered others to look into your parentage. I hear that Flambard has started to poke the fire to see what he can find in the ashes, but I will ensure that he finds nothing.'

Darius poured the wine as Conn sighed, 'So what do we do now, Piers?'

'You are to do nothing. Stay out of sight here at the inn—your men will no doubt be glad of the rest. Darius and Edvard will be your eyes and ears, for I want you to steal a ship; I seem to remember that you are both particularly good at that.'

This made Georgio smile while Darius had frozen, still holding the wine jug aloft.

'Steal a ship? Don't they hang you for that?' he exclaimed. They all laughed, except Edvard, who cuffed him hard for speaking out of place again. But it broke the tension in the room.

'A wide-bellied cog has been in for repairs for several days. They will hopefully be finished sometime tomorrow afternoon. You will take your men and horses there just before dawn. Edvard has arranged for the captain and crew to be engaged elsewhere, and only one boy is sleeping on board her. I have engaged a pilot, a man I have used before, who will be waiting on the quayside for you, and will take you to England. When you land, Conn, you will ride to Pevensey to find Henry, who's moving his forces there as we speak. He will welcome you with open arms, especially when you offer your services to train his cavalry as Horse Warriors, as your father did for his father before you.'

Conn nodded in understanding, but with a rueful smile.

'As usual, Chatillon, you always plan well and make it sound seamless until something unexpected and dangerous appears.'

'Ah yes, we can't always plan for the unexpected. Georgio, I want you to take Darius and ride to London. I have a friend called Jacob, an apothecary and physician on Seething Lane. Go and find him—he expects you. Ensure you are not followed. He'll give you a small package. Keep it close, keep it safe, and keep it hidden, and I'll send you further instructions as to its use. There are one or two people around Henry who may prove to be an obstacle to our plans, and may need removing,' he explained, taking a mouthful of wine.

'Poison, no doubt,' whispered Darius under his breath, but only Georgio heard him and sent him a frown as Chatillon continued.

'I have at least half a dozen informers in Henry's court—some close to the King—but most will steer clear of you. However, there is one who is above suspicion and will take your messages and give you any from me. Only contact me in the direst circumstances, as we must appear to have severed all contact. She takes many risks, as she is no supporter of Henry. Her name is Rohese, and she is the daughter of Hugh Grandesmil, the Sheriff of Leicester, who died a few years ago. He was a long-time supporter of Robert. However, she is married to Sir Robert de Courcy, the trusted royal steward of Henry and Matilda's household. As such, she's in a position to hear and share much information. From what I remember, she's also quite pretty, which will give you an excuse to pay her attention.'

CHAPTER FOUR

At that, he stood and clasped arms with Georgio and Conn, smiling up into his protégé's eyes. 'It's unlikely that I will see you for a while, so I thank you for this. Consider your debt paid, and godspeed to you all.'

With that, he was gone, Edvard moving like a shadow in his footsteps behind him.

Still holding the wine jug, Darius sank into the nearest chair and stared at Georgio for some time; the room seemed oddly empty without the Papal Envoy's presence.

'You promised me intrigue and danger, but now we're stealing a ship, not to mention collecting poison. Do other squires undergo this training?' he asked in a soft, concerned voice.

Georgio smiled ruefully as he slapped the young squire on the shoulder.

'Only the best ones, Darius, only the best! Now let us snatch a few hours' sleep before we exercise the horses in the morning.'

Deep in the shadows opposite the inn, a figure had stood for hour, and was now moving from foot to foot to keep warm in the damp, dark passage. He had been satisfied to watch the arrival of Edvard and Chatillon at the inn, and had made his way to the archway into the courtyard, so he saw the candle being lit in the upstairs room. He waited and then returned to his hiding place. Now, he sank much further into the depths of the alleyway, into a doorway, as he heard them emerge from the inn and make their way along the thoroughfare back to the castle.

It was rare that he undertook missions himself. In England, he had a dozen men to do his bidding, but this was too important to leave to a new minion here in Rouen. He had wanted to see what happened with his own eyes, and he was elated that it had played out as expected. Initially, he had been surprised at Chatillon's treatment of the Horse Warrior, but as he'd watched, he'd become suspicious. He knew the tragic events in Aggio, outside of Genoa, had occurred, but could it destroy such a friendship? Malvais had followed Chatillon's every order in England last summer. He knew that, somehow, this was part of a bigger plan by Chatillon, and he needed to put the pieces together. He waited a considerable time before setting off after them and returning to his room in the castle, his mind working overtime. He decided to put a watch on all of them as he peeled off his cloak and mounted the steps to his room.

In the darkness of the long stone corridor, Edvard emerged from a dark window embrasure and smiled—he knew exactly who had followed them and why, and now waited for him. Chatillon would not be surprised who it was watching them, and with luck, it would hasten the slitting of his throat. As Flambard's hand reached for the latch of his door, an arm came around him, and a blade was at his throat. He gasped in shock as a deep voice hissed in his ear.

'Do you think you're invisible, Flambard? Do you think you can watch a man such as Chatillon and not be seen? I do not know exactly what you are hoping to find, but I know you are poking your nose into a business that is not yours, and I'm sure you are aware that people who interfere in Chatillon's plans do not live long. I've wanted to slit your throat for some time, and Chatillon holds enough evidence and documents against you that it would justify me doing that now.'

Flambard frantically searched for a reply. 'It was not

Chatillon I was watching—it was the Horse Warrior. By chance, I saw Piers arrive. I swear I'll not breathe a word,' he croaked.

Edvard gave a harsh laugh at such a poor attempt at an excuse. 'You'd never breathe again if I had my way. I'll be watching you, Flambard. You have run out of chances.'

With that, he was gone, and Flambard collapsed, gasping against the door. He staggered into his room and, with shaking hands, lit the candle and rubbed his hand across his neck. It came away with blood where the skin had been pierced. He was not cut out for this—he would use other people in future. But he was more convinced than ever that something was afoot.

Chapter Five

June 1101 – Rouen

The Horse Warriors had muffled the hooves of the big War Destriers as they rode out of the streets of Rouen and down the long wooden wharves that stretched west on the banks of the Seine. These had been built by Duke Robert over ten years before, for his previous disastrous invasion of England against William Rufus. Fortunately, they were some distance down the river from the city, so there was little chance of them being seen. In the soft filtered light just before dawn, Conn could see the ship at the far end of a wharf. It was lucky that the tide was in and the ship was riding high—it would be easier to load the horses, which could often prove difficult.

As they reached the wide-bellied cog, a figure detached himself from the nearest warehouse doorway and bowed. Three other men were standing behind him.

'I am John Mason. I have been engaged to guide you to the south coast of England. Three crew members have been instructed to bring the cog back to Rouen.'

Conn nodded and smiled. Truly, Edvard thought of everything—the boat was borrowed and not stolen.

CHAPTER FIVE

'I'm pleased to see you, John Mason. We need to load the horses, and then we can sail on the tide.'

At that moment, a sleepy and confused young crewman emerged from his palliasse bed under the stern deck, having heard the last words.

'The Captain isn't here, Sire. I was not aware that we were sailing today,' he mumbled, rubbing his eyes.

'You are now, young man. Come here and pass me the wide planks you use for livestock, and you can help us load and secure the horses. I promise you there'll be extra silver for your trouble. Gracchus, you and two of the men set up the tarpaulins. I can see them over there. We'll cover that end of the deck; the horses are always more settled undercover when they can't see the motion of the waves.'

The new crew members jumped aboard to lend a hand and get the large cog ready to sail. Most of the big Destriers were willing enough to step onto the planks and follow their riders; they had done so several times before. Diablo, however, took exception to everything and fought Darius and Georgio every inch of the way. At the same time, the pilot, John Mason, watched in dismay as the huge horse planted his feet firmly, and refused to budge towards the planks.

'You'll never get that wild horse on there, and if you do, how will we control him at sea?' he asked in a worried voice.

'He has made a trip like this at least half a dozen times before—he's just playing games,' Conn answered, seemingly unconcerned as he climbed the planks to the wharf, and, taking the bridle from Darius, he gave it a hard shake and spoke sternly to the horse. Diablo showed the whites of his eyes and shook his head in protest, but finally designed to walk calmly down the planks after Conn onto the deck of the wide cog, where he was tethered under the now-secured tarpaulin.

A short while later, they were sailing out of the mouth of the River Seine. Conn stood on the stern and looked back at the receding land behind them, as Georgio came to stand beside him and rest his hands on the gunwale.

'I wonder when we'll set foot here again, for this plan of Chatillon's sounds long-term, especially if Henry wins,' mused Conn.

'It might only be a few weeks if King Henry has any suspicions about us!' exclaimed Georgio.

Conn laughed. 'Ever the optimist, Georgio, we must ensure we are convincing. I like Henry; we spent much time together when I was in London, and part of me admires his ambition and daring to take the crown against difficult odds. He must have known that when Robert returned from Jerusalem, he would come to take it back.

Georgio turned and regarded his friend in surprise.

'Having heard the details about the forces Duke Robert has gathered, I can't see how Henry can take him on in battle and win. Robert and his nobles are all experienced veterans, while Henry appears to have an army of peasants. Where does that leave us? We'll fight for the usurper, Henry Beauclerc, against impossible odds, and be part of a ragtag defeated army.'

'Highly likely, Georgio, and I assure you that I'm a realist. But, I'm sure that Chatillon will have a way out for us; he will not let us languish in an English prison if Robert takes the throne back. In the meantime, we must regard this as a very lucrative venture. For now, both Chatillon and King Henry will be paying for our services. I must go and speak to our pilot,' he said, leaving Georgio shaking his head.

Conn climbed the short ladder to the foredeck and stood

beside John Mason, who nodded at him.

'Where exactly are you planning to land us?' he asked, gazing at the calm sea ahead. It was a beautiful summer's day with just enough breeze behind them to fill the sails as they headed north towards England.

'I'm heading for Newhaven. We'll sail a short way up the River Ouse. There are small wharves there, old but serviceable, that they use for the wool and sheep exports. It's near your destination; I hear the King is moving his forces down to Pevensey, and I know you are joining him there.'

'And you? Where are you based, and which side do you plan to support, John?' asked Conn.

John gave the Horse Warrior a wary sidelong look but could see the genuine interest in Conn's face.

'I am from Rye, Sire, one of the chartered portmen. We supply ships for the King, no matter who is on the throne, as do many other ports on the south coast. Twenty ships are out in the channel now, and you may see some of them soon as we sail north before swinging west. As to whom I support, that isn't for the likes of me to say. I will take money from whoever asks for my services.'

Conn nodded, pleased at the man's honesty and liking him for it. He squinted north, but he could see nothing yet on a horizon obscured by a low band of summer mist. He wondered if Chatillon and Duke Robert knew of the fleet waiting for them, and then realised they would. A dozen pigeons a day flew into the coop in Rouen with messages for the Papal Envoy. He would be aware of every move.

Conn frowned as he stared ahead. He may have given Georgio a confident answer, but he was not as certain as he made out. The friendship he had developed with Prince

Henry was bound to be different now that he was the King of England. He had to both win back and keep Henry's trust. He was also banking on their shared comradeship in planning and facilitating the murder of William Rufus. However, he was not naïve, and knew this was a double-edged sword, for he was one of the few people who knew of Henry's involvement in the assassination. How would Henry regard him, he wondered. As a loyal compatriot ready to risk everything to support him, or as a threat because of his knowledge—a threat to be removed to keep him safe?

There was another consideration—he had always had Chatillon's protection in the past. This was well known, but now he was arriving as a refugee from Robert's court, having lost that friendship. It wouldn't take long for the story of that night to find its way across the English Channel. This meant his only protection for Georgio and his men in the English court were his wits and intuition. He prayed they would be enough.

Late June 1101 – Pevensey

Several hours later, Conn and his men, having waved Georgio and Darius off on the London road, headed east towards Pevensey. The locals at Newhaven told them that a great force was now camped at Rickney, a league or so above Pevensey Castle. For Conn, it was good to feel the wind in his face and have a good gallop with Diablo after their confinement on the ship. He gave the big horse his head as he galloped over the downs that hugged the coastline. Eventually, he slowed, and his men caught up. Staring into the distance, he could see what must be Pevensey Castle.

It was an impressive structure which King William Rufus had taken and fortified after the rebellion of 1088. As they trotted slowly in that direction, Conn recalled that it was here that Finian Ui Neill had met his ferocious wife, Dion, an exceptional archer. Now, it belonged to William De Mortain, the Earl of Cornwall. He was a firm supporter of Duke Robert, so they needed to avoid it.

They turned northeast, and before long, they could see the thin trails of smoke from numerous cooking fires ahead of them. As they crested a small hill, King Henry's camp was spread out in front of them. Conn noticed the King's standard on the far hill and rode through the camp towards it. He noticed the lack of large pavilions that the nobility would set up. This reinforced his view that the King's army would be made up of the fyrd, duty-bound freemen and villeins who owed their local lord or abbot allegiance, and who had now been called to fight for their king. They would be poorly trained and equipped. As he rode past their fires, he saw they had clubs, pitchforks or hastily made pikes. He didn't rate Henry's chances highly if he hoped to face hundreds of Robert's trained knights with this ill-assorted rabble.

He headed for the King's standard and found several nobles, and an older priest with a large cross hanging on a gold chain around his neck. They had gathered on stools and camp chairs in the morning sunshine. They watched his arrival with interest as he dismounted and led Diablo towards them before knotting the reins and handing him to Gracchus.

'God's day to you. I am looking for the King—is he within?' he asked.

Suddenly, there was a loud shout behind him. 'Malvais!

Thank the Good Lord, for we are in dire need of you and your men,' shouted Richard de Clare as he slapped Conn on both shoulders and then clasped arms with him. 'The last I heard, you were lost in the wilds of the East. How is it that you are here?'

'It is a long story, De Clare, and one best told over a large jug of wine,' laughed Conn, pleased to see his friend. Gilbert Fitz Richard, Baron of Clare but always known as Richard de Clare, had been a close compatriot when he was last in England. A friend of Chatillon's, he had been involved in the plot to kill William Rufus. Walter Tirrel, who fired the fateful arrow, was his brother-in-law. He had ridden with Conn and the King's body to Winchester, and was one of the few people who knew that the King was still alive when they put him in the cart. However, Conn had learnt to trust him with his life.

'Henry will be overjoyed to see you, but first, I'll make you known to His Grace, Anselm, the Archbishop of Canterbury, who was out of England when you were here last.'

Conn bowed to the seated prelate, who nodded and gave him his blessing.

'I have heard much of you, young man, not only because of your famous name, but from my namesake, Archbishop Anselm of Milan. I believe you facilitated the crossing of the Lombard Crusade over the Bosphorus into Anatolia. That cannot have been an easy task with over twenty thousand of them.'

'Indeed, Your Grace, it was challenging. Fortunately, they are now the concern of Raymond of Toulouse,' answered Conn.

'I believe you have met Henry Beaumont, the Earl of Warwick?'

CHAPTER FIVE

'Yes, I had that pleasure several times when I was last in the English court.' Conn bowed as he respected the elder Beaumont brother.

'I am glad to see you have brought some of your Horse Warriors with you, Malvais; they'll be worth five of our slapdash cavalry,' he said, waving his arm at Conn's men, who were still mounted.

Conn bowed his thanks as Richard led him away to one side.

'The King is with the troops. He insists on training them himself, which is madness, I know, as he is not a soldier. But, we must admit some of his advice is working, and they are so overwhelmed he's spending time with them that they listen. I'll take you to him. My man will find accommodation for you, your men and the horses,' he said, waving over a small, smooth-faced individual who seemed overly obsequious as he repeatedly bowed to Conn. As he indicated where the man would find Gracchus, Conn thought there was something very familiar about him, but assumed he had come across him at Winchester last summer.

'Bernard is invaluable—he can obtain virtually anything we ask for, even out in the fields and countryside,' said Richard as they walked to the large meadow below the camp.

Bernard, meanwhile, avoiding Gracchus and the stamping snorting Diablo, walked beside one of the young Horse Warriors, Andreas, who had dismounted.

'I'll arrange several tents for you and grazing for the horses. I presume the black beast needs to be separated.'

Andreas laughed and nodded. 'Lord Malvais will need a larger pavilion if you can lay your hands on one.'

Bernard gave a smug smile and nodded. 'Of course. Are you

49

his squire?' he asked, smiling up into the face of the dark-eyed young man as he led the way through the camp.

'No, that's Darius. He has gone with Sir Georgio di Milan to London,' he replied.

'Have they indeed? I wish I were back in London instead of in fields that'll turn to churned-up mud as soon as the rain comes. Will they be back soon? I presume they'll share the pavilion,' he asked, opening the meadow gate to allow them through.

'I think so. I heard they're to go and pick up an important package.'

'That's enough!' shouted an annoyed Gracchus. 'Lord Malvais does not need to have his business known and spread about the camp by the likes of you,' he growled at Bernard, while a red-faced Andreas moved out of range. He had felt the fist of Gracchus on several occasions, and he realised he may have been indiscreet with this stranger.

Bernard bowed. 'I assure you I'm the soul of discretion. Ask my master, Sir Richard, if you're unsure. Now, there is a small area by the stream where the stallion can be placed.'

Gracchus dismounted, glaring at Andreas and throwing him the reins of his gelding as he led Diablo away to ensure he was secure.

Conn stood on the sidelines with De Clare and watched King Henry as he taught a line of twenty yeomen how to use their pikes against cavalry. After listening briefly, Conn had heard enough and walked forward to stand behind the King to speak to the men.

'I would ignore that advice if I were you, for every trained pikeman knows you have to sharpen the other end of your pike and drive it a foot into the ground first, before planting yourself at an angle to drive it into the chests of the horses galloping at you. Otherwise, your pike will have no purchase, snap or just be knocked out of your hand, and you will be a trampled bloody mess on the ground.'

Henry, red-faced, turned to find out who on God's earth would have the audacity to take his advice to task. Then his eyes widened in surprise as he saw the tall Horse Warrior behind him with a laughing Richard de Clare.

'Malvais! By the Holy Face of Lucca, I can't believe you are here. I heard you were fighting for Emperor Alexius.'

'I was, but then I heard you were recruiting and thought you might need my help.'

Henry clasped arms with Conn; he may now be a king, but in Paris and London, they had become fast friends, and formality went out of the window.

'I do need help, Malvais. As you can see, I'm working with raw, untrained men, and I have no idea how long we have before my brother lands.'

'I may be able to help you with the latter of those problems if we can speak privately later. However, let me help you with this first,' said Conn, grinning.

In moments, he had the men gathered around, and he showed them how to race together when attacked, and form a hedgehog of spikes to keep the cavalry out. Henry stood back and watched him with satisfaction.

'Has he brought any men?' Henry asked Richard.

'Half a dozen, I think, and his comrade Georgio di Milan, who will arrive in a day or so. He will be just as useful organising the training of your cavalry. He reminds me of his uncle, Morvan de Malvais—he completely reorganised Robert's forces at Gerberoi. He was a strategist. As you know, we rode out of that fortress, with Morvan riding beside Robert, and defeated your father. He did the same thing to help your brother, Robert, defeat King Malcolm at Falkirk. It's as if they see things from above, a bird's view. I am convinced this makes the Malvais warriors so effective.'

'I had forgotten about Gerberoi, one of my father's only defeats. It took his pride a long time to recover from that, and I saw the change in him. But Morvan was originally my father's man—he set up a full cohort of Horse Warriors for him in Caen. I used to watch them training. I was spellbound. And then, Morvan suddenly left Caen to fight for Robert. I could never understand why.'

Richard realised that his admiration for Conn had encouraged him to say too much, for he had been Morvan's closest friend and knew the secret of Conn's parentage and why Morvan left.

'Those days are long past, Sire, and now Conn has crossed a continent to be at your side—that is certainly a sign of loyalty.'

Henry nodded. 'I'll be interested to hear what he has to say. He implied he had information that may help us.'

On the far side of the camp, Bernard almost ran to the outskirts, where a group of Welsh mercenaries sat around a campfire with several skinned rabbits roasting on spits. He shouted their leader over—a stocky, weathered-looking man called Owen.

'I need a man to ride for London immediately—someone clever, with their wits about them.'

Owen nodded and returned to the fire. 'Brynn, come hither. Bernard has a job for you!'

Bernard hissed in annoyance. 'Do not use my name, Owen. These are dangerous dealings in dangerous times.'

CHAPTER FIVE

He regarded with interest the scar-faced mercenary who came over. He had the black hair and light blue eyes often found in Wales, but his good looks were ruined by an old, jagged scar from his left eye to his mouth. Realising he was staring, Bernard quickly handed Brynn a pouch of silver.

'For any expenses, such as accommodation, fresh horses and your time. We expect a job well done for this type of payment.'

The man tested the weight of the pouch in his hand and nodded before slipping it safely inside his doublet.

'I need you to ride like the devil for London. It may sound as if you are looking for a needle in a haystack, but the man you seek is distinctive. He is a Horse Warrior, with the trademark laced leather doublet and crossed swords on his back. Not only that, but he and his squire are riding War Destriers, huge horses of eighteen hands or more that will be noticed. I want to know where he is, where he goes and who he meets. I am sure I do not need to mention that he should not be aware he is being followed or watched.'

Again, the tall Welshman nodded and, snatching a rabbit from the spit, he stuffed it into an old leather bag, picked up a small sack of wine, and headed for the horse lines. He smiled as he tacked up his large, rangy chestnut gelding—this sounded like easy money for him. Finding Horse Warriors within the city walls should be no hard task, and he knew the city of London well.

Moments later, he was galloping north while Bernard, knowing his master would be well pleased, headed back to the pavilions.

Chapter Six

July 1st 1101 – Rickney

Conn spent some time grooming and settling Diablo before joining his men around the campfire.

'I never thought I'd say this, but I truly miss Darius, particularly his ability to find plump chickens or geese in the bleakest of places. This sheep must have been at least twenty years old and in its death throes when they slaughtered it!' exclaimed Gracchus.

Conn laughed as Gracchus tore at a lump of tough mutton, just as a squire arrived to summon Conn to dinner in the King's tent.

'I'd lay a silver penny that they don't have this tough meat at the King's table,' he added, but stood and followed Conn, flinging the lamb away to be fought over by the camp dogs.

'Are you here as a replacement squire or as my bodyguard?' he asked Gracchus, in an amused tone.

'Neither, Sire, just a quick word of warning. That man, Bernard, was digging for information today. He was clever and picked on the youngest. At first, I wondered if it was the boy's pretty face, and that was where his preference lay, but then I realised he was questioning with intent. He wanted to know where Georgio had gone and why. Unfortunately, Andreas told him before I could intervene.'

Conn stopped and stared into the distance, considering what he had been told.

'It may be useful if Andreas develops a friendship with Bernard, but not one that would endanger him. I want to know more about Bernard because I'm sure I've seen him before. You're right to be suspicious, though, for something about the toadying little man makes the hairs stand up on the back of my neck. Let's see what Andreas uncovers. Well done, Gracchus.'

Despite being in a field near Pevensey, the King's pavilion was full, and he was entertaining in style with a dozen nobles around two wide trestle tables. A seat had been kept for him beside De Clare, and despite the threat of invasion hanging over their heads, it was a boisterous gathering with much banter and laughter. Large chunks of roast venison and goose adorned the table, accompanied by at least a dozen side dishes and desserts, courtesy of the King's Royal Steward, Robert de Courcy, who always ensured the best was at hand. Once the serious business of eating and drinking was over, Henry called for Conn to tell of his exploits in Byzantium.

In as shortened a version as possible, Conn described the richness and grandeur of the Emperor's palaces in Constantinople, for he knew that many around this table would want to know of them. Then, he described the forces of Alexius and the danger of riding against Seljuk warriors.

'And you served the Megas Doux, John Doukas—I have heard much of this man. What was he like?' asked Robert Beaumont, the younger of the two brothers.

'Most of what you hear is true. As a soldier and a commander, he is formidable; he gives no quarter and will put whole towns to the sword if they will not surrender, somewhat like your father,' said Conn, bowing his head to Henry, who returned a rueful smile.

Henry knew he had much to do and prove if he wanted to earn even half of his father's reputation.

'He was obviously impressed with you, Malvais; I hear from the Archbishop that he promoted you twice and finally to the high rank of Topoteretes in Nicomedia. Yet, you left all of that to cross Europe to be here with us, and I'm eternally grateful, as you'll be training my slipshod cavalry. We applaud you for your decision to return,' declared King Henry as the men in the pavilion banged their cups or fists on the tables in acclamation.

However, Conn saw the frown and annoyance on the face of Robert Beaumont, who was in charge of the King's cavalry—the last thing he needed was to make an enemy of one of the powerful Beaumont brothers.

'I believe you also have news of my brother, but you can share that with only my council present. Now, tell us of this Crusade of the Faint Hearted; the Archbishop tells me you beheaded rebel crusaders on the beach.'

This got everyone's attention, and many, including Robert Beaumont, stared down the table at Conn with growing respect.

'Only half a dozen, Sire—the rest I had flogged and branded,' answered Conn, as one noble spluttered into his wine at those words, and the rest regarded him with new respect.

CHAPTER SIX

July 1101 – London

It was Sunday morning when Georgio and Darius finally rode through Southwark to cross London Bridge while the bell of St Olave's church summoned worshippers to prayer. However, when they saw the bridge, they could see a long line of waiting carts blocking it. They could hear voices raised and threats shouted as Georgio reined in and sighed. It had been a frustrating few days as his horse, after only three hours on the road, had bruised the bulb of its heel when slipping down a gravel bank to a stream. This had developed into a limp, which meant they had to put up at the inn at Hardcross, kicking their heels and wasting time, while they put a cold pressed poultice on the injury before they could go further.

Neither had been to London before, and they were full of anticipation. As expected, the streets were teaming with people, but their time in Constantinople had prepared Georgio for anything, while Darius had spent a few years as an accomplished street rat. Being mounted, they could see over the heads of the crowd to the altercation taking place in the middle of the old bridge.

'Run through and find out what's happening, Darius. See if a coin or two will help to resolve the problem,' he ordered as he sat and waited.

A small crowd gathered to stare in awe at the large War Destriers. In no time at all, Darius returned.

'They've now righted the overturned cart, and I scattered a few coins into hands to encourage them to reload the sacks of grain. Being in the Malvais livery helped—I told them that a noble lord was becoming very angry at the delay,' he said, grinning as he remounted.

'You are incorrigible, Darius. I suppose I have to scowl at them when we ride through.'

'That would help,' he laughed as he pushed forward, yelling, 'Make way, make way for his lordship!'

As they reached the end of the bridge, Darius shared that he had found them an inn. A merchant on the bridge had recommended the Bridge Inn, a good hostelry with ample stables. Once again, Georgio thought how lucky he had been to find Darius, a squire who thought ahead without being told. A short while later, they trotted through a stone arch into the cobbled yard of the Bridge Inn. Dismounting, Georgio was impressed as several well-dressed boys ran forward to take the horses. The large two-story inn was unusual, with a wooden gallery that ran outside the second floor, and a staircase leading to the rooms. Within minutes, alerted of a knight's arrival, the innkeeper came bustling out bearing a welcome cup of cool ale.

'We'd like a large room for my master and myself, for one night initially, but it may be two. We go to fight for the King, so we cannot stay longer,' announced Darius.

Georgio spluttered in his ale at the audacity of his squire. So much for keeping a low profile, he thought, but the innkeeper was impressed as he led him up the staircase while Darius unbuckled the saddlebags and followed behind.

A tall figure had watched all of this from the shadows of the large archway. The Welsh mercenary, Brynn, had made good time and arrived in London well before them. An initial search of the better inns had revealed nothing, and he was just about to try the monastic houses when he spotted them crossing London Bridge. Being eighteen hands high or more, their horses were distinctive as they turned off the bridge into

CHAPTER SIX

the busy streets. He could easily lose himself in the crowd to follow behind them. Now, he needed to wait and see where they went. He crossed to the opposite side of the small square and positioned himself between two market stalls to enjoy some banter with the women selling their produce, from where he would clearly see the two men emerging.

He didn't have long to wait, for Georgio was impatient—he wanted to ride south to rejoin Malvais by the next morning. They headed for Byward Street following the innkeeper's instructions, who told them that Seething Lane ran north from there, although he expressed surprise that they intended to go there. Before long, they were striding along the north bank of the River Thames, where numerous wooden hovels and small jetties had been built. Suddenly, Darius stopped, transfixed by what rose shimmering in the bright July sunshine—King William's great white Tower of London.

'Is this the famous tower Flambard escaped from?' asked the young squire.

Georgio, who had also stopped to stand and stare at the impressive structure, nodded.

'Yes, we were told that he had a rope smuggled in and, having drugged his guards, he climbed down and escaped.'

'That was some feat; it's far bigger than I expected. He must be a braver man than I gave him credit for,' answered Darius.

'Or he was a desperate man who needed to escape—they were about to behead him,' added a laughing Georgio.

They pushed on but had difficulty finding their destination until they asked one of the workers sitting on the banks of the river. Darius was surprised to see that the group of men wore country smocks, which you would see on farms, and they were covered in dust and small pieces of straw. They were a rowdy group, partaking of breakfast ale and pieces of cheese and bread wrapped in kerchiefs or a torn cloth. However, at the sight of Darius in his livery, and Georgio in the Horse Warrior regalia, they quietened for the squire's question.

'Seething Lane, my lad? It's behind you just over there, but you might get those nice boots muddied, as it's no more than a narrow path between all the threshing barns.' Darius thanked him and threw a small copper coin in the air, which the man deftly caught.

The men were right; the high walls on either side kept the narrow path from drying out, and the tramping of numerous threshing workers had churned up the mud and slime underfoot, which was treacherous.

'Are you sure this is where he lives, Sire? There seems to be nothing but grain stores and threshing floors. I can see no houses ahead, and it seems an odd place for an apothecary.'

'Chatillon never gets his information wrong, Darius; he will be along here somewhere,' responded Georgio, pushing ahead while using his hands on the walls to keep himself upright in the glutinous mud. Darius slipped and only just prevented himself from falling full length by clinging to a jutting stone in the wall. He frowned back at a laughing Georgio behind him, but then noticed a tall, dark figure silhouetted at the end of the lane. He appeared to be standing and watching them, but Darius could make out no features, so he shrugged it off as one of the workers.

'I think this path may be the route for a small stream or spring,' spat Georgio as the space widened and the noise of voices came to them. On their right, a dozen workers sat in the sun on a low stone wall, helping themselves to ale from large stone jugs being passed around. Women and men

CHAPTER SIX

were throwing ribald comments and insults at each other and laughing, their flails propped beside them. Then a shout came, a handbell was shaken, and they all began to move back to the hardened threshing floor, where high piles of corn and grain awaited them. Darius took the opportunity to wave over the man collecting the jugs.

'We're looking for an apothecary who supposedly lives somewhere on this path. Do you know of him?'

The small, thickset worker struggled with Darius's words and strange accent, so Georgio shouted over. 'A physician, he lives here somewhere.'

'Ah, old Jacob, best physicking in the whole of Lunnon, they say. Treats the likes of the poor and us for a few eggs in payment and such. There are two cottages at the top of this lane—Jacob has the large one at the top.'

Georgio shouted his thanks while Darius dug in the purse and, digging out another coin, threw it to the man. Georgio shook his head.

'At this rate, we'll have no coins left to pay our reckoning at the inn.'

Darius was shocked; he was enjoying being a benefactor for the first time in his life. Georgio laughed at the expression on his face.

'Come, let us move, or we'll be covered in this,' he said, gesturing towards the clouds of chaff from the corn rising around them.

As they returned to the path, Darius automatically glanced behind him, but no tall, dark figure was on the path. Before long, the path had widened and dried considerably, and they reached the pair of detached stone cottages, which were long, low buildings, older and larger than Georgio expected. They were set back from the road, and the larger one had a tiled roof.

'These have been here for some time, probably from the days when these streets and grain sheds were meadows.' Each sat in its own patch of land, but the tiled cottage had several larger outbuildings. The door to the dwelling was low, made of thick oak and covered in iron studs. He noticed the windows were small and barred—heavy, weathered shutters could be seen inside.

'It looks more like a gaol than a house, but it is reassuring to see this here; it means we have the right place,' murmured Darius, reaching out to run his fingers over the carved wooden sign firmly nailed to the door.

'What is it? Do you know?' asked Georgio while hammering on the door.

'It is the rod of Asclepius—see the entwined serpent. Asclepius was a deity who dealt with healing and medicine. Most physicians in Greece use the same symbol.'

The sound of bolts being drawn reached them, and the door was pulled open by an attractive woman. She looked them up and down and smiled a welcome.

'Master Jacob is expecting you,' she murmured, indicating they should enter.

It was cool in the stone-flagged house as she led them along a long corridor, through several rooms, and out into a large walled garden. Georgio was surprised that it was full of fruit trees, and more were fanned out on the south-facing wall. As they walked across the soft grass beneath the trees, they came to what was clearly a physic garden, full of herbs and exotic plants. Georgio was immediately taken back to the home of Chatillon, his chateau south of Paris, which had an almost identical garden with a similar long stone workshop like the one ahead. On a sunny bench sat a tall, thin, older man who stood to welcome them. His face may have been lined, but his eyes were bright and shone with intelligence.

'Georgio di Milan, I presume, one of the famous Breton Horse Warriors. I have followed the story of you and your brave friend, Conn Fitz Malvais since you were snatched and taken as boys.'

Darius was wide-eyed that this old physician, in the backstreets of London, knew so much, while Georgio smiled.

'I am honoured to meet you, Sire. I know you to be an old and dear friend of our mentor, Piers De Chatillon, and no doubt one of his chief informers in London.'

Jacob laughed and called for refreshments while waving his servant, David, over to take their boots. 'I see you came the long way from the south,' he laughed, pointing at the calf-high glutinous mud.

They sat in the sunshine and talked about many things. Jacob was very interested in the events in Constantinople, where he had once lived for several years, and was keen to hear of their adventures, but he had news for them as well.

'I'm afraid that your friend, Raymond De Toulouse, now leading the Crusade of the Faint Hearted, is heading into disaster. Instead of travelling south to Jerusalem, he has turned north. They captured Ankara, but I have heard that the Seljuk Turks have joined forces and formed an enormous army. It will not end well.'

They sat in silence for a while, all three of them lost in their thoughts and sadness for the thousands of defenceless, unarmed pilgrims who were marching into danger.

'However, let us talk of more pleasant things. I hope you'll stay and eat with me, and you can tell me of my friend, Ahmed. Is he still living in Chatillon's chateau?'

As the heat rose in the high-walled garden, Georgio nodded as they walked to a long wooden table in the shade. Darius noticed that the back of the house was just as locked and barred as the front.

'It is like a small fortress,' he murmured.

There was certainly nothing wrong with Jacob's hearing as he whirled around on Darius and nodded vigorously.

'It has to be, young man, for us Jews are blamed for every misfortune, from floods to poor harvests and plague. They turn on us often, forgetting any good we may have done. They burnt me out six years ago—that is why I now have a heavy, stone-tiled roof.'

'Yet you stay!' exclaimed Darius.

'I like it here. I like the people. London has been my home for nearly fifteen years. But it's the same in most cities across Europe—more attacks, especially since the fervour around the crusades.'

They spent a pleasant afternoon discussing many things, including King Henry and Duke Robert, until finally, their clean boots were returned, and Jacob led them to his workshop at the end of the garden and unlocked the door. Like Ahmed's workshop, shelves lined the walls full of pots, vials, and coloured glass bottles, while various containers stood on tripods bubbling gently over a low candle. Having never seen such a workshop, Darius was mesmerised and wandered around the room, peering into containers and pots. He was about to lift a basket lid when Georgio hissed, 'Snakes!' Darius jumped back in alarm, and Jacob laughed aloud.

'No, only fresh Belladonna leaves and berries, but I know all about Chatillon's wife, Isabella, and her snakes. As you know, Chatillon was here in London last year, and he was telling me that the big one, Octavian, was nearly six feet long now. I believe she has tamed him.'

Georgio smiled and nodded. 'She carries him around the garden when she walks with Ahmed, and all the servants stay away.

'What is this package I am to pick up, Jacob?'

Jacob led them to a bench on which was a tiny stoppered pot and two very small leather drawstring bags. One had a circle scorched onto it and the other a red triangle.

'You spent some time working with Ahmed, so you will recognise these and know their effects. The one with the red triangle is powdered fly agaric. As you know, it can be added to soups and stews. The difficulty is ensuring it is in the victim's bowl and not given to the whole family.'

'Two pinches will deliver delirium and death in days—a small pinch looks like fever or even drunkenness,' added Georgio.

'The bag with the circle is arsenic, a favourite of every assassin,' said Jacob.

'Why?' asked Darius, leaning over to stare at the bags with morbid fascination.

'Because it has no smell, taste or colour. The smallest dose will cause cramps, diarrhoea and vomiting. Given daily, it will cause confusion and, finally, paralysis of the lungs, then death. I know whom Chatillon intends you to target, and it may be difficult to access his household. So the bottle is a special oil I have produced for the task. It is essential that you wear gloves and take care not to get a spot of it on your skin. The oil is infused with monkshood—you may know it as aconite or wolfsbane in Greece,' he said, looking at Darius. 'It needs to be poured carefully, hence the small opening and stopper. Only a few drops into his gauntlets or boots will suffice to cause pain over a few days and then suffocation. You could put it on the hilt of a sword, but make sure a squire will not hand it to him.'

Jacob glanced at Darius' horrified, pale face, who swore he would wipe the hilt of every sword from now on.

Jacob carefully placed the items into a leather pouch and handed it to Georgio.

'Never let this out of your sight while you travel; keep it hidden. Once you stay somewhere for any length, bury it beneath your pavilion or in a nearby garden.'

Georgio saw the stern, serious expression on the physician's face and reassured him.

'Do not fear, Jacob. I will relate your instructions to Conn, and we'll follow them to the letter.' He took a red leather pouch of silver from his doublet and handed it to the physician, but Jacob smiled and waved his hand away.

'I need no payment. Chatillon has done me several favours over the years, and he and Edvard saved my cousin and his family in Rouen during the riots several years ago. I still owe him far more than I can ever repay.'

The sun was beginning to set as they rose to take their leave, but Jacob's manservant came in and whispered a few words to his master.

'It seems as if you may have been followed; a man has been watching the house for some time. We have to be constantly vigilant here. I may be wrong, for he may be watching me and who comes and goes to my house, but just in case, I will ensure that David lets you out at the end of the garden. He will lead you through the grounds of an old chapel and into Mark Lane, a wider and far less muddy thoroughfare,' he said, smiling.

'Sire, I think you may be right, for I thought I saw a dark figure following us on Seething Lane, but then he disappeared,' said Darius.

'Godspeed, and I hope I may soon meet you both again, for you have entertained me well and given me much to think on.'

It was a clear summer's night, and before long, they were back at the inn, where Georgio hid the leather pouch under a floorboard beneath the bed. The inn was full when they went downstairs for food, but the innkeeper found them a table. It was a few hours later, having demolished a hearty fish stew, that Darius noticed a dark, hooded figure in the shadows of the doorway. He could feel his eyes on them as he finally came in and walked to the small counter to demand a jug of wine. Darius nudged Georgio, who was wiping his mouth with the back of his hand and reaching for his wine.

'Look at his boots,' he whispered as the man, with his hood still up, walked with his wine to a table at the back. Georgio followed his gaze and saw the distinctive yellowish mud from Seething Lane that had been cleaned from their boots.

Georgio glanced back to where the man sat. It was darker there, and his hood was still up—unusual in the summer, but even with his face in the shade, he could see the man was staring at them. 'You may sleep on the floor before the door tonight, Darius, with your sword close to your hand,' he said grimly.

Chapter Seven

July 1101 – London

Surprisingly, Georgio had an uninterrupted night's sleep. Not so Darius, who had pulled his palliasse across the door and spent several hours listening to every creak in the gallery. When Georgio shook him awake and opened the shutters, he felt he had hardly closed his eyes.

They had a long ride ahead of them to Pevensey, so they went to find some food and drink before they set off. Georgio ordered the grooms to give the horses a good bran mash and some oats, as they opened the inn door to the smell of freshly baked bread. The innkeeper's wife came bustling in with platters of warm bread, cheese and cold meats that lit up the face of the young squire, and he tucked in as if he hadn't eaten for days. The innkeeper came over to hover as they were finishing.

'Will you be leaving to join the King today, Sire? They say he has an immense army waiting in the south.'

Georgio, his mouth full of food, nodded.

'Well, I suggest you take the road east along the river and not the road south over the bridge, as I know that large convoys

CHAPTER SEVEN

of victuals, fodder, wine and weapons are heading south for the King's camp. The road is narrow in places with several old bridges, which will slow them down. It will take you twice the time.'

He pulled up a stool and, dipping a finger in the ale, drew a quick map of the route on the wooden table.

'There's a horse ferry here at the Isle of Dogs—it is only a few coins and goes back and forth all day.'

It was some time before they took their leave and thanked him for his help. The large cobbled yard was empty, but Darius could see the grooms brushing down the horses before they tacked them up, hoping for a tip. They mounted the staircase to their room and immediately saw the door was ajar. Darius drew his long dagger and kicked it wide open, followed by Georgio. No one was there, but the room had been ransacked. Their saddlebags lay open on the floor, the contents and spare clothes scattered. The palliasse had been slit and searched, as had the stuffed mattress on the bed.

Georgio waved Darius to help him move the heavy bed, and he prised up the floorboards. To his relief, he saw that the leather pouch from Jacob was still there and untouched. He held it tight and then walked to the open window. The offshoot roof just below faced north, and moss had grown on the thatch. He could see the marks where someone had climbed up and slid back down to jump into the yard below. He turned back to Darius, who had sheathed his dagger.

'Pack our bags, Darius, and then summon the innkeeper and tell him what has happened.'

Later than expected, they left the inn and headed east for the horse ferry.

'It was a clever move—no one saw him come and go,'

commented Darius.

Georgio turned and raised a questioning eyebrow at his squire.

'Well, he was a lone man, so would not risk breaking into the room while we were there, so he watched and waited. I questioned the grooms; they saw nothing, and neither did the serving girls. He stole nothing, so he was purely trying to find out why we went to see Jacob,' explained Darius.

'What we need to know is who hired him? Somehow, he knew we were going to be in London. Only a few people had that information: Conn, John Mason, the pilot, the crew of the cog. None of these seemed viable. Maybe Conn can shine some light on the matter,' he murmured.

July 1101 – Pevensey

At that moment, Conn was entering the King's pavilion to inform the King and his council what he knew about Duke Robert's plans.

Henry welcomed Conn warmly, and the Horse Warrior bowed to the other nobles in the room. As he took the proffered seat, Anselm, Archbishop of Canterbury, and both Beaumont brothers, Richard de Clare and Robert Fitz Hamon, regarded him with interest and respect after the previous evening's revelations.

'So, what do you have to tell us, Malvais?' asked the King.

'I would imagine, Sire, with the numbers of informers I believe you already have in place in Robert's camp, you will know most of it,' commented Conn.

Henry smiled and acknowledged that with an inclination

of his head. 'Accurate numbers would help us.'

'Robert now has over two hundred ships in the harbour at Treport; more than your estimate, I believe. Most have already been converted for carrying large numbers of troops and horses, and all non-perishable goods have been loaded. He has an immense store of weapons, and thousands of men are camped in the fields around, ready to board when the order comes.'

Glances of concern were exchanged between the nobles, and Henry frowned.

'I am aware that my brother has a great deal of support,' he murmured.

'I was only in Rouen for a short time, but more nobles were arriving daily with large retinues; the castle and city of Rouen are bursting at the seams,' added Conn.

'Do you know when he will sail or where he intends to land?' demanded Henry Beaumont.

'From what I heard and saw, I would say it will be another week, maybe longer, before he leaves. Only a few trusted people know the destination of the invasion fleet; he keeps that very close to his chest, and I have heard discussions of everywhere from Hull to the Blackwater in Essex. Taking York was mentioned at one point.'

There were a few gasps at this new information.

'God's blood, Henry. Are we in the wrong place? Should we have stayed at Westminster and protected London and Winchester?' shouted a red-faced Robert Beaumont.

'I still think he'll aim for the southeast, my lord, as Count William of Mortain is very powerful and influential and already has a thousand troops, or more, at Pevensey Castle. He is advocating for a landing in the south.'

There was silence in the pavilion as they all considered the information.

'We have our fleet in the Channel and our horsemen and beacons on the coast. If Robert's fleet is sighted, we will know, and we should have time to deploy our forces as he must land, unload and deploy his,' declared Henry Beaumont.

'Duke Robert is aware of that, and as you know, he now has Flambard at his side, who has detailed all the defence measures you will use, Sire. Flambard now sits in on council meetings—not at the table, but he helps supervise the invasion fleet's logistics,' added Conn.

The Archbishop spluttered in rage and thumped his fist on the table. 'That treacherous worm. I told you to execute him, but you let him sit in that tower for too long, and he got away!'

'If it's any consolation, Sire, they use him, but he's still seen as untrustworthy and looked upon with contempt. Chatillon has him watched constantly.'

'And what of the Papal Envoy? I had counted him a friend. I know he is at Robert's court—what is his position? Which way is he leaning?' asked Henry.

Conn had expected this question and had discussed it with Piers.

'Chatillon is watching and waiting, then reporting back to Pope Paschal. The new pope is inexperienced in politics and diplomacy; he's a religious academic and is indecisive, so he is fence-sitting as his position is a difficult one. I hope you will not mind me saying this truthfully, Sire—in Europe, you are seen as an oath breaker, which means that Pope Paschal cannot openly support your cause. But he is satisfied with your promises to defend the Church in England, and the fact that you have Archbishop Anselm back at your side, reflects

CHAPTER SEVEN

well on you. Chatillon recently told Duke Robert that the Pope would not give him the Papal Banner of support and endorsement. This was a blow to the Duke and his supporters.'

Again, there was a gasp around the table as this was not known, and Conn saw the triumphant expression on Henry's face as he sat forward and placed both hands palm down on the table.

'So, in reality, the Pope is supporting neither myself nor my brother, which could work in our favour,' he said, looking at Anselm for confirmation. The Archbishop nodded sagely.

'Paschal is a tricky character, Sire. What Malvais says is true, but if anyone can control him, it will be Piers De Chatillon.'

Henry met the eyes of Malvais and Richard de Clare. All three of them knew that the Pope had given his support for the assassination of William Rufus, and it was in the Pope's interests to ensure that the truth of it never came out. It was also in Henry's interests, for he had initiated the assassination, so keeping Chatillon on his side was important.

'You must send a message to Chatillon and thank him for his continuing intervention with the Pope, Malvais.'

'I am afraid that Chatillon and I have parted ways. I have little or no contact with him anymore.'

Henry's face reflected his surprise at this news. 'You can tell me more of that later as now we appear to have a few weeks grace, so let us use that time effectively to train the men we have and raise more. Hugh of Chester is leaving in a few days to join us, bringing a large force to swell our ranks. Let us hope that he arrives soon.'

Conn's ears pricked up at that; this was the man he must assassinate, the man who must be killed at all costs, and he was determined to find out all he could from De Clare as they walked back to the training ground.

'Tell me of this Hugh of Chester. Will he bring cavalry? I have heard the name, but he was not at Westminster when I was there, and I know nothing of the man.'

Richard de Clare gave a harsh laugh and shook his head before replying.

'What can I say? Hugh d'Avranches, Earl of Chester, nicknamed Le Gros, because he is very fat, and The Wolf, after his ferocity against the Welsh. I dislike the man intensely. He's a glutton, a lecher, and a drunkard but, at the same time, a superb soldier and strategist. He rules most of northern Wales. His position at Chester is highly important as he keeps the Welsh forces at bay and seems to be constantly at war on the borders. He was a loyal supporter of William Rufus and is now the same for Henry. He's unpleasant and is now so fat he can hardly walk, but he is crucial to the holding of Wales.

'I own that I am surprised he is riding to join the King—he's so large that he rarely rides anywhere. I clashed with him during and after the rebellion against William Rufus in 1088. He was leading the forces of the King while my father and I were trying to hold Tonbridge. He made sure my family suffered for our role in the rebellion, and we were imprisoned for six months. My father's health never recovered from that, and he died shortly after. However, my brother-in-law, our friend Walter Tirrel, pleaded for me, and William Rufus pardoned me, much to Sir Hugh's disgust. I avoid the man as much as possible.'

CHAPTER SEVEN

July 1101 – Rouen

The sun was beginning to set and it was raining as Ranulf Flambard trotted into an inn, a league or so to the south of Rouen. He had taken a circuitous route, doubling back on himself several times and stopping in small copses of trees to watch the road behind. He knew that Chatillon had him watched and followed, but as he cantered over the bridge on the River l'Iton into the village of Evreux, he felt confident that no one was behind him.

A boy took his horse, and he entered the substantial hostelry. He had not been there before, but the person he was meeting had assured him of its comfort and the innkeeper's discretion. He entered the large taproom, which had half a dozen occupants—locals by the look of them—including a shepherd in his full-length smock with his dogs by the fire, and a travelling peddler in the corner with several baskets of his wares gathered around his feet.

The innkeeper greeted him and waved him back into the large hall. 'You are expected, my lord; the lady has booked two rooms, one to be used as a parlour, and my good lady will serve dinner there.'

Flambard nodded briefly in satisfaction and followed the man up the stairs. Once there, he knocked on the door, waved the man away and entered the room, closing the door tight behind him to keep out prying eyes.

Meanwhile, in the taproom, Jean Baptiste took off his colourful peddler's hat and ran his hands through his thick hair. He walked over to the counter and slid several small coins towards the innkeeper.

'Can I have a bowl of your finest stew, and, as I cannot go

further in this downpour, can I spend the night on the wooden settle or, better still, in your hay loft?' he asked with a smile.

Hearing the jingle of coins in the man's purse, the innkeeper leaned forward on the counter.

'For one or two more, you can have the little box room at the top of the stairs—it has a palliasse, which would be more comfortable.'

'That's very kind of you, sir, as I have to be up early and on my way to Rouen tomorrow. I hear the city is full to bursting, and some of those soldiers might want to buy some ribbons and gee-gaws for the girls in the town,' he said, grinning.

The innkeeper had played right into his hands, and Jean smiled, gave him the extra coins, and then sat back to enjoy his food and wine.

Jean Baptiste had originally worked as a happy-go-lucky young man in Paris for Ahmed, delivering messages and potions and collecting information. As he grew older, he became almost a ghost on the city's streets—he was a master of disguise and excelled in not being noticed. Since Ahmed moved out to live at Chatillon's chateau, Edvard, recognising the young man's value, had employed him full-time and used him in various cities and locations.

Jean had recognised Ranulf Flambard immediately, but his target was Agnes de Ribemont. He had followed and watched her and her servants for some time in Rouen since Duchess Sibylla had lost the baby. He quickly discovered that Agnes was a cunning and malicious woman, and he didn't doubt, after Flambard arrived, that they were planning to do somebody harm.

In the chamber upstairs, Agnes de Ribemont, Countess of Buckingham, smiled and waved Flambard to a seat beside a

CHAPTER SEVEN

small fire. It was a damp and misty evening outside.

'This is an unexpected pleasure, my lord, although the innkeeper will be surprised as the men I entertain here are usually much younger.'

Flambard gave a thin smile and took the chair proffered. Her eyes never left his face as she poured him a goblet of wine. Ranulf Flambard never arranged assignations such as this without good cause.

'So, my Lord Prince Bishop, what is so important that we meet and hide away like this rather than strolling in the castle grounds in Rouen?' she asked, leaning back and watching him warily.

She had known him for many years; he was a snake, the type to be held tightly behind its head so it couldn't strike. However, he could be a useful snake at times, and if possible, he could help her get Duke Robert back into her bed.

'For once, *I* need *your* help, my lady, in a matter that may benefit both of us,' he said and smiled.

She gave a short laugh, for she had seen that charm offensive used on so many people before, usually people of power. She was flattered and raised her goblet in a toast to him.

'Tell me more,' she whispered as the rain lashed against the window.

Chapter Eight

July 1101 – Pevensey

Conn was pleased to see Georgio and Darius ride into camp late that afternoon. However, when he heard their news, he was perplexed that they'd been followed, and he couldn't see any reason why or who would be behind. He tentatively accepted the leather pouch from Georgio.

'Is there a chance you have this wrong? Could Jacob be the one they were watching? The Church would no doubt like to find him handing out such packages. They would demand his death at the stake.'

'Possibly, but as nothing was taken from the room, we can't know that,' answered Georgio.

'No, he was following us, probably from the inn. Have you forgotten that I saw him silhouetted at the end of Seething Lane? He is a big man, almost as tall and broad as you, Sire. Also, he was cloaked and hooded in July yet the city had no rain, and it was warm,' added Darius.

'I will think on it, but be watchful because it sounds as if someone is interested in what we are about, and that could prove to be dangerous, especially now we have this pouch.'

CHAPTER EIGHT

'I'll get a spade,' said Darius, leaving them alone while Georgio explained each bag and bottle's contents and effects.

'Hugh of Chester will be here in several days, so we need to find a way to use one of these. He can't die immediately, as that will look like poison, so we need a gradual process; he must become ill first,' explained Conn.

'A small amount of arsenic on the rim of his drinking cup would do that. Then a few days later, a drop or two of the oil infused with monkshood in his gauntlets or boots,' suggested Georgio.

'We'll have to see what opportunities present themselves,' murmured Conn as Darius returned and, cutting out a square of turf, began to dig a hole near the pavilion wall.

Georgio checked that the bottle was still tightly stoppered and then placed the pouch in the hole. The soil and turf were returned, and Darius tamped it down before placing one of their shields to cover it.

They were just in time, as Richard de Clare arrived moments later to take Conn and Georgio hunting.

'The King wants to hunt. He has declared he is tired of saltmarsh lamb.'

Conn was pleased for the distraction, and it was a lively party that rode east towards the forested hills. They left Darius behind, as Conn had sent a messenger pigeon to Chatillon about the position of the English fleet the day before and now hoped for a reply. Darius wasn't disappointed as he had several hours of work seeing to their tack, which hadn't been cleaned since they left Normandy.

The sun was beginning to set outside, but it wasn't dark enough inside the pavilion to light a candle. Darius was pleased with his work—he had been industrious and had cleaned and polished all three heavier battle bridles until they shone. He hung them on the end of the sword stand and decided to take a well-earned rest until the others returned. He glanced at his thin palliasse on the floor and, without a second thought, went to lie on Georgio's more comfortable canvas camp bed. He had hardly closed his eyes when he heard a noise—someone had entered their pavilion. It had two rooms, as was usual for a lord, and Darius was in the sleeping area. He thought at first it may have been a messenger, but he knew they would have shouted a welcome, so he moved to the doorway and peered into the larger room at the front. Someone was bending over the saddlebags, so he leapt forward and shouted, drawing his dagger.

'What do you do in here?'

The man jumped, almost fell, and straightened as he stared at Darius in dismay. Then he arranged his features into a smile and gave a small jerky bow.

'I am Bernard, servant to Lord Richard de Clare. I have been helping your master until his squire arrived—I presume that is you.'

Darius reluctantly sheathed his dagger and nodded. 'What do you want?' he demanded.

'I was seeing if there was anything your master needed. I can always lay my hands on many useful items.'

Darius stepped back and regarded the small, smooth-faced man. He felt an instant wave of dislike and mistrust. 'I'll see to the needs of my masters from now on.'

The man bowed again, and then he was gone, leaving Darius staring at the untied and open flap on the saddlebags.

Not long afterwards, Conn and Georgio returned in high spirits. They had taken several bucks and a young boar and

CHAPTER EIGHT

listened, somewhat sceptically, to the tale of Bernard's visit.

'He has supplied us with everything we needed, although I admit I find him unctuous and too willing to please,' said Conn.

'Devious and suspicious were my thoughts—I'm sure he blatantly lied about why he was here,' spat Darius.

Georgio laughed. 'We see bogeymen everywhere since London—even in friends' servants.'

Darius shrugged, seeing they were not taking it seriously, but he vowed to keep an eye on Bernard.

The next day, Conn was with the council when an exhausted messenger galloped in from the north.

'My Lord King, I bear a message from the Earl of Chester,' he said, bowing and holding out a folded piece of vellum. The King broke the seal and read the contents before swearing long and loudly.

'God's wounds, the one man I need here with his forces is stalled at Oxford,' he stormed, flinging the vellum on the table for others to see.

'What is to do? I heard the shouting,' asked the Archbishop, rushing into the pavilion.

'Hugh d'Avranches has brought half his forces south as promised, but is now halted at Oxford. He has a wound on his thigh which has festered. The ride south has exacerbated this, and his physicians have told him he can ride no further for at least a week while they apply poultices, or he may lose the leg,' growled Henry, pacing back and forth in exasperation.

'By then, Robert's forces may have landed, and we'll be short of the thousand men he promised us!' exclaimed Robert Fitz Hamon.

It was deathly quiet in the tent while they considered the

impact of this disaster.

'I can ride there and march them south,' declared Henry Beaumont.

'No! I cannot spare you, Henry. I need you to check on the fleet tomorrow and try to raise more ships. Money is no object, for this could be the key to stopping my brother in the Channel by sinking his troop ships.'

'What of my brother, Robert? He could go,' suggested the Earl.

'As you know, I have sent Robert and his men to Pevensey. He is watching Mortain's forces to ensure he does not suddenly march north and take us by surprise.'

Conn stepped forward. 'I can go, Sire, and I am sure our friend De Clare will ride with me. With his permission, we'll take control of the Earl of Chester's forces and bring them south.'

Henry stared at Conn in surprise for a few moments, and then smiled.

'You would do this for me?'

'Of course, Sire. I came here to assist you in any way possible, and despite De Clare's antipathy to Sir Hugh, I am confident he will come with me,' he said, turning and grinning at Richard de Clare, who was shaking his head.

The King laughed at De Clare's sour expression.

'You will need to leave at dawn. Ride hard and persuade Hugh to hand over his command. I'll give you my seal to show you have my authority. March them south as soon as possible.'

Conn nodded. 'Five days at the most, Sire, which is all we'll need.'

Henry banged his fist on the table and then raised his goblet.

'They have butchered and are roasting the joints of boar.

Let us now drink and enjoy the evening. A toast: godspeed to Malvais and De Clare, for they may well be our saviours.'

July 1101 – outside Rouen

Agnes de Ribemont was intrigued by Flambard's request that she arrange this meeting, but years in the courts of Europe had taught her to wait for him to show his hand. She talked of court gossip and lightly flirted with him while they had dinner, and she waited for his opening gambit. He needed her, she was sure, but for what?

Finally, replete, he stretched out his legs before the fire and gave her a measured stare while she twirled the wine in her goblet.

'I've always admired you, the way you have single-mindedly taken everything you wanted and manipulated the men in your life, until now, of course,' he said.

'I will get him back; this is only a temporary aberration. He'll soon be bored of bedding her, and I have a plan,' she said bluntly, meeting his gaze.

'I don't doubt that you will, but it will take time. I may be able to help that process along. I think that between us, we have information that will allow us to manipulate him and his brother.'

Agnes sat forward, her eyes narrowed—now he had her interest.

'I need you to cast your mind back, to around twenty-three years ago. You were in the throes of your early love affair with Robert Curthose when he was estranged from his father, King William. The years must be memorable, for I believe you gave birth to William of Tortosa, the son you and Robert share, in 1079.'

Agnes felt a slight shiver of apprehension at those words, for she would kill anyone who threatened her son or his reputation. Flambard saw the eyes narrow and the lips thin, and he smiled.

'Do not fear. This is not about you or yours; I need your memories of those times. Memories of the men at Robert's side and the events that took place.'

'Gerberoi,' she murmured.

'Yes, the battle of Gerberoi, when Robert unbelievably defeated his father, King William, who was the greatest warrior in Europe.'

'Just tell me what you need to know,' she said impatiently.

'In the summer of 1078, Morvan de Malvais abruptly left King William's service to join Robert Curthose and the rebels to help him fight for the dukedom he thought should be his. You were in Caen at that time. Can you cast any light on why he did that?'

Agnes cast her mind back to those heady days when she and Robert were besotted with each other, and she had been one of Queen Matilda's ladies-in-waiting.

'Morvan stayed with Robert for years afterwards. I remember he went to Scotland with him to fight King Malcolm. Robert was back in his father's favour, as his mother, Queen Matilda, had interceded for him. However, I seem to remember a split in the Malvais family. The two brothers had always been very close, and then suddenly, he and Luc De Malvais were estranged. Morvan was a very angry young man in those days.'

'Angry at what? At the King or at what Luc De Malvais had

done? We know that Luc betrayed his wife and had a bastard son around that time—Conn Fitz Malvais—we saw him a week ago in Robert's court. Who was the mother, though? Is it possible it was one of Robert's sisters, because Belleme knows something we don't? That much was obvious in what he said in court,' asked Flambard. He leaned forward in his enthusiasm to the extent that he gave himself away, and she smiled slightly.

'Ah, I see. You hope Conn Fitz Malvais is Robert's nephew, albeit illegitimate, but just as importantly a grandchild of King William. That could be very useful.'

Flambard sat back, regretting his openness, and he shrugged, so she decided to play his game.

'Robert has four sisters. Adeliza is older than me, and I know little of her, though I believe she married well. Cecelia was given to the Church as a small child. She is at the Holy Trinity in Caen, so you can discount her. I remember Constance was close to her brother but was suddenly sent to Brittany to prepare for her marriage to Count Alan. She is dead now, and rumour has it that he poisoned her. Finally, there is Adela, who I always found too commanding and imperious. Adela married Stephen of Blois and made his life miserable—she still does. He is only away on crusade again because she gave him no choice. A frightening woman.'

'Coming from you, that is praise indeed,' he said, laughing, but she froze him with a cold glance.

'Luc De Malvais could have met any one of them during his many visits, but I own myself surprised that he strayed—he was besotted with his beautiful, blonde Saxon wife.'

They sat silently as he considered what she had told him.

'Why did he poison her? Constance,' he asked.

'I'm not sure, but my maid has been with me since I was a girl, and servants talk. We think they're invisible, but they know so much. She may remember something,' she said, trying to bring Constance to mind.

Suddenly, an image of Constance came to her—Constance riding out every day from the courtyard at Caen. She was exceptionally beautiful, with long waves of honey-golden hair and bright blue eyes. Suddenly, she sat up straight.

'Morvan! She rode out with Morvan de Malvais almost every day. They were friends, and he seemed to act like her bodyguard.'

Flambard smiled, and he reached over and took her long white fingers in his.

'I knew you would prove to be extremely useful. Now I have one person to see who might confirm this—Robert de Belleme. If it proves true, then we'll decide how to use it.'

He stood and stretched as if to go, but she got up from her chair and stood before him in one lithe movement. Her left hand slid up under his tunic onto his chest while her right hand moved between his legs and fondled his manhood. His breathing became faster as he looked down into those unusual violet eyes.

'I had heard you were of a good size down there, my lord, and I see it is true. We have these rooms to ourselves before we return to the circus in Rouen where eyes will be upon us. I also know you prefer more adventurous bed sport like me, so let us use this time to enjoy ourselves.'

Flambard rarely mixed business with pleasure, but it had been too long since he'd swived anyone, and she was still a very attractive woman—and very accomplished between the sheets, he'd been told. He smiled and pulled his tunic over his head while she dropped to her knees and untied his chausses and braies.

Agnes smiled as she fondled him and then used her tongue to excite him further. She glanced up and watched him close his eyes and throw his head back in pure pleasure. Another one was drawn into her web. A wasp to be sure, but she had him now and would use him.

Chapter Nine

July 1101 – Pevensey

Conn returned to his pavilion that evening, very pleased with how things were falling into place. He needed proximity to their target, and now he had arranged to get it.

Georgio, Darius and the men were still sitting outside the large tent with Gracchus and a few of the men, as it was a warm summer's night. A few skins of wine had been consumed, and they hailed him warmly. He informed them they would all be riding for Oxford early on the morrow.

'You may want to read this before you take that decision,' said Georgio, handing him a tightly rolled thin strip of vellum in a small wooden tube. Conn took it into the pavilion, lit a candle, and scrutinised the message from Edvard in Rouen. Georgio had followed him in and read it over his shoulder.

'They want us to go and find John Mason, the pilot, as soon as possible and make an offer to him to change sides and pilot Robert's ships. This could be crucial if he accepts the offer. He told us he lives in Rye and was going to his home for a week or two as he farms there, so he should still be there,' he said as he read it for a second time.

CHAPTER NINE

Georgio nodded. 'You need to go to Oxford, but I will ride out to Rye. Take Darius with you, as you'll likely need him for the task ahead. Squires are somewhat like servants and are often ignored or unseen. You're clear on what to use—the amounts of poison and its effects?'

'Yes, and I'm sure that Darius will keep me right—he seems to absorb information like a sponge,' he said, and they laughed.

At that moment, Darius entered and looked from one to the other, perplexed, as he had heard his name and knew they were talking about him.

'What is it?' he said in a resigned tone.

'Nothing bad. You're to ride to Oxford with Malvais. I'll ride in the opposite direction to somewhere on the coast called Rye.'

'It is one of the ports that supply ships to the King; I talked to the pilot on the cog when you were dozing. It is only six or seven leagues away, a day's ride, but who will you take with you, Sire?'

'Take Andreas. He is young but eager and a good swordsman. I do not anticipate any problems, but you must keep your destination secret. Most people will think you have ridden out at my side. I believe your friend, the slippery Bernard, will be with us, Darius. He is Richard de Clare's servant, so he'll not be here to watch you, Georgio,' added Conn, as he stretched out on his camp bed. Toast after toast in the King's pavilion had taken its toll, and he was soon asleep.

Darius, however, lay awake, full of anticipation. He knew their task was to assassinate someone, and he felt excitement, but then shuddered when he thought of what his mother would say if she knew. She was proud he had become the squire of a famous commander and had even accepted that her only son was going across the world to England, but she would be horrified that he was involved with nefarious practices such as poisoning someone. However, as the first rays of dawn hit the pavilion, he was the first up, preparing the tack and equipment they would need.

Georgio was up and dressing, but Conn took a few shakes before he swung his legs to the ground and held his head in his hands. Without being asked, Darius brought out the spade and retrieved the pouch. He had cleverly prepared a smaller drawstring bag for the bottle and the small bag of arsenic. He had no sooner replaced the pouch and stamped the turf back into place than De Clare was heard shouting for Malvais.

They emerged from the tent to find that Bernard had laid out quite a spread for Malvais and his men to break their fast. He stood back with a satisfied smirk as Darius glowered back at him, more determined than ever to watch this man and take his revenge on him in some way.

Richard noticed that Georgio was not eating. 'Are you not hungry? We have a long ride ahead of us.'

'I'm not coming, Sire. I have an errand somewhere closer, so I'll let you have your fill and enjoy any leftovers when you leave.'

Conn, concerned that Georgio might have said too much, jumped in. 'Leftovers? With Gracchus and the men here, if there *is* anything left, it will be stuffed in their doublets to take with them,' he said, laughing before adding, 'I've asked Georgio to take a good look at the castle at Pevensey—he has a lot of experience of sieges, and it may come to that.'

'Good idea,' said Richard as Bernard suddenly muttered in his master's ear and disappeared off through the camp.

Darius watched and, after a few moments, followed him. At

first, it looked like he was returning to his master's pavilion, weaving in and out of the tents as the large camp began to wake up and fires were kicked back into life. Then he disappeared. Darius whirled around, breaking into a run between the tents, jumping over men still sleeping. He looked in every direction, but there was no sign of the man. Reluctantly, he headed back. As he returned to the pavillion, he met Georgio's eyes, who had seen him follow the manservant, and he shook his head and shrugged. Not long afterwards, Bernard reappeared, apologising to Richard for a few items he had forgotten, but as he turned away to stuff them into his already bulging saddle bags, he looked straight at Darius, raised an eyebrow and smiled as if taunting him.

An hour later, Georgio and Andreas rode out of the camp and initially turned south for Pevensey. An hour later, they could see the first forces of Lord Robert Beaufort, who was maintaining a watch on the castle in the distance. They turned east into a low-lying area of wetland grazing meadows that took some care to cross, for many spots were brighter green, indicating areas that could suck the horses in. This slowed them down considerably, but Georgio found Andreas an interesting companion. He was mesmerised by this green wetland, for they had nothing like this in his homeland. Then he talked happily of his parents' farm in the hills and valleys above Constantinople, where they grew olives, bred horses and kept large herds of goats, producing what he proudly said was the best cheese in the area.

'What did they think of you becoming a Horse Warrior, Andreas? Did they not need you on the farm?' he asked.

'I was never a farmer. I always helped, but I spent hours gazing down at the city shimmering far below us. As a child,

I would run out to stand and wave at the Emperor's cavalry as they rode by. Then, when I was about seventeen, they stopped for water and to buy food, and I was training some of our horses in the paddock. Their captain came to watch and said they were looking for recruits. He could see I was a good rider. He spoke to my father, who shook his head initially, but could see the hope on my face. An hour later, I rode out with them, my mother's sobs following me. I can still hear them. But my father said we only have one chance, and we all have to choose the pathways in life that are the best for us, and I had chosen this.

I was happy in the Emperor's cavalry and visited the farm twice a year. Then Malvais came. I had never seen horses like his or such skill with a sword. From that day, I swear I was his disciple. When he fought that Pecheneg warrior in Nicomedia, I never doubted for a second that he would win. I train as many hours as possible to try and be as good as him.'

Georgio felt a warm rush of emotion sweep over him at this story and had to turn away for a second, pretending to look for the path ahead.

'Yes, Malvais has that effect on people. There are some men who are natural leaders, and he is one of them—and he is fearless. You met his father and uncle in Morlaix, and you can see where he gets it.

'I can see firm ground ahead; let us push on.'

Soon, they were back on the coastal track that led to the southeastern ports. The road was busy, and they were forced to slow to a walk, but they took the opportunity to talk to the traders and iron smelters from the Weald, who sold their wares in the ports. Soon, they could see Rye in the distance on a higher piece of land. The tower of the Norman church

CHAPTER NINE

overlooked the town, and they stopped a local who told them that John Mason had a large cottage overlooking the River Brede.

They arrived late afternoon. The cottage was easy to find. Mason was not home, but his wife directed them along the river. It was some distance to where the river split into shady, deeper ponds, and they found John, his braies tucked up high, knee-deep in the river, teaching his eldest son to tickle trout. Several fat fish in the basket on the bank showed their success. His face showed his surprise at seeing them as he straightened and bowed his head to Georgio.

'Is it another boat or ship you're after?' he asked, assuming they were returning to Rouen.

'Neither. Is there somewhere we can talk without fear of being overheard?' asked Georgio.

Looking thoughtfully at Georgio, John climbed out of the river and gave a hand to his son to pull him out before answering.

'Come back to the cottage. I will send Mary and the children to her parents' house in the town, and then we will be undisturbed. Trout for dinner, gentlemen,' he said, picking up the basket while his son stared at the impressive horses in awe.

Without hesitation, Andreas dismounted and, lifting the gangly youth, swept him into the saddle and handed him the reins. The boy's mouth dropped open, and then he turned and grinned at his father in delight as they headed back along the river. Georgio watched Andreas running and laughing alongside as the boy kicked the great horse into a trot.

The pilot had done well for himself; it was a large cottage with several rooms and outbuildings. He dropped to his haunches on the river bank below, brought out his knife and quickly cleaned the fish as Andreas tied the horses to the paddock fence over the water trough. Georgio commented on the lushness of the land and then listened to the pilot's plans for purchasing more meadows along the river for a small herd of Sussex cattle, which could also be used as draught oxen to plough the fields.

'We might be able to help you with that,' commented Georgio as the pilot led them into the cottage where his wife, a pretty dark-haired woman, had laid out refreshments.

The family left for the town sometime later, and only three of them sat around the table in the main room as dusk fell. John Mason lit several candles and placed the trout on a griddle over the fire before taking his seat and meeting Georgio's eyes.

'I'm sure you haven't ridden all this way to help me buy land and cattle, so what do you want of me?' His head slightly tilted as he sat back and regarded them.

Georgio knew from his previous dealings with the pilot that he was dealing with an astute and clever man—no one became a respected master pilot without years of hard work and training.

'What I am going to tell you cannot leave these four walls,' responded Georgio, reaching into his doublet, bringing out a soft red leather purse, and setting it on the table between them. It made a satisfying thud with the weight of the coin inside.

'This will be yours if you can help us. I have a similar purse for the money you might have to spend. This money and request come from the man who hired you in Rouen.'

'Chatillon,' whispered the pilot as he pulled the purse

towards him, untied the drawstring and gave a low whistle. 'Silver—true pure silver at that. Why do I feel that I might not live to spend these coins, for that much silver usually means high risk and danger?'

'There is an element of danger, that is true, but only if you speak of what we ask. If you share the information with a few trusted friends of yours who are also pilots, then no one else will ever know of your involvement, and as for us, we were never here. Are you prepared to listen and decide whether to take the risk?'

Outside the cottage, a tall, black-haired man had positioned himself below the top of the river bank so that only his head was showing above it. The cottage's windows were small, but the shutters were open on this summer's evening, and with the candles lit, he could see all three and hear the hum of conversation. A local in Rye had told him who the cottage belonged to, and now Black Brynn, as he was known, tried to work out why the Horse Warriors were there.

Inside, the pilot looked at the handsome, curly-haired Horse Warrior before him. He had an open face, and he had grown to like both of the Horse Warriors on the sailing from Rouen. Their exploits at such a young age had taken him aback, but he had instinctively trusted them. He nodded and put his hand on the purse of silver. Removing it from the table, he placed it inside his doublet.

'Tell me what you want me to do,' he said while serving the fish onto wooden trenchers and pushing a platter of fresh bread and butter towards them.

Outside, Black Brynn slowly raised himself and ran in a crouch to the corner of the cottage. Noticing the hunting dogs tied up in the paddock, he crept closer, not making a sound—he needed to hear what was said.

Inside, Georgio was explaining. 'The English fleet is on patrol in the Channel. We want to know if anyone will take money to change sides and fight for Duke Robert. I suggest you use a go-between so they don't know it comes from you. We also need four or five pilots who will go to Rouen almost immediately to guide the Duke's invasion fleet back so that it avoids the English fleet. They intend to land in Portsmouth, but few people know, and this must remain a secret on pain of death.'

Brynn heard the last part of the conversation with satisfaction, as Bernard's master had suspected they were spies for Duke Robert. He smiled at the thought of the silver this information would be worth, although, as usual, he would have to share it with Owen, who always took half despite him taking most of the risk. Suddenly, a thought occurred to him: why couldn't he take this information higher, to one of the Beaumont brothers, or even to the King himself? Surely, they needed to know that these Horse Warriors were their enemies. Being Welsh, he had no love for the Norman kings, but he needed their money. He nodded his head—he would go to the King.

He was so preoccupied with this thought that he took a step forward instead of back, and his leg connected with a large water pot and dipper. He fell forward with a crashing noise. The dogs began to bark, and shouts came from within as he scrambled to his feet and raced back up the track to where he had tied his horse in the trees. He drew his dagger as he ran. His sword was hooked on his saddle so it would not impede his movement—now, he regretted leaving it there as he heard the pounding of feet close behind him.

CHAPTER NINE

Andreas had been the first out of the door. He had seen the shape of the man in the light from the window, and he knew he couldn't be allowed to escape with such information. Fit, young and fast, he caught up with the man just as he put a foot in the stirrup. As Andreas grabbed the neck of his doublet and pulled him backwards, the man whirled and stabbed Andreas in the chest. The young Horse Warrior gasped and staggered back, bravely pulling the knife out and flinging it away. Georgio arrived seconds later and roared with rage as he saw Andreas fall to his knees, blood running through the fingers he had pressed against the wound.

'See to him!' he yelled to John Mason whilst facing the intruder, who had drawn his sword.

Brynn was afraid. He had seen the Horse Warrior training sessions, but he thought he knew their style of slashing their enemies from the saddle with their heavy, long blades. He had a shorter, wider sword for thrusting at close quarters in a shield wall to gut a man. So, he surged forward, stabbing with all his might at the Horse Warrior, but suddenly, he wasn't there. He heard the whoosh of the sword as it came down for his head, and flung himself to the left, but it hit his shoulder, the deadly sharp blade slicing through his leather doublet, cartilage and bone so that his left arm now hung useless.

He felt the sweat running into his eyes as he turned and faced his attacker, launching a flurry of blows at Georgio that were easily deflected.

'You followed us to London. Tell us who hired you, and I may let you live,' he shouted.

Brynn laughed as the blood was freely dripping from the fingers of his left hand, and he knew his death was near.

'All I want is a clean death. I am only small fry; I do not

know who hired us. Bernard is their errand boy, but we are only mercenaries,' he gasped. He lurched at Georgio again, hoping to catch him off guard, but Georgio sent the sword flying from his hand and then ran him through. He looked at him for a second as he pulled his sword out, wiped it clean on the man's braies, and then turned to the scene behind.

'How is he?' he asked, dropping to his knees beside Andreas, who was deathly white.

'I can send for the physician, but he is lung stabbed, and blood is now coming from his nose and mouth,' John said in a low voice.

Georgio felt his eyes fill with tears at the loss of this young Greek man who had such great hopes and had wanted to come with them for adventure. Andreas reached out and gripped Georgio's hand tightly.

'I did as Malvais asked. I followed Bernard last night. He met with a group of mercenaries at the edge of the camp. Tell Malvais, won't you, that I did as he asked,' he gasped.

'I will, Andreas. I swear I will tell him,' said Georgio, stroking the curly black hair from his friend's eyes, as with one choking and shuddering gasp, he was gone. Georgio, raising the young man's hand to his cheek in farewell, gave a cry of anger and loss that turned into a racking sob, before folding the young warrior's arms on his chest over his sword.

Chapter Ten

July 1101 – Oxford

It was late afternoon on a perfect summer's day, as Malvais, Richard de Clare, and his men rode towards Oxford. The weather had been kind, the ground firm, and they had made good time.

'I know nothing of Oxford, but by God, this is some of the richest farming country I have ever seen—every meadow full of fat sheep and cattle, and every strip waving with corn as far as the eye can see,' said Conn.

'Yes, it sits at the confluence of the Thames and Cherwell rivers, and the land here is well-watered and managed. Oxford was once the largest town after London and had a large population that needed feeding, but it was subject to several attacks and people left. Recently, the religious foundations have moved to the city's outskirts, and it's becoming quite a seat of learning for clerics. The Benedictines dominate the area; they have a lot of influence and have several abbeys and priories here.'

'Who controls the castle and city now?' asked Conn.

'You may have heard of Robert d'Oyley? He rode at Hastings

with your uncle. He was tasked with building the castle here. He improved the old Roman defences and built Saint George's Tower and a solid stone bridge over the Thames. His younger brother, Nigel d'Oyley, took over as castellan after his death.'

It seemed that De Clare would say more, but he stopped and was quiet for several moments before, with a sigh, he finally continued.

'I must admit, Malvais, I have few pleasant memories of Oxford. It was here in 1088 that William Rufus held his Royal Council after the failed rebellion. Hugh d'Avranches insisted that I be dragged forth in chains, that my lands be forfeit and I be imprisoned,' he explained with a slight shudder.

Conn reined his horse to stop and looked at his friend.

'De Clare, I'm sorry. I didn't realise what I'd done by insisting you come with me to Oxford. I was selfish, thinking of the good company and your wise council. Instead, I'm subjecting you to painful memories and a man you hate.'

Richard laughed it off. 'Do not fear, Malvais. It was a long time ago, and I learned to grow a thicker skin. Fortunately, my friends and family stood by me and fought for my reinstatement.'

'Do you find it difficult to justify your position now?' Conn asked. 'Duke Robert, the man you nearly gave your life for, is coming to invade again, but you are on the other side fighting for a different brother.'

Richard stared off across the wetlands for a while before answering.

'Loyalties shift for many reasons, Malvais. I'm climbing towards fifty, and your outlook on life changes with age. You think more about self-preservation and your family rather than being ruled by the emotions that pushed you to rebel when you were younger. I think with my head rather than my heart. But I still consider Robert a friend.'

They rode on and before long trotted over the stone bridge at Grand Pont into the city, which had spread and grown outside its original defences. The sprawl of streets was busy with dozens of stalls. Having a thousand men camped close outside the walls brought a brisk trade to the local merchants and traders. Despite the bustling streets, many people stopped and stared at the body of knights and armed men riding towards the castle, especially the Horse Warriors on their large steeds with their crossed swords on their backs.

The castellan, Nigel d'Oyley, and a woman Conn presumed was his wife, welcomed them warmly and promised to find them rooms in the nearest houses in the town, as Sir Hugh, Earl of Chester, and his entourage had taken all of the rooms in the castle. Their men were offered refreshments in the Great Hall while they followed Sir Nigel up to the solar.

There were many people in the solar as refreshments were brought. A stern, gaunt, older Benedictine sat in the window seat while two women and a young girl sat with their needlework.

'I thank you and your wife for your hospitality,' said De Clare and was surprised when laughter broke out.

'This is not my wife—this is Lady Adeline d'Ivry, eldest daughter of the late Sir Hugh Grandesmil. She's a family friend who has managed the house for me since my wife, Agnes, died. This is her younger sister, Rohese, who is visiting for a while.'

Conn's eyes immediately went to her face, and she gave him a slight smile before dropping her own as the castellan continued with the introductions.

'And this is Abbot Columbanus. He is here at Sir Hugh's request. You may have heard of him, for he is a great healer.'

The two men bowed to the assembled company.

'I presume you're here to see Sir Hugh?' asked the castellan as he waved them to seats.

'We carry the King's Great Seal, Sire. King Henry has ordered us to take Sir Hugh's men south, as he cannot do so, we believe,' explained De Clare, but he saw the castellan's concerned frown.

'Do you foresee a problem with that, Sir Nigel?'

'Do you know the Earl at all, my Lord De Clare?'

'Unfortunately, yes,' he said with a rueful smile. The castellan and the ladies laughed. The Benedictine frowned. 'Well, then, you know how difficult he can be. Part of the problem is that he has almost created an independent kingdom in Chester and the Welsh Marches. He does as he pleases, keeps the Welsh at bay, defeating and punishing them, and thinks of himself as Lord of the West. Don't get me wrong—I'm not questioning his loyalty, for he is the King's man as long as he can rule his territory with minimal interference.'

Malvais met the gaze and open face of the man opposite, and he instantly liked and trusted him, so he decided to be open with him.

'I appreciate your openness and honesty, Sir Nigel, but we're here for a purpose that is crucial for the King to be able to repulse this invasion. Henry desperately needs these forces, so I must do what I can to persuade Sir Hugh to either ride back with us or give us permission and his blessing to take his men south. Can you arrange for us to see him as soon as possible?' he asked.

CHAPTER TEN

'He rarely misses dinner; his servants carry him down in his chair as his appetite for food and wine is still prodigious. I'll introduce you tonight and arrange a private audience with him for noon tomorrow. He will not rise from his bed before then.'

Richard de Clare snorted in exasperation at the delay. 'Like a king indeed! Why do we have to wait to seek an audience with the Earl when we're here as the true King's envoys, on the King's business? We do not have time, and the King does not have time to wait on Sir Hugh's pleasure!' he exclaimed.

The Benedictine frowned and stepped forward at that point. 'You do not understand, my lord. Sir Hugh is not a well man, and I have given him a strong sleeping draught to still the opposing humors of his body, for they are not in balance. There is too much yellow bile, which isn't allowing the wound in his leg to heal as it should.'

Richard rolled his eyes at Conn but had no choice other than to subdue his frustration and follow Lady Adeline as she took them to the steward, who showed them their lodgings. Conn was pleasantly surprised at the size of the house and the rooms. Even his men had a large room to share on the ground floor, and there was ample stabling for the horses. Conn saw to Diablo himself as usual and sent Darius to unpack, while Richard stood leaning against the stall and watched.

'I resent that we're forced to kick our heels here—we *do not* need *any* delay.'

'We will no doubt leave tomorrow afternoon and make good time marching them back,' answered Conn, shouting for the boys to fill the water buckets.

'I love your eternal optimism, Malvais. I presume I must've been like that at your age,' he said with a cynical twist of his mouth.

Malvais laughed but then became serious. 'What did you make of the Benedictine?'

'I know him by reputation. He is a powerful prelate in the order They own large amounts of land and, of course, the abbey of Eynsham, where he's based. He is very influential among knights and lords for forty leagues around. He does have a reputation as a great healer, and the word 'miracle' has been murmured at times, which means that the lower orders travel for miles hoping he will lay his hand on their sweat-soaked brows.'

'Do I detect a touch of cynicism or even disbelief, De Clare?' asked Conn, assuming a suitably shocked expression.

Richard shook his head. 'I've as much faith in the Holy Trinity as the next man, but I baulk at these so-called healers who sell relics. There must be enough fragments of the Holy Cross across Europe to rebuild hundreds of them.'

'Blasphemy! Come, enough of this. Let us go and rest for an hour and then dress in our finery for tonight. I own I am now curious to meet this Sir Hugh, Le Gros.'

The Great Hall was full, and, as expected, they had been given seats at the top table on the left of Sir Nigel. At present, there was a gap on Sir Nigel's right as they awaited the arrival of Sir Hugh. The tables on the dais were shaped like a capital E, the middle leg being for the large joints and platters of meat that would be served. To Conn's left, sat Lady Adeline d'Ivry and her sister, Rohese de Courcy. Both bowed their heads in welcome to the guests as they were seated. Sir Richard being deep in conversation with their host gave Conn time to study Rohese.

CHAPTER TEN

Chatillon was right. She was very pretty, with dark green eyes and long, dark, curly hair, constrained by a wide, green silk band which matched her dress. He judged her to be only a year or so older than himself, but her bearing indicated she was certainly aware of her position as the wife of the King's Royal Steward, and of her heritage. Her family, the Grandesmils, were among the great Anglo-Norman families who came over with King William and fought at Hastings.

Suddenly, a horn sounded, and everyone's eyes went to the procession, which was making its way down the staircase led by Abbot Columbanus. Knowing that all eyes would be on him, Sir Hugh, in a large chair carried by several men, waved a regal hand in greeting. To De Clare's disgust, applause broke out amongst the Earl's retinue in the hall. He met Conn's eyes and shook his head as the Earl was placed at the table.

'We are delighted you can join us tonight, my Lord Earl, and may I introduce our guests, although I'm sure you know Lord Richard de Clare.'

The castellan had no chance to say more or to introduce Malvais, as Hugh d'Avranches launched into a violent, loud diatribe against De Clare, which shocked everyone on the dais and stopped conversation in the hall.

'That treacherous dog, De Clare? What is he doing at this table? He should be down there with the other dogs in the rushes scrabbling for bones. I take insult that you expect me to share a table with him, d'Oyley. I'm minded to return to my room because of the noisome smell of treachery and betrayal coming from the other end of this table.'

The Earl's face was bright red with anger as he thumped his fist on the table. There must have been a hundred in the hall, but the silence was complete. The Benedictine abbot on the other side of Sir Hugh put his hand on Hugh's forearm as he spoke quietly to him so that only the top table could hear his words.

'My Lord, those events are well in the past, and De Clare has proved himself to be a loyal and faithful follower of King Henry. Remember that Christ preaches forgiveness; it's one of the main tenets of Christianity. Soon, but hopefully not too soon, you will stand to answer for things you have done in your life, and I hope you will be able to count the forgiveness of former enemies amongst them.'

The mention of his own mortality, and the possibility of judgement coming sooner rather than later, seemed to affect the Earl, who sat back, his face becoming a lighter hue.

Abbot Columbanus stood and raised his hands. 'Now let us say grace.

'Bless this feast and thank the Lord for the bounty we will receive.'

After this, the conversation began again, the dinner returned to normal, and the entertainment began. Sir Hugh ignored the existence of the two guests and applied himself to piled platters of food. Conn could see why he was nicknamed Le Gros as roll after roll of fat sat under his chin, and he was almost as round as he was tall.

The musicians began to play, and Sir Nigel called for Rohese to sing, which she did with no false modesty, stepping down to join the harpist. She had a beautiful, lilting voice that matched the clear notes of the harp, and Conn applauded as loudly as any when she was asked to sing another. After that, the other musicians struck up, and there was dancing.

Conn leaned over to De Clare. 'Ask Adeline d'Ivry to dance.'

'What! She's a widow and would no doubt have to refuse.

CHAPTER TEN

I'd make a fool of myself, and I think I've had enough attention for one night,' he declared.

'You're still a handsome man—how could she refuse? Come, I will ask Rohese.'

'Ah, now we get to the nub of the matter. You are indeed your father's son, Malvais,' he said, chuckling.

To his surprise, Adeline immediately rose to her feet and let him lead her onto the floor, but it soon became clear that she felt sorry for him and was somewhat responsible as a hostess for what he had endured from Sir Hugh. However, he made the best of it, and soon they were laughing as he whirled her around in the dance. She was an attractive woman and hadn't danced since her husband's death.

Meanwhile, Conn had taken Rohese by the hand and engaged her in conversation during the dance.

'Rohese. Now I wonder where I may have heard the name before, my lady?' he asked, but she did not smile, and he presumed she had decided not to give herself away that easily.

'My husband, Sir Robert de Courcy, is in the King's camp. He is the King's Royal Steward and may have mentioned me.'

He tried a different tack. 'Like De Clare, you must find the current situation difficult. I believe the Grandesmil family have always fought for Duke Robert in the past.'

Her eyes flashed in anger at him, and as they turned around each other in the dance, she hissed at him, 'That is not the type of thing spoken of in the present climate, my Lord Horse Warrior, especially not in this company.'

With that, she pulled her hand away and left him standing alone, the other couples dancing around him. He had no choice but to look after her in surprise and then return to his seat, wondering if Chatillon had got this wrong. She could surely not be his messenger and contact. He had also been hoping for her help with his task, but now he was unsure what to do.

'So, the Malvais charm didn't work. Now that's a thing you rarely see,' said Richard, slapping him on the shoulder and laughing, whilst Rohese pointedly ignored Conn for the rest of the night.

Chapter Eleven

July 1101 – Oxford

Darius had enjoyed the evening at the castle; the drama, even at the expense of Sir Richard, had been exciting. Conn's attempt at flirtation had made him smile, for as De Clare had implied, Conn was rarely, if ever, rebuffed. But his triumph had been when they entered the Great Hall behind their masters. Darius had arranged for Gracchus to steal Bernard's velvet tunic, who then took it to the stables to rub the horses down. So Darius had stood behind his master in the Malvais livery while Bernard had fumed beside him in a plain, borrowed tunic.

These pleasant thoughts helped him to drift off to sleep, but a soft knock woke him. He scrambled up from his palliasse and opened the door. To his surprise, Rohese, the dark-haired, pretty woman from the castle, was there. Conn had woken immediately and swung his legs out of bed as she entered the room.

She turned on Darius. 'Get out! We will call you when we are finished.'

Conn smiled at her authoritative tone to his servant. 'Go

down to the kitchens. We may be some time,' he said, lighting the candles.

As the door closed behind his squire, she turned on him.

'What do you think you are about?' she snapped at him.

Conn, who had moved forward to greet her, stepped back as she moved forward.

'I was told you're fairly new to this, but tonight you nearly gave us both away with your pointed questions loud enough for everyone to hear. I have worked very hard to build up my cover and my network of informers over here, and I am not going to let your clumsy posturing ruin that.' Her voice resonated with emotion and anger.

To say he was taken aback was an understatement, the words clumsy and posturing ringing in his head, so he did the only thing he could in the circumstances—he pulled her tightly into his arms and kissed her. She pushed against his chest and fought at first, but then he felt her relax in his arms, and he reached up and untied her cloak, which dropped to the ground.

'I'm sorry I disappointed you, my lady, as that was not my intention. I was merely flirting with you, as Chatillon said that would be a good cover. He said that I should be suspected of being an admirer or, hopefully, a lover.' His fingers moved up into her thick, curling hair, and cradling her head, he kissed her again. When he let her go, her breath was coming in short gasps. He stepped back, waving her to a chair, and filled two goblets from the jug of wine left on the table. Then he looked down at her.

'Shall we begin again, Rohese?' he asked softly.

She nodded, her eyes travelling over him. He was naked except for a pair of fine linen braies that did nothing to hide his powerful thighs or the fact that he had obviously enjoyed kissing her. She was in a loveless marriage with an arrogant, ambitious man, and the thought of letting this man make love to her was exciting, but too much of a risk. A light flirtation to explain their meetings could be set up, but she could never have any other type of attachment to one of her contacts. Conn came and sat opposite her, the candlelight playing across his broad-muscled chest.

She raised her eyes to his, and he gave a rueful smile as if he knew what she was thinking.

'I'm a quick learner; I will follow your lead. I believe you've been told why I'm here and what I intend to do?'

She quickly nodded. 'It will be difficult as the Abbot Columbanus rarely leaves his side.'

'Why is that? I did not get the impression that the Earl is a godly man,' he said with a cynical twist of his lips.

'He has promised the Benedictine that he will give him a grant of land for their new abbey, but Columbanus is trying to persuade him to fund the building of the abbey as well, saying it will be dedicated to him. These have been just words, so the Abbot has drawn up the paperwork and pressures the Earl to sign it. But I've seen his eyes; he is amused and is playing with the Abbot, although he will grant him the land.'

Conn nodded in understanding. 'How do you know so much?'

'Did your friend, Piers, not tell you how good I am? I have informers amongst his servants. I have the head almoner at Eynsham Abbey at my feet, literally,' she said, laughing. 'I was given these pretty features, so I unashamedly use them, and of course, I was taught by the best,' she added.

'Chatillon,' whispered Conn, shaking his head. He knew

asking the next question was wrong but could not stop himself. 'So, was he your lover?'

She laughed at the expression on his face.

'Only once, when he recruited me—he knew how useful I could be. After that, I resisted him, for I could see how easily I might fall for him as he was exciting to be with. He laughed and said I was right to do so, as it would have led to complications. We are now firm friends.'

'I like your honesty, Rohese, and I admire your strength of character—I've watched the way women are drawn to him.'

'Your audience with Sir Hugh is at noon. I will try to help by drawing the Benedictine out of the chamber. My sister, Adeline, will help—she loathes and despises both of them. We might have to produce a servant who is near to death,' she said and then laughed and crossed herself for tempting fate.

'It will be a difficult meeting, for he hates De Clare,' said Conn.

'You also need to ensure that sleek turd, Bernard, is nowhere near the meeting. Leave it to me. I will dose his food so he cannot leave the privy tomorrow.'

Conn looked at her in surprise. 'We suspected he was watching us and spying for someone.'

'Oh, he is worse than that. Underneath that smiling countenance, he is devious, cunning and a killer. You know who his master was and who he is still working for?'

Conn frowned and shook his head.

'Ranulf Flambard. He has been on that man's payroll since he was sixteen and provides him with information from all quarters. He runs a dozen of his own informers or hired thugs. It was well known in court that he provided Flambard with other services, but Flambard was clever—he never openly acknowledged Bernard as his servant. He worked in the shadows but was often used as a cupbearer at the notorious parties held by William Rufus in his early years as king.'

'Does De Clare know this?' asked Conn, now thoroughly alarmed at what his friend might have shared with his servant.

'I doubt it. Bernard has the habit of making himself invisible and indispensable. I would warn him immediately. Now I must go. Let me know if you need help with your task tomorrow.'

He stood and walked her to the door, opening it for her. As he did, he noticed a sudden movement in the moonlit corridor and saw that a door, further along, was slightly ajar. He pulled her into his arms and kissed her deeply before indicating with his head that they might have an audience.

'That was a thank you. I understand your rules, no strings, and no involvement, but let us not deny ourselves all pleasure,' he whispered softly into her ear.

'I will join the King's court in a week or so. I look forward to seeing you there,' she said loudly. He smiled and kissed her fingers in farewell as he heard the door further along close, and a weary Darius came grumbling up the stairs.

July 1101 – Rouen

Edvard made his way to an inn on the outskirts of Rouen. It was quiet with only a few customers, but the pedlar, wearing his colourful hat, sat in the corner with his baskets of wares.

'Well met, Jean. I haven't seen you for an age. How is it with you, my friend?' he asked in a voice loud enough for the others to hear.

'Very well. I've almost sold all of my stock to the soldiers; love is indeed blossoming in Rouen,' he said, grinning.

Edvard laughed as he knew this was just one of his many disguises, and the sales of ribbons and satin posies were a bonus. He liked that Jean Baptiste was a master at this game and would stay in that role for the whole of his stay in Rouen. It allowed him to watch and listen, becoming almost invisible as one of the many street pedlars, both in the castle bailey and the city. They drank a few tankards of ale, talking of other things, and then both stood to leave. Once outside, the pedlar lounged at ease while Edvard led out his horse. Only then did he come forward, after the groom had gone, to stroke the horse's neck as Edvard mounted.

'That's a goodly horse you have. It must have cost a pretty penny. Where did you buy him?'

Edvard leant forward as if to answer him as Jean whispered, 'Flambard met Agnes de Ribemont at an inn south of Rouen. They had business together. I heard the odd name, and they mentioned Malvais, Gerberoi, and Belleme, but I heard little else as they had soft voices. Then he swived her, or maybe she swived him, for some goodly time. It was impressive,' he said, then laughed aloud at his joke and Edvard smiled. 'They left separately the next morning, an hour between them. They are taking care not to be seen together.'

Edvard nodded and slid a purse of silver into his hand. 'Stay in Rouen for a few days; I may need you again,' he said, and then he was gone, leaving the smiling pedlar to count his reward.

CHAPTER ELEVEN

It was rare that Lord Robert de Belleme, Earl of Shrewsbury, was surprised by anything, but later that afternoon, he certainly was when Ranulf Flambard was admitted to his chambers. He regarded the fugitive courtier with a wary eye and the habitual sneer that adorned his face.

'And to what do I owe this unexpected pleasure, Flambard?' he asked as he noticed Flambard seemed uncomfortable and uncertain—something that was rarely seen in this man, who had spent a decade behind the throne and almost ran England for William Rufus.

'I have some information, my Lord Earl, which, given your recent outspoken comments, you may find of interest.'

Belleme stared at the man he had always detested, and when he had made him stand long enough in silence, he waved him to a seat.

'I own that I was more than interested in your comments about the parentage of the Horse Warrior, Conn Fitz Malvais.'

Belleme steepled his fingers and regarded Flambard with hooded eyes. He saw his hatred of Morvan de Malvais as a personal vendetta. He aimed to damage the Malvais family in some way in revenge, but he did not want anyone else to interfere with the plans he had in place.

'Go on,' he said in a voice that Flambard did not find encouraging.

'There are two things: I met with Agnes, the Countess of Buckingham; if anyone would know about events surrounding the birth of Conn Fitz Malvais, it would be her. You may remember that she rarely left Robert's side in those days. She was in the heart of the family as a lady-in-waiting. Between us, Agnes and I think we know who both his mother and father were. However, there are some facts we still need. We don't have the evidence as yet, and we thought you may have the answers because you certainly have your suspicions as well.'

Belleme felt a rising wave of annoyance that Flambard had dug so deep, but he blamed himself for stirring the pot. He leaned forward and pinned Flambard with a penetrating stare.

'So, tell me what you think you know,' he said in a cold, cynical voice.

Flambard hesitated. If he were wrong, he would be ridiculed; if he was right, he could put himself and Agnes in danger. Finally, under Belleme's unwavering stare, he murmured, 'Morvan de Malvais is his father and…..'

Again, he hesitated, for this name could have him back in a cell if he were wrong. Duke Robert would never forgive him for blackening his sister's name and reputation.

'Spit it out, Flambard,' shouted Belleme, making him jump.

'We believe it may be Constance of Normandy,' he said in barely a whisper.

Again, there was silence as Belleme considered killing Flambard where he sat, and then he wondered what excuse he could give for doing so. Instead, he gave a harsh laugh to indicate the ridiculous nature of the information.

'Are you mad?' he asked.

This was not the response Flambard expected. Then, without warning, the chamber door opened, and his squire announced, 'The Papal Envoy, Piers De Chatillon, my lord.'

The name had a similar effect on both men as their eyes slid to the tall, dark, elegant figure who strolled into the room, smiling as he regarded the two men, who were equally shocked by his appearance. As expected, Belleme recovered his composure first as Chatillon spoke.

'Now, here's a sight I never thought to see: a dangerous lion sitting down, listening to a hyena. You are keeping dubious company, Belleme. I own I am astonished at you.'

'I find myself equally surprised twice today by two guests I did not expect. What makes me so popular now, I wonder?'

Chatillon laughed. 'Ah, but we are old friends, Belleme. We've worked successfully together so often for our shared interest in Robert, whereas the hyena here is always hungry, scavenging for what scraps he can find to serve his own interests. Where will his next meal come from? Could it be from the equally rapacious Countess of Buckingham?'

Chatillon moved closer to Flambard and put both hands on the arms of his chair. He leaned forward so that his face was close to his.

'I've heard on good authority that the meal you are planning at the moment is of such rich food that it could make you seriously ill—it could even poison your gut, Flambard. If I were you, I'd stick to plainer fare. Do we understand one another?'

Flambard could feel the sweat on his brow. He knew a threat when he heard one, and Chatillon never made threats lightly. He nodded, and Piers straightened up, but his black eyes never left Flambard's face.

'Now go! Belleme and I have more important things to discuss than your night in the bed of Agnes de Ribemont.'

A shaken Flambard got to his feet bowing to both men, and made for the door. He gave a nervous glance back into the room as he went to pull it closed and saw that Belleme was shaking with laughter.

Chatillon sat down in the chair recently vacated, and folding his hands in his lap, he stared at the Earl of Shrewsbury.

'It has to stop, Belleme, this hatred of Morvan de Malvais. It is beginning to turn you into a bitter man rather than an amusing cynic. if I can see that, then others will, too. When the likes of Flambard come looking to use someone as powerful as you to meet their ends, that should tell you something.'

For the first time, Chatillon saw something in Belleme's face that gave him hope, so he pushed the message home.

'Despite our occasional differences, I still call you a friend, Belleme. We have fought on the same side for many years and hopefully will do so for many more.'

Belleme looked across into Chatillon's face and nodded, and for the first time in years, it was with a rueful smile rather than a sneer. Because of that, Piers took a risk he would not normally take.

'I am going to do something I hope I will never regret, but Robert trusts you—he sees your loyalty, and so do I. It would do Robert no good to know of Conn's parentage. Knowing how much he loved Constance, it would sadden him, especially as it led to her murder. Conn is my protégé, as you know, and in some ways, you played into my hands with your accusations, for it led to a public split between us, which I wanted. Conn is now with Henry Beauclerc in Pevensey.'

Belleme nodded. 'I suspected as much when I heard that he had flown the coop, stealing a ship on the way.'

Chatillon smiled. 'I ensured the ship was returned, but Conn is working for us, Belleme; reporting back information and creating mayhem and obstacles where he can. At the moment, he's permanently removing an individual Henry desperately needs, one who could have hampered the invasion's success with his thousands of men.'

'Who? One of the Beaumont brothers? ' he whispered. 'I heartily dislike both of them.'

'I will tell you no more, for the less you know, the better. But you're astute, Belleme—when the news breaks, you'll know immediately who the target was.'

Standing, he placed a hand on Belleme's shoulder in comradeship before leaving him to consider everything that had been said.

For once, Belleme was flummoxed by Chatillon, as he had never known him to share confidences, and although honoured was by far too strong a word, he felt gratified that he had been trusted enough to hear them.

Back in his room, Flambard found that he had to down several cups of wine to calm himself. He felt his stomach knot when a knock came on the door, but it was only one of the Duke's messengers who handed him a sealed document. He recognised the papal seal at once, and for a while, he sat and stared at it on the table. He knew that Archbishop Anselm was working against him; he had learnt from friends in England that Anselm had written to Rome asking for papal support to punish him. Now the Pope had written directly to him. He sighed and tentatively broke the seal before rolling it out on the table and weighing it down to scan its contents. It was worse—far worse than he expected.

He had not only been dispossessed of his lands at the Pentecostal Court at St Albans, but he was no longer the Prince Bishop of Durham with all the power and wealth that entailed. Pope Paschal now demanded that Flambard return to England to answer the charges against him. If he did not do so, he would be defrocked by canonical sentence.

Flambard sat and stared at those words in shock. He had never thought for a moment that they would do this to him. He had lost everything, and now his ecclesiastical career was in jeopardy. If he was to have any future in the Church anywhere in Europe, his only hope was Anselm, the Archbishop of Canterbury,

He dropped his head in his hands, for that was impossible; Anselm was the architect of his destruction. He and King Henry were the very enemies Flambard was helping Duke Robert fight against and defeat, so he could see no way he could persuade Anselm to reverse his decision.

For an awful moment, he realised that he had chosen the wrong side. He should have stayed and used his skills. He could have thrown himself on King Henry's mercy. He could have shown him how to stop Duke Robert from taking the crown back.

Was it too late? He began to pace the room, desperately seeking a solution, any way out of this situation, but he could think of nothing. He stopped, beat his fists against the wall and let out an angry cry of despair.

Chapter Twelve

July 1101 – Oxford

It was still very early when Conn awoke. He lay thinking about the events of the previous day and night as the first fingers of dawn penetrated the shutters. His task from Chatillon was twofold: initially, he was to prevent the Earl's troops from reaching King Henry, and then, to remove the Earl so the Welsh would take advantage of the situation. Chatillon thought they would seize the opportunity while there was such a gap in ruling the borders. This would give Henry an additional problem, particularly if they attacked Chester, and especially if the great bastion of the North West fell to them.

The problem they had was how to get the poison into Sir Hugh's room. They had not expected him to be virtually chair-ridden, so a different method had to be employed for the first, gradual stage, which Jacob had recommended. It had to look as if Sir Hugh's illness had developed slowly, and then, finally, he would succumb to a larger dose of undetectable poison.

It was no good. He would have to take De Clare into his confidence. He had helped facilitate the assassination of William Rufus; surely, he would also help with this, as he hated Sir Hugh. At that point, Conn remembered he had other information to share with his friend, and he leapt out of bed, nudging Darius awake with his foot.

'Go to De Clare's room and tell him I need to see him on his own as soon as possible. Then find us some food and ale,' he ordered. A sleepy Darius pulled on his tunic.

Not long afterwards, Richard de Clare appeared with a grin. 'My man tells me you had a pleasant visitor last night.'

Conn slowly shook his head in annoyance. 'Does he spend his life with his nose stuck in the crack of a door watching and listening to the affairs of others?'

Richard could see that Conn was annoyed but was unsure why as he sank into the chair.

'Tell me, Richard, what do you know of him, this Bernard?'

'He came to me when my old manservant broke his leg. I believe he was a servant in the King's court. He's a very resourceful man,' he answered, perplexed.

'Oh, I don't doubt that he is, for he was taught by one of the best. He is Flambard's man and has been from a very young age. He's still working for him now and sending information back to him. If you looked into it more closely, I would lay silver that your servant breaking his leg was no accident. In a flash, there was Bernard at your side, obsequious and always willing to help.'

Richard's face darkened. he was shocked at how he had been duped, and then angry.

'I will kill him,' he said, getting to his feet.

Conn raised a hand. 'No, let us not be hasty; let us think it through,' he said as Darius arrived with a large tray of food and ale.

'I must have had half a dozen questions from your man,

Sire, and he tried to take the tray from me at one point. He's hovering outside.'

Conn met Richard's gaze and nodded, as Darius looked from one to the other, knowing something was afoot.

'Let us use this situation to our advantage and ensure we feed him the wrong information. However, I need him out of the way today. Can you find an errand for Bernard, which takes him away while we see Sir Hugh? Rohese offered to dose him, but that might take too long. Can you do that now, as I have something of more note to tell you?'

Richard nodded but then looked worried. 'More important than what you have already told me? Now you have me worried, and I wonder exactly what Flambard's game might be. A spy, certainly, in the heart of Henry's camp, but is it for information to impress Robert, or is he hoping to hear something to use against us?' he whispered.

'Flambard is certainly no friend of any of us or Chatillon, so I imagine it may be both,' replied Conn as Sir Richard opened the door.

'Ah, Bernard, you're here. Good. I need you to take a message to my sister in Banbury. We will not have time to call in and see her as I originally intended. I think I mentioned that she's great with child and cannot travel. Give me a moment, and I'll write and seal the note.'

'Sire, surely one of the men can do that? I'm sure I'll be of far more use at your side when you meet Sir Hugh today,' Bernard protested.

Richard drew himself to his full height and looked at Bernard in astonishment.

'You are expecting me to entrust a private matter, a personal family message, to one of the common soldiers? What would my sister think? You are also questioning my decision. What has come over you, Bernard?'

Standing at the door, Darius saw Bernard's shoulders slump as he became resigned to his fate. He apologised to his master, bowed repeatedly and followed Sir Richard to his room.

Darius closed the door as Conn stood gazing out of the window with a thoughtful expression.

'This is too difficult, Darius—to achieve what we had originally intended to do with the wine and the cup. We are leaving too much to chance and making it far too dangerous for you. Go to Lady Rohese—she knows what we are about to do. Speak privately with her and ask for her help or suggestions.'

Richard returned with a grin. 'I have never seen anyone looking as dejected as he rode out.'

'Do you even have a sister in Banbury?' asked Conn with a laugh.

'Yes, a much younger one, who I care for dearly. Now, tell me what you are about. I would lay silver it is something for Chatillon.'

Conn inclined his head. 'You are right. I intend to kill the Earl of Chester on his orders.'

Richard's mouth dropped open briefly, and then he shook his head in astonishment.

'I don't know why I feel taken aback at the enormity of that prospect. After all, we were all involved in the death of William Rufus; if we can kill a king, what chance does a mere Earl have? This must seem like small fry after that. How do you intend to do it, for the Benedictine rarely leaves his side?'

'Poison. We have two types with us: one slow and debilitating, which will be administered first, and then the second,

CHAPTER TWELVE

which should kill him within a day or so.'

Richard watched his young friend and admired how he could coldly discuss this death. He was indeed becoming the protégé Chatillon hoped for.

'I have no objection to you killing him as, honestly, I'd dance on his grave if I could, after the way he treated me and my family. I presume this has to do with the delay in troops reaching the King? If they reach him at all.'

'Yes. Given your new loyalty to Henry, do you have a problem with that, Richard?'

'No, I'm really only hedging my bets with Henry, as last time, Duke Robert let us down, abandoning us to our fate. He sacrificed us all by deciding not to sail and join us—including his uncle, Odo of Bayeux, who lost everything in England. If Robert comes this time and wins, then I will rejoice and join his ranks. If not, then I was at Henry's side. Do you need any help with this task today?'

'No, Richard, you have helped enough by removing our spy, and I have help from another quarter. I need you purely to be a witness that Sir Hugh was almost bedridden when we arrived, and we did everything we could to persuade him to relinquish control of his troops to us, which we both know he'll refuse. He may not physically lead them but he wants the glory of sending them into battle for the King.'

They were to meet Sir Hugh at noon, and as the hour approached, Conn worried that Darius had not returned. However, with only a short time to go, he appeared, bursting into the room, out of breath and with a basket on his arm.

'A present from Lady Rohese, baked by her own fair hands— and if I may say so, they are delicious, Sire,' he said, taking the cloth from the basket. They both peered in to see half a dozen small cakes, each covered with a sprinkling of honeyed almonds.

'Ah, Gastelet aux Armandes. My mother's favourite; a real taste of Normandy,' said Richard.

'Apparently, they are also Sir Hugh's. I've brought a wooden platter from the kitchen, and I will mark it ever so slightly on the rim, hardly noticeable. The two cakes close to that will be for Sir Hugh,' he said, making a small slit in the side of the cakes and, using the tip of his dagger, sprinkling a tiny pinch of arsenic into each.

He then liberally smeared honey from the top over the sides. He covered them with the patterned linen cloth and then stood back with an expression of pride, which made Conn smile.

'Well done, Darius. I swear you will be well rewarded for this. Now, do you have the bottle?'

Darius took the pouch from within his palliasse. The bottle was very small, hardly the length of his little finger, and fitted easily into the palm of his hand as he placed it into the pouch on his belt.

Richard watched all this, fascinated. 'How is that to work?' he asked.

'Darius will come with us, and having presented the cakes, he will retire unobtrusively to the back of the room where Sir Hugh's accoutrements are stored. In the worst-case scenario, Sir Hugh sends him out of the room, and we are left to find another way. If it works, Darius will deposit a few drops into each of the Earl's boots. As soon as he pulls his boots on, it will still be intense and strong enough to penetrate the skin of his feet. It is aconite—what you know as Wolfsbane,' explained Conn. 'Now we must go!'

CHAPTER TWELVE

A short time later, all three were apprehensive as they stood outside the door of Sir Hugh's chamber. Conn knocked, and Abbot Columbanus answered, bowed and ushered them in. He made to stop Darius, but Conn insisted, explaining the platter was a gift for the Earl.

Darius bowed to Sir Hugh, whipped off the cloth and placed the cakes on the table within reach of the Earl, who sat in his large carved chair.

Hugh d'Avranches regarded the small cakes with pleasure, but then turned a wary eye and sour expression on his guests.

'You wish to speak to me, I believe. Not that I want to hear any of the lies and falsehoods that will come from that man's mouth,' he said, pointing at De Clare.

Conn stepped forward. 'Sire, we carry the King's seal,' he said, taking it from his doublet and holding it high.

'King Henry trusts Richard de Clare and chose us to visit you. The King is aware of your injury but hopes you are recovered and will proceed south with all haste as soon as possible. The King needs you, Sire. If you cannot lead them, he asks us to take your troops south in your name.'

The Earl looked at them in patent disbelief, then turned to look at the Abbot, standing at his shoulder and gave a great guffaw of laughter.

'You honestly expect me to hand my troops to this proven traitor, so that he can turn on King Henry and allow his friend and true master, Duke Robert, to take the crown?'

'There are two of us appointed to this task, my Lord Earl, and I would trust De Clare with my life. Only Richard and I cared enough to wrap William Rufus's body in our cloaks and take him back to Winchester. Only De Clare stood vigil with his body all night in the cathedral. The other nobles were too busy thinking of themselves and their lands.'

The Earl looked surprised at how this upstart knight, this Horse Warrior, spoke to him.

'Who are you that I would believe you or let you take my troops?' he demanded.

'Malvais, my lord, Conn Fitz Malvais.'

The Earl looked taken aback by that, and looked at the Abbot, who raised his eyebrows but inclined his head to confirm it.

'Malvais!' exclaimed the Earl in surprise. 'I knew the Malvais family—Bretons who could ride like the very devil. They rode with us at Hastings. The father died on Senlac Hill, trapped under his horse. The young son was at the front, cutting down the Saxons as if they were corn.'

'That man was my father, Sire, Luc De Malvais. He still rides and fights like that, but mainly defending the borders of Brittany.'

'Well, you come from a good line,' he grudgingly admitted.

Conn felt the atmosphere change in the room, and blessed his family name as the Earl now seemed to be in a trance of memories from those days. Conn watched in satisfaction as the Earl absentmindedly popped another two cakes into his mouth. Now he prayed the Abbot would be summoned, as he was very close to Sir Hugh's shoulder and could be offered a cake meant for the Earl, who waved the two men to sit and asked the Abbot to pour the wine.

'These are delicious—my favourite. Try one if you wish,' he offered, as a knock came on the door.

The Lady Adeline appeared while Conn and Richard took a small cake each from the safe side of the platter and ate them.

'I apologise for disturbing you, but we urgently need the

Abbot's ministrations. One of our faithful servants has been stricken by the bloody flux and is crippled by painful cramps. There seems to be much of it in the town.'

'Not the plague, is it?' the Earl asked in concern.

'No, Sire, we don't think so, but the Abbot will know at once,' she answered, escorting the Abbot from the room.

'You need to know, Sire, that I was recently in Rouen. Duke Robert has hundreds of ships and thousands of men. If Robert lands on the south coast, without your help, the King cannot keep the crown, having an army of predominantly peasants

'I see you have inherited your father's traits—he too was direct and tenacious. I must admit I feel better today due to the ministrations of the Abbot, and I own I don't wish to miss the battle, so it is likely that I will travel with you and my men on the morrow. I will take Abbot Columbanus with me,' he said, eating the last two cakes on the plate.

Conn smiled. 'The King will be highly relieved, Sire,' he said as they stood to go. Darius came forward, picked up the empty platter and cloth, and opened the door for them.

'Did you succeed? I did not dare glance in your direction in case I gave anything away,' whispered De Clare to Darius as they descended the staircase.

'Yes, Sire. It was easier after the Benedictine left. Before then, I could feel his eyes on me constantly.'

That night, Rohese was woken by the sound of running feet and voices in the corridor, but she stayed in her bed. The next morning, she met an exhausted Adeline on the stairs.

'Is it Sir Hugh, Sister? He did not look at all well at dinner.'

'Yes, he seems to have succumbed to the bloody flux and is blaming the Benedictine for bringing it back on his clothes and hands. He is not an easy patient, and will certainly not be leaving today,' she said, rolling her eyes in horror.

Rohese smiled as she tripped down the stairs to take the message to Malvais. Their plan had worked. Sir Hugh and his troops would be going nowhere, and she admitted to herself that she was pleased the Horse Warrior would be here for a day or so longer.

Chapter Thirteen

July 17th 1101 – Rouen

After the arrival of the papal letter, Flambard was distraught. Things seemed hopeless; all of his plans were in ruins with no future in sight. But, on the third day, a message arrived for him from Agnes de Ribemont that they needed to meet.

The castle was in disarray with people rushing hither and thither, as the Duke's fleet was to sail the next day. Originally, Flambard's plans meant he hoped to pack his chests and not return to Normandy. He had hoped to find a way to build bridges in the English court, but the letter from Pope Paschal had destroyed that hope. His fortune confiscated, he now saw only a bleak future ahead as a low-level courtier, living at the favour and bounty of a duke or king who only tolerated him and could dismiss him at will.

Agnes had arranged to meet him by the large loop of the River Seine, and as Duke Robert and his entourage had already transferred to Sir Henry of Eu's castle at Le Treport, she thought there was little chance of them being seen. However, Chatillon and Edvard were still in residence in Rouen. Due to his difficult position as Papal Envoy, Chatillon had arranged to sail for England a few days after the invasion fleet. Hopefully, the Duke's camp would be established by then, and he may even have seized Winchester, so Piers knew he needed to be on hand to guide Robert.

Chatillon was sitting at leisure in the Duke's solar, wondering how his protégé was faring in Oxford with Sir Hugh, when Edvard arrived, an amused smile on his face.

'I have been informed by one of her servants that the Countess of Buckingham is meeting Flambard later this morning on the large loop of the river. As you know, we have been watching her for weeks.'

'As expected, Edvard. People are so predictable, are they not? I must be losing my touch, for they don't appear to have heeded my warnings. Perhaps I'm becoming too subtle or soft, Edvard. God forbid!'

Edvard laughed. 'I did tell you to slit his throat, and I knew you'd regret not doing so, for that leopard will definitely never change its spots.'

'I truly believe that Flambard is on the verge of despair after recent news, making him a desperate man and inclined to take risks. There is a thick copse of trees close to that loop in the river. Take my dark roan, for he will merge into those trees, and you can wait and watch them. When they look to be finishing their conversation, ride out into the thinner trees so they can only see a dark hooded figure watching them. Let us frighten them a little, Edvard, for we must take our pleasures where we will. I will see to the Countess, leave her to me,' he said with a thin smile, as Edvard bowed and went to do his bidding.

CHAPTER THIRTEEN

'You took your time!' snapped Agnes de Ribemont, as Flambard reined in by the river bank.

'I doubled back several times; I had to ensure that I wasn't followed. Chatillon knew all about our tryst at the inn. I swear that man can see through walls.'

Agnes paled at those words. One did not make an enemy out of Piers De Chatillon if one could avoid it, and he'd already warned her off. But she was desperate to get Robert back so she would take the risk.

'Let us make this brief and then go our separate ways,' she said.

'You have something for me, I believe,' said Flambard, constantly looking over his shoulder, although he had placed his squire at a distance who would warn him if anyone approached.

'Yes. A few days ago, I finally found and spoke at length with my old maidservant. She is not in good health, but God be praised, her memory was unimpaired. She remembers that summer well, for the scandal swept around the servants' quarters. Lady Constance was in love with Morvan de Malvais, and they openly rode out with each other almost every day. However, it came to the Queen's notice, and she refused to let her marry him, as King William had already arranged an alliance with Count Alan of Brittany. Constance was part of the plan to strengthen the ties between the two families. Constance refused and told her mother and her maid that she was with child. The Queen panicked and kept it from the King, as he would have killed Malvais with his bare hands. Constance was sent away in seclusion to Falaise to have the child. Morvan discovered this and rode out to join the rebels, causing him to break his oath to the King and create a rift with his brother. Constance married Count Alan, and my maid seemed to think the Queen smuggled the child away to a family in the north.'

Flambard gave a shout of joy, and standing up in the saddle, he punched the air, which made his horse whirl. He brought it under control and moved it so that his knee was touching Agnes de Ribemont. His hand slid up her thigh as he moved his face close to hers. She could see he was in buoyant spirits now.

'I knew I could depend on you, Agnes, and I look forward to continuing our liaison in every way, for we were right—Conn Fitz Malvais is the nephew of Duke Robert and King Henry, and, more importantly, the grandson of King William. You will demand an audience with Duke Robert because you fear for his life. You have unearthed a dark plot to replace him with Conn Fitz Malvais, and then we unleash the truth of his parentage. I will tell King Henry something similar: we only have their interests at heart as he threatens both of them. However, we must keep this quiet until we see our moment, for this is important enough to propel us back to where we should be, in a position of power, by the autumn.' He almost shouted the last part, and she grinned back at him.

'I will see you in England,' he said, moving his horse away as a dark figure emerged on the edge of the copse close by. He had obviously been watching them. Flambard went cold, and his heart sank.

'Fly Countess! Fly! I will ride straight for Le Treport,' he

CHAPTER THIRTEEN

shouted, whirling his horse around and galloping along the river bank, his squire racing after him.

Agnes cast a worried glance at the dark figure in the trees and kicked her horse into a canter.

The Earl of Buckingham had always had a large house on the edge of the town that backed onto the river. She clattered into the yard and, throwing the reins to the groom, shouted for her steward who came running.

'We're leaving! We sail for England, so find a boat to take us there in two days. We will travel with only a dozen chests, my maid, and two manservants. I will go to London, wait there and see how this invasion plays out,' she said, murmuring almost to herself. She put her foot on the step when he spoke.

'I will see all is done, my lady, but you have a visitor—he is in the garden,' said the steward, bowing and leaving her in the wide hall.

It could not be the dark figure from the trees, for she knew she had arrived ahead of him. She walked through the house into the garden and, standing in the doorway, shaded her eyes from the bright morning sun. At first, could see no sign of a visitor until a soft voice beside her made her jump, and she turned. Piers De Chatillon was sitting on the bench against the wall under the climbing rose that dripped with summer blooms. He was not in his papal regalia, which alarmed her, for this was clearly a private visit.

'Come and sit beside me, Agnes. I'd forgotten how lovely this spot could be in the summer.'

She found her mouth was suddenly dry as she did as he ordered.

'I'm somewhat puzzled, my dear Countess, not only by your new choice of companion, for I had thought you more discerning, but also by your change of heart. You told me that you loved our friend, Duke Robert.'

'I do,' she whispered.

'Yet, you not only kill his unborn child, you go on to plot against him with a man who would happily destroy him without a second thought. I can only presume that these are the actions of a woman scorned—a bitter woman, who wants revenge,' he said, turning his piercing gaze on her. For once, she had no answer.

'I told you recently that I would not let you see your next name day if you persisted in this vendetta against the Duchess Sibylla. Did you think that I did not mean that, Agnes? Did you think I would let you live purely because my friend once loved you and you share a son? I assure you, I do not have a sentimental bone in my body.'

His voice was ice cold, and she felt real fear, rather than apprehension, for the first time. He put his hand inside his black leather doublet, and she shrank back, thinking it was a dagger, as she had no doubt he would kill her. Instead, he brought out a small scroll and gave a thin smile.

'Surely, you don't think I would kill you here, Agnes. When have you ever known me to be so clumsy? Also, it is many years since I stooped to having the blood of my victims on my hands. I have so many other talented people to do that for me. However, I must admit the antipathy and dislike I feel for you could easily persuade me to slit your throat, and I know it would give me immense pleasure.'

Agnes was aware that her hands were beginning to shake, and she clasped them tightly together as he unrolled the small vellum scroll.

'You are no assassin, Agnes; you are careless and leave too

CHAPTER THIRTEEN

many trails for people to follow. This small scroll would ensure you are beheaded in the castle courtyard tomorrow if I wished, but I feel I like the thought of keeping that axe hovering over your head for a while yet. This is a signed confession from your young maidservant, Magdalena.'

Agnes could feel the sob rising from within her, but she could do nothing to prevent it.

'Edvard had an interesting conversation with her. Not only did she admit to administering and mixing the potion, on your orders, before lacing Lady Sibylla's food, but she also gave him details of where to find your old maidservant. Edvard found her as well. I know what information she gave you, but I'm afraid that she was very ill and, sadly, is no longer with us.'

Agnes found that she had a pain in her chest, and she began to gasp for breath.

'You killed her!' she cried out, but Chatillon laughed.

'Edvard may be just as ruthless as I, but he does not usually kill dying old women. No, the village priest was there and about to give the last rites, and Edvard asked for five minutes alone with her. You no doubt shared what she told you with Flambard. Am I right?' he asked and, hanging her head, she nodded.

'So, not content with destroying Robert's life, you are maliciously trying to destroy the life of a young knight. But this time, you got it wrong, Agnes. The baby that Constance bore was exposed to die on a hillside on the orders of Count Alan, who was consumed with rage and jealousy that Constance had given herself to Morvan. I can produce both the Count and the squire, now a grown man, who checked on the cold, blue body of the child the next morning. Conn Fitz Malvais is the bastard son of Luc De Malvais, who will, as you know, also take your head from your shoulders if I choose to tell him what you have been trying to do to his son.'

Agnes reached over and clutched at his hand, begging for her life, but Chatillon shook her off and placed the scroll back inside his doublet.

'You will cancel any plans you have to go to England. You will stay here, and you will send an urgent message to Flambard telling him you have discovered the story you gave him was untrue, much of it servant gossip. You now know for certain that the child Constance bore is dead. In a month or so, you will retire to your estate in Buckinghamshire to spend the rest of the year with your husband and legitimate son. I swear I *will* produce this document if I see you again in Robert's or Henry's court.'

At that, he stood and left without a backward glance at the sobbing and cowed woman on the garden bench.

There was a spring in his step as Chatillon returned to his chamber in the castle. Edvard awaited him with a message from Rohese in Oxford that simply read.

Task accomplished.

Chatillon smiled. The strands were coming together, and with Sir Hugh out of the picture, there was no way Henry had the forces to take on Robert, even if he called out the whole southern fyrd of England. Robert's hundreds of trained knights and their troops would cut his peasant army to pieces. Henry would have to negotiate; he had no choice but to compromise, hopefully without a spear being thrown or a sword taken from its scabbard.

'I think we both deserve a goblet of our best wine in my favourite Venetian glass for this, Edvard,' he said, settling into a chair while Edvard poured.

'And the Countess?'

'I want her dead, Edvard—not quite yet, but before next summer. I want it to be a long, debilitating illness—something painful that begins before Yuletide. I also need her wits to go so no one believes any wild ramblings she may come out with. She deserves to suffer for what she has done. What shall we use?'

Edvard looked thoughtful before replying. 'Water hemlock is the best for that. We know it affects the mind; we have used it before, and the tiniest drops in her food or wine regularly will suffice. Within a few months, her painful limbs will not obey her commands, and her mind will become a grey fog of jumbled thoughts.'

Chatillon smiled at the thought and raised the beautiful green Venetian goblet high in a toast.

July 17th 1101 – Le Treport

Duke Robert found an Englishman, and a missive from Chatillon, waiting for him as he entered Sir Henry of Eu's castle after inspecting his fleet. John Mason stepped forward and bowed to the Duke.

'I have brought a dozen English pilots with me, Sire. They will, of course, all have their quadrants, but we have also brought charts, which your captains are now copying. I have been instructed to guide your fleet south instead of north, then we will turn and sail west. By doing so, we will completely avoid the English fleet of fifty or so ships in the Channel. It will mean a longer sailing time, but they'll not know we are even there, as you will not be in sight until we sail from the south into Portsmouth.'

Robert's face lit with a smile, as did the faces of those nobles around him, as he opened the message from Chatillon.

> *Use the pilots wisely: they know what they are about and have been well paid.*

The message was not signed, as usual, and Robert held it to a nearby candle flame.

'Chatillon. Only he could manage to turn the loyalties of the sailors from the English fleet,' murmured Belleme with a smile.

Robert smiled with pleasure while thanking John Mason and sending him off with Count William de Mortain to scatter the pilots across the grouped ships of the fleet.

Behind them stood Flambard, who had ridden in an hour before. His fists were clenched in anger as he heard the conversation because, for weeks, he had been mentioning the possibility of this, but the Papal Envoy had dismissed the idea as impractical. Now, Chatillon had put that very plan in place. He burned with hatred for the man who was always several steps ahead of him. A messenger touched his arm, and they stepped over to one side. He read the message from Agnes with mounting fury.

CHAPTER THIRTEEN

Do not use what I gave you for I have found that part of it is untrue, just gossip amongst the servants. I now know that her child died; in fact, he was murdered by Count Alan of Brittany.

He crumpled the message and flung it back at the servant who waited.

'No reply,' he growled and returned to the group around the Duke. The future looked just as bleak as before, and he had to find a way to somehow take back the initiative.

Early the next morning, crowds gathered all along the harbour and coast around Le Treport to watch the fleet sail out—over two hundred ships, nearly three hundred knights and their men. It was a considerable undertaking and certainly an impressive sight. The whole sea seemed full of ships as far as the eye could see as their sails billowed, and they set sail to invade England. Robert stood on the bow of his flagship, his closest, most trusted nobles gathered around him.

'We go to take back the crown of England, Sire. In our minds, you are already the King, and I will place the crown on your head myself!' shouted Mortain, to great cheers from the packed boat, that echoed from the closest following ships.

'Thousands more loyal men wait for us in England, Sire. The Oathbreaker will stand no chance!' shouted Henry of Eu.

It was a clear summer morning. Chatillon and Edvard had crossed the River Seine and ridden north to the coast. They now reined in, high on a bluff, to watch the fleet sail past Rouen before it turned west for England.

'It fair takes the breath away, Sire, and I'm not easily moved. It will take nearly all day for them to leave Le Treport, but surely Duke Robert must succeed this time with such a force,' declared Edvard, his eyes fixed on the multitude of ships approaching and turning.

'One would think so, and we have done everything in our power to increase his odds. Now it is all up to him and the nobles at his side. However, as we know to our cost, Edvard, there is often a slip between cup and lip.'

Chapter Fourteen

July 1101 – Rickney, north of Pevensey

Conn and Richard had been kept waiting in Oxford for a further two nights as Sir Hugh's health wavered. On day two, he appeared to recover. Although pale and sweating, he had kept to his room, admitting no one except Abbot Columbanus and Lady Adeline.

Early on the third day, the castellan, Sir Nigel, had strolled with them and the Lady Rohese in the gardens. He brought what he presumed would be unwelcome news to them.

'Sir Hugh is leaving; he's decided to travel back north. The Abbot has convinced him to pray and have his confession heard in the religious foundation of St Werbergh in Chester. Only then will the flux clear, and he can lead his troops south in triumph.'

For the sake of the castellan, Conn had shaken his head in frustration. 'I told him that time was of the essence and how Henry needs those troops now! He is putting his pride and wishes before the defence of his king and country!'

'I would like to be in the room when you tell him that. Honestly, I'm not sure he knows what he's doing—he is dosed with so many tonics and potions. You have done your best, both of you, but he is a very stubborn man, and if God wills, he may recover and still march south,' Sir Nigel responded.

'You know what this is. The Abbot sees how ill he is and wants him back in Chester to sign the land grants and leave a legacy to build the abbey,' Rohese whispered.

Sir Nigel had given a wry smile and nodded. 'I think you are right, but it is out of our hands; Abbot Columbanus has taken firm control.'

'When we left, Duke Robert's fleet was almost ready to sail. By my reckoning, we have only days left at the most. It will be too late for Sir Hugh's troops, but we must take our leave of you and return to lead our men. We thank you for your hospitality,' Conn had said, bowing.

The castellan understood, swore he would stand witness to their attempts to get Sir Hugh to relinquish his troops, and said farewell. Rohese had let Conn hold her hand far longer than was normal as she whispered, 'As soon as I have further news of him, I'll let you know. I have notified Chatillon that you succeeded.'

Conn had smiled, kissed her fingers and bade her farewell.

As they rode south, Bernard, back at Sir Richard's side, had made several ribald comments to Darius about Conn's affair with the lady, which Darius had ignored. Conn was pleased with how things had gone, and Richard was happy that his nemesis, Sir Hugh, was not long for this world.

CHAPTER FOURTEEN

Two days later, they rode back into Henry's camp at Rickney. Darius saw to the horses while they made their way to their pavilion, carrying their saddlebags. Georgio arrived soon afterwards. Conn knew something was seriously amiss when he saw his friend's face. Georgio was pale and drawn with dark shadows under his eyes.

'What has happened? Tell me!' he exclaimed, taking him by the shoulders.

Georgio related the events at Rye and the death of Andreas, the young Horse Warrior. Conn closed his eyes for several moments, pulled Georgio into a bear hug, and held him before releasing and holding him at arm's length. He looked into his face.

'I know you will have done everything possible to save him. You say he followed Bernard at some point?'

'Yes, he discovered that the man who followed us in London was one of the Welsh mercenaries, and he saw Bernard paying him. I found and confronted their leader, Owen and told him his man was dead. At first, there was surprise and shock on his face, but then he shrugged and denied any involvement. He said Black Brynn was a loner who picked his own jobs if they paid well. I could do or say little more, for I had no reason to explain why we were in Rye, and that also meant that I couldn't take it any higher—I heard that Robert Beaumont had hired them. We had to bury Andreas in the churchyard in Rye; we couldn't take the risk of bringing him back here; there would be too much explaining to do. I paid for several masses to be said for his soul.'

Conn was sad for the young man, and he nodded in understanding to reassure Georgio that he had done the right thing.

'We know who is behind this and need to warn Chatillon. We know Bernard hired Brynn, and he, in turn, is still employed by Flambard. Now, Darius, I need you to find Richard and get him to bring Bernard here with him. We have proof he is working for Flambard and Duke Robert, and that gives us every excuse to slit his throat in revenge for Andreas. I'll go and break the news of the young man's death to the men.'

Darius returned with Richard de Clare, but Bernard was nowhere to be found; his belongings and horse were gone. Conn swore loudly.

'Owen or one of his men got to him first. One day, we will catch up with him, and I will make him pay, I swear. Meanwhile, I will go and confront Owen and find out what he knows and who he is working for. De Clare, come with me. you have had dealings with the Welsh.'

'I'm coming as well!' exclaimed Georgio, but Conn stopped and placed a hand on his arm.

'Do you think that is a good idea? I can see that the hurt of Andreas' death is still very near the surface, Georgio.'

'He died in my arms, Conn, only because these Welsh mercenaries were paid to follow and possibly kill us. I owe it to him to be there when you confront him.'

The Welsh mercenaries had built their camp and horse lines northwest of the main camp. They kept themselves to themselves. Conn had seen a group of them watching the Horse Warriors train on horseback at the paddock, but they had never taken part. Therefore, he had had no reason to give them a second thought. However, with lands in Wales, De Clare was a mine of information.

'I was surprised to see them down here with Henry as they

CHAPTER FOURTEEN

hate the Normans. This means they must be getting paid a considerable amount of silver.'

'Henry's not short of money, De Clare; he has the Treasury at his disposal, and, due to Flambard's management, the chests in Winchester are overflowing with silver. What of their leader, Owen? Do you know anything about him?'

'He has a hard and ruthless reputation like most Welsh clansmen—they are born with a sword in their hands. Owen had it tougher than most, for he is the bastard half-brother of Gruffad ap Cynan, the man they call 'The King' in the north of Wales. They both spent several years languishing in the dungeons of Sir Hugh, but they escaped. For some reason, a falling out between them led to a feud, so Owen became a sell-sword. I believe he has forty or so men with him, supposedly to fight for King Henry, but he has no scruples about taking money from the likes of Bernard.'

Conn frowned. 'So, you're saying this is in no way personal; they are just earning their silver where they can.'

'Yes. You may not like that, but as you should certainly know, that is what mercenaries do. They rarely invest themselves in a cause. I will agree to come with you, as he knows who I am and may likely not cause trouble if I am there.'

The Welshmen were preparing their evening meal when they arrived at the camp, and several fires had plump grouse or skinned rabbits already on spits. Owen was sitting on one of the large logs they had dragged around the fires, and with his dagger, he was whittling a stick to thread another rabbit onto. He glanced up at them as he saw their approach, but then looked down again. He made no move to welcome them or to ask their business.

Conn stood an arm's length away. De Clare and Georgio

were close behind him.

'I am aware, Owen, that Georgio told you your man, Black Brynn, was killed, but I want to know why he was following Horse Warriors who were on the King's business?' asked Conn as the man glanced up again.

'Ah, but was it on the King's business, Malvais? Yes, I know exactly who you are, and I am not looking for trouble between us, but that toad, Bernard, seemed to think it was *not* the King's business,' he declared while continuing to whittle the stick with his dagger.

Conn gave a harsh, short laugh and sneered, a gesture of contempt, which got Owen's attention as he put down the stick but kept his dagger in his hand.

'You are telling me that you had no idea who Bernard was or who he is working for, yet De Clare tells me the Welsh are supposed to be clever and cunning.'

Owen stood up, his dark eyes narrowed. He was not tall, but he was thickset, broad and solid.

'I simply took his generous purse; we are not concerned with the arguments of kings and dukes,' he growled.

'Yet, you take King Henry's silver whilst you are working for the spies against him. I wonder what the King or Robert Beaumont will think when they hear that. Bernard was Flambard's man and sent all the information he gathered from you and others back to Normandy. We have ample proof of that, and it would take seconds to convince King Henry and the Beaumont brothers that you are turncoats working for Duke Robert,' said Conn in an accusing tone.

At that point, Georgio could no longer stay quiet and stepped forward on Conn's left.

'I believe you are perched here on the outskirts of the camp

CHAPTER FOURTEEN

so that you can join the Duke's army as soon as it lands. Opportunists, robbers and cold-hearted killers are what you are. Our friend, De Clare, tells us that even your own family will not have you,' he spat at the Welshman.

Richard placed a hand on Georgio's arm, gripping it, warning him that he was going too far, but he shook it off. Conn raised a hand to quieten his friend, and Georgio reluctantly stepped back just as Owen attacked.

Conn was already waiting for him as he had seen the man's muscles tense at Georgio's words, and in turn, he flung himself at Owen's upper body, shoulder-charging him while grabbing the wrist with the knife. Conn was hoping to use the log behind the Welshman's knees, and it worked as he went backwards with Conn on top, pinning him down as he wrested the knife from his hand and held it at Owen's throat. The other Welsh mercenaries sprang to their feet, drawing their weapons, but De Clare raised a hand to keep them at bay.

'It is their quarrel, not ours; let them fight it out,' he ordered.

Conn now straddled the Welsh leader, the knife still at his throat.

'One of your men killed one of mine, a young man from Greece, who was only just beginning to learn our trade. In revenge, Black Brynn was killed, and his body was dumped in a cesspit, for he deserved no better. I will track and find Bernard, and he'll pay for his actions. As for you, stay away from me and my men, or I swear you'll join him.'

With that, he flung the leader's dagger into the trees, stood and, with a slight smile at a worried De Clare, the three of them left without a backward glance.

Two of his men pulled Owen to his feet. To their surprise,

he laughed. 'A worthy opponent indeed, who cleverly caught me at a disadvantage. But it will be a different story if we meet again, especially in the heart of battle, for those Horse Warriors are marked men. Marked men for us all, do you hear me?'

A resounding cheer of, 'Owen! Owen!' echoed over the trees as they raised their daggers and swords and stamped their feet.

It was a long time before Conn slept that night, so many images from the past week in Oxford kept coming to him. Then, there was the face of young Andreas, full of enthusiasm as he rode in the mock battles in Constantinople, often ending on the ground. Still, the young Horse Warrior was tenacious. Laughing, he would repeatedly throw himself back into the saddle, determined to be one of them and earn their respect. Now, he was gone because of Bernard.

Finally, he drifted off but was roughly shaken awake by Georgio.

'You were shouting loud enough for the camp to hear. You were shouting her name repeatedly. It is a while since you had those nightmares, not since we left Anatolia.'

Conn put his hand to his cheeks, and he felt the tears. He had been dreaming of Marietta, running towards her to stop the blade that would pierce her chest, but he couldn't get to her in time, and the blood bubbled from her lips as he held her. He sat up and wiped his face on his linen shirt.

'It must have been the death of Andreas that triggered it. Such a waste—such an awful pointless loss of a young life, just as her death was,' he said, almost apologetically.

Georgio sat on the camp bed with him, put a hand on his friend's shoulder, and shook his head in sympathy.

'I know. I couldn't stop the tears as I cradled Andreas while he died, but his last words were to send a message to you, to make sure you knew that he had done as you asked. You were everything he wanted to be, Conn,' he whispered as he stood for a few moments and then returned to his bed.

Conn stared bleakly ahead as the pavilion wall began to lighten with the first rays of dawn. He wondered if he would ever live up to that reputation, to their faith in him, for Belleme was right in one way: people did die around him. When Chatillon's wife, Isabella, was taken, the Papal Assassin, raging at his loss, swore that he was cursed, that the women he loved were lost or died because of him. He had now chosen the same path, to be at Chatillon's side, but he needed to do more to ensure his friends and those he loved were safe.

July 20th 1101 – Portsmouth

Duke Robert's fleet landed totally unopposed on the south coast of England. The pilots had excelled in bringing his fleet from the south to glide out of the early morning mists through the narrow entrance to the wide, natural harbour of Portsmouth. Robert jumped into the shallow water and strode up the beach, where he was greeted, as if he was king already, by the loyal nobles, who had been informed at the last minute, where and when he was going to land. Nearly thirty leagues to the east, Henry had no idea his brother was on English soil as Robert's ships docked at the wharves and began unloading thousands of men and horses.

His numbers were swelled hourly by more men arriving to support the rightful King of England, having been persuaded by Robert's staunch allies, such as young William de Warrene, to break their promise of fealty to King Henry. Even Belleme was seen to give a triumphant smile as he helped Mortain set up camp, setting sentries and dispatching outriders to spread the word.

Finally, one of the local fishermen who had fled east at the sight of such a huge fleet emerging from the south, landed in Littlehampton, and told everyone of the great sight he had seen. Within an hour, a message was sent to the nearest sheriff, who declared it impossible—it must be an exaggeration. He decided to go and see for himself when he had broken his fast before sending any foolish messages to the King.

A few hours later, shocked at the hundreds of ships that filled the horizon as far as he could see, he sat on his horse and watched in disbelief as dozens of ships continued to sail into the harbour, in turn, to unload their cargoes of men and weapons. He sent a messenger galloping east to find King Henry and his army, for Duke Robert had landed with a huge force.

Chapter Fifteen

21 July 1101 – Rickney, north of Pevensey

Henry was in good spirits on this bright morning, as they had been hunting since dawn. De Clare and Malvais had joined the group and it had been fast and furious through the forest, chasing a stag and his hinds that the dogs had lifted from their early morning grazing. The dogs had finally held the stag at bay, and Henry had, again, shown his skill with a bow. Conn found himself beside the King as they rode back to the camp.

'That brought the archery competition and the events that followed it to mind. Do you ever think on it?' he quietly asked of Conn.

'No, my Lord King. I was lucky to have Chatillon as my mentor for several years before we parted ways. He has a very straightforward view on such things: that was then, this is now; no ruminating on past events ever and no regrets; leave everything in locked boxes in your mind.'

'Ah, I see what you are saying, Malvais—I should never seek to open *that* box.'

Conn inclined his head while shifting the subject slightly; this was not a topic for discussion in the open, with others around them straining to hear what was said.

'Hunting has always been your forte, Sire. You may not have been a warrior like Robert, but while your brothers were away, you spent valuable time hunting with your father. I was told he was also an excellent shot. You have inherited his skill, wisdom, foresight, and ambition. If I were you, I would think more on that.'

The King laughed aloud, and many heads turned to wonder at how the Horse Warrior was amusing him.

'You are becoming quite a courtier, Malvais; Chatillon taught you well. I hear that you had a falling out with my Welsh mercenaries. Should I be concerned?' asked Henry, turning his gaze on him.

Conn smiled. Henry had also learned from Chatillon and had informers all over the camp.

'Use them for you are certainly paying them well, but watch them. I will do so, for I do not trust them.'

'Needs must, Malvais. Needs must. Especially as Sir Hugh has still not arrived.'

'As De Clare told you, we did our best, but Sir Hugh remained obdurate despite our pleas. He had a gaunt, older but influential Benedictine at his side, who seemed to have his ear. I was somewhat concerned at the constant sleeping draughts he was giving him.'

Henry frowned. He had a difficult relationship with the Church. Archbishop Anselm may be on his side, but these Benedictines seemed to think they had a higher right to do as they pleased, and many of their foundations took their orders straight from Rome, rarely notifying the Crown of their plans and schemes.

'I will look into it, Malvais, or maybe it's too late, for I see

CHAPTER FIFTEEN

that Lady Rohese and her entourage have arrived ahead of us, and by her expression and that of her husband, De Courcy, it doesn't look like good news.'

Conn's eyes flew to Rohese, standing deep in conversation with her husband, Sir Robert de Courcy, at the door of the King's pavilion. They dismounted, and the King greeted Rohese with a long kiss; he enjoyed every pretty woman despite their husbands standing by.

'I hope you're not bringing me bad tidings, my lady. We expected you to travel south with Sir Hugh's protection.'

'I'm afraid I do, Sire. We left Oxford as we knew Sir Hugh would be a week behind us. As you may have heard from Richard de Clare, the Abbot Columbanus ordered Sir Hugh to go on a pilgrimage to St. Werbergh before he went into battle. The Abbot promised him that if he did, God would ensure he would ride out triumphant with an angel on his shoulder. However, we've just heard that Sir Hugh collapsed when he reached the religious foundation in Chester and was carried inside by the monks. The messenger said his heart was beating out of his chest, and he screamed with the pain in his limbs. They tell me he lasted only a few hours. The great Earl of Chester has gone, Sire,' she said, producing a very realistic sob.

Henry covered his face with his hands and groaned.

'And his men, the troops we desperately need, where are they?'

'They are still camped outside Oxford, Sire. Their commanders await instructions. The problem lies in the fact that his heir, his son Richard, is only seven years old. The boy's mother, Ermentrude of Clement, is setting up a stewardship, but she is a mouse of a woman, and if you do not mind my view, I believe she'll have no idea what to tell the troops.'

'Not at all, my lady. I met her a few times and never heard her speak. He was not a man any woman would want to be married to—he treated her abominably. But we must not speak ill of the dead. God rest his soul.'

He turned to Henry, the Earl of Warwick. 'This gives us an immediate problem, for we must have those men, but the loss of Sir Hugh now leaves a gap in the North West that the Welsh will take advantage of as soon as they hear the news.'

Henry Beaumont shook his head. 'One problem at a time, Sire. We can deal with the Welsh afterwards.'

Just then, a dust-covered messenger cantered through the camp towards them, shouting at people to get out of the way. His horse had been hard-ridden and was blown, gasping for every breath. The man almost fell from the saddle as he abruptly stopped before the group.

'My Lord King, I have ridden all night with a message from the Sheriff of Portsmouth. He says to tell you we are undone, Sire, for they have landed. There are thousands upon thousands of Duke Robert's men at Portsmouth, hundreds of ships as far as the eye can see.'

Conn watched as the King's face froze in shock, and then his shoulders slumped, and he turned to the Lady Rohese and the Earl of Warwick with a slight smile.

'*One problem at a time, Henry*, is what you said. Well, it is now too late for anyone to reach us from Oxford in time, so we will have to use the troops we have. God help us. Fitz Hamon, ride forth with your men and see if these wild numbers are true. Also, it might be one of several landings in different places on the coast, and I do not want to send what forces we have west until we know the truth. Henry, send a message to your brother at Pevensey to send out vedettes to search the south coast. Tell him it's urgent, and tell him what's happened. He must pack up his and the Archbishop's camp so they are ready to march at a moment's notice when the order comes to move west.'

'Portsmouth.' murmured Fitz Hamon, pulling on his gloves. 'He must be aiming for Winchester Sire. He intends to seize the Treasury with only Queen Matilda there to defend it. God help her!'

The King paled at his words. 'Of course, it is only a day or more's march from there. Fitz Hamon, send a messenger back to us with what you see at Portsmouth, but then ride north. Go to Winchester and protect the Queen, for she is with child. She is carrying the heir to the throne!'

There was immediate surprise on the faces of the assembled group, for this had been known to only a few of Henry's closest advisors.

Fitz Hamon bowed. 'With my life, Sire, I swear,' he said, running for the horse lines and calling for his knights and their men to mount up.

'I am blessed when I have men like the Lord of Gloucester, am I, not Malvais? Get my cavalry and Horse Warriors ready to ride for me—it looks as if we'll need them sooner than we thought,' he said, slapping Conn on the shoulder.

July 22 1101 – South of Winchester

Robert and his large army were ideally placed to move on Winchester as they had camped a league or two to the south. Winchester was important to both sides; it had a special significance in the kingdom as King Alfred's old capital city and the home of the Treasury. They did not expect it to be too heavily defended, and Robert could take and hold it while his forces lined up to defeat Henry, who was still far to the east. The English barons, such as William of Warenne, who had flocked to Robert's banner once he had landed in person, brought the news that Henry had a much smaller force, perhaps only a third of theirs. Belleme greeted the young noble with the usual cynicism.

'Well met, Warenne. Tell me, are you not dizzy from changing sides so often, back and forth, back and forth, violating any previous promises or oaths made? Or is this just the result of a broken heart?'

It was well known that Warenne was a bitter young man who had wanted the hand of the Scottish Princess, Matilda, himself, before King Henry carried her away from the abbey and married her. Now, he smiled at the jibes made at his expense; he knew it was a waste of time and breath rising to Belleme's barbed comments as it only gave him satisfaction if one did.

'My family are here to support the true king against the Oathbreaker, Henry Beauclerc, who has no right to the crown. I have brought over a hundred men to fight for Duke Robert.'

'Good! We are to march on Winchester in the morning, and we expect the sight of the huge force of arms arrayed around the city walls will lead them to hand over the keys without a sword being taken from its scabbard,' answered Belleme.

'No, my lord, you have that wrong. I now know the city will fight to the last man because Queen Matilda is in residence there alone. It is she who will defend the city, and they say she is with child,' stated Warenne.

CHAPTER FIFTEEN

Conversation stopped in the crowded pavilion at that news, and Robert de Belleme's eyes went straight to Duke Robert's face.

'Surely, Queen Matilda will not be on the battlements of Winchester with a sword in her hand. We can take the city, ensuring she is unharmed. We can even offer her safe passage, Robert,' suggested Belleme.

Flambard, who, as usual, was lurking at the back, stepped forward.

'If you do not mind me saying so, my Lord Earl, you do not see the wider picture and implications. Duke Robert is Queen Matilda's godfather, an honour given to the Duke when she was only an infant, and as such, he swore to protect her. How will it look if we attack Winchester and she is harmed, or even worse, miscarries the child she is carrying due to shock or fear? All of that will be laid at the Duke's door. At present, he is the wronged party, fighting against the Oathbreaker. But as we all know to our cost, that could change in an instance if something happened to the Queen because of his actions.'

This point of view effectively silenced everyone in the large tent, as Flambard hoped it would, and Robert paced the floor until he finally turned and faced his nobles.

'Leave me! I will think on this in peace,' he said, and the pavilion emptied. Belleme and Flambard were the last to go.

'Do not do anything rash, Robert—this is purely a ploy by Henry Beauclerc. He knows you will need the Treasury and Winchester, so he has shamelessly used his wife to protect it,' said Belleme with a worried frown, for he knew they had to take Winchester, no matter the cost.

Flambard hovered for another moment to reinforce his argument.

'You have a formidable force assembled here. It is in your power to seize Winchester after you have defeated Henry, but now you can be the righteous one who chooses not to attack the Queen. After all, you are a Christian crusader, the saviour of Jerusalem, Sire.'

Robert, who had always hated making decisions, dropped into a chair to think this through and waved Flambard out.

As he emerged from the pavilion, he felt satisfied that he had done as much as possible to influence the Duke. Belleme was waiting for him outside and bore down on him immediately, forcing him to step back in alarm.

'What are you up to, Flambard? What agenda are you following, or should I say whose? Are you, in fact, in Henry's camp? Was your miraculous escape from the Tower of London a setup so you could flee to Normandy to be at the Duke's side, dripping poison into his ear?' he growled.

'I swear, my Lord Earl, that you have this wrong. I am only trying to help the Duke, for I can see how this could damage his reputation and lose him followers. The Queen is much loved and respected in England,' he babbled as Belleme's intense, menacing stare seemed to reach into his soul.

It was true that Flambard did not want the Duke to seize Winchester and the Treasury, as that did not fit in with his plans at all. It was most opportune that Bernard had returned to his side so that he could send him to Warenne with the news about the Queen. He had been pleased to see his highly talented servant when he'd suddenly appeared earlier, and more importantly, had brought information that Flambard could use to his advantage.

However, Belleme was not finished with him yet, as he grabbed him by the neck of his tunic and tightened it into a knot around his throat.

'If I find you have been false to me, Flambard, I swear I will tear your liver out with my bare hands and force it down your lying throat,' he said, letting him go suddenly and pushing him backwards.

Flambard managed to keep his feet and nodded, standing suitably cowed as Belleme spat on the ground and moved away.

'So many threats, so many enemies—but I will rise again above them all,' he muttered as he watched Belleme limp away.

The next morning, Belleme headed for Robert's pavilion early, hoping to catch him on his own, but there were already several nobles sitting outside, breaking their fast. Robert was amongst them.

'Have you made a decision about Winchester, Sire?' he asked, dropping into a camp chair and accepting a tankard of ale from a servant.

'Yes. For once, I believe that Flambard is right. I cannot tarnish my reputation by attacking a defenceless queen. I must be chivalrous in this instance, Belleme!' he proclaimed.

'Chivalry, in my view, has always been overrated, Sire. Let us hope you do not regret this decision, for my men tell me that Fitz Hamon and a hundred more men rode in to defend her overnight, so I would certainly not call her defenceless, Robert.'

There was silence at Belleme's news, as there was little to be said, and many there agreed with Belleme that Winchester should be taken. However, most of them also knew how stubborn Duke Robert could be once he had made his mind up on something.

Mortain had heard enough, and as he stood brushing off

the crumbs of his repast, he announced, 'We also have news that Henry is on the move. They have dismantled their camps at Pevensey and Rickney and are marching northwest. We think they could well be heading for London, Sire. This could be a clever move by Henry, as the city invariably comes out for the King, and it would be a difficult city to attack because of the River Thames.'

Robert also stood. He tried not to meet Belleme's accusing and disappointed gaze as he waved them into the pavilion.

'Gather around the map table. I have decided to move the camp to Warnford. I'm told by a local knight that there are ample meadows there for grazing and, of course, water for the horses. It's not too far, and by the time we have pitched camp, we will know where Henry is heading and can plan accordingly. Now let us sound the horns to alert the camp and look to your knights and retinues, my lords.'

Everyone filed out, including the Duke, leaving Belleme, staring at the map weighted down on the table, and shook his head. Where was Piers De Chatillon when you needed him? This decision was pure folly, and he knew that Robert would have listened to the words and sage advice from the Papal Envoy.

Belleme prayed that Chatillon would sail to join them before it was too late.

Chapter Sixteen

July 1101 – The Weald

The King's army was indeed moving, but not to London. Instead, they were moving in a wide sweep, north and then northwest. The idea was to place themselves between London and Duke Robert's army to keep him from the capital and Westminster Palace.

Moving an army this size was a great undertaking, even at a good marching rate. Having summoned the fyrd, Henry had over a thousand foot soldiers, but there were also hundreds of carts and wagons carrying supplies, pavilions, tents, and spare weapons. It stretched for leagues. Mortain's route took them up into the High Weald Downs, which slowed the men and wagons further on the difficult slopes.

Concerned at the terrain before them, the King summoned Henry Beaumont to his side and called a stop.

'One of our knights has much land hereabouts, does he not?'

'Yes, Sire, Philip de Braose. His father, William, died recently; he rode with your father at Hastings and was rewarded with the land known as the Rape of Bramber. It runs from Surrey down to the coast. He also has land in Powys in Wales. He is one of our Marcher Lords and often fights on the borders with Sir Hugh and his men.'

'Send him to me. He will know these lands far better than Mortain, who has us climbing mountains.'

A short time later, the second Lord of Bramber appeared. Conn had halted the Horse Warriors and cavalry as ordered, leaving Georgio in charge, and had ridden back to find De Clare to ascertain what was happening. He arrived at the same time as a concerned-looking Philip de Braose. The King greeted the young man warmly, ensuring his words put him at ease.

'I remember your father, Philip. He came to Caen when I was young,' he said.

'Sire, we have always been loyal supporters of your family, and now our banner flies in your camp. I have brought nearly a hundred men to fight for you.'

Henry inclined his head in recognition and waved him to a table where a map was spread.

'I believe we are here,' he said, pointing to the Weald, 'but these hills are slowing us down and proving almost impossible for the heavier wagons. We need somewhere to pitch camp tonight, and we need your advice, as I hear you know these lands well.'

Philip stared at the map momentarily, and then, with his finger, he pointed out a route.

'I suggest we follow this lower ridge we are on now as there are no more steep slopes, and then drop down into St Leonard's Forest at the western end of the ridge. Several trails through the forest are wide and well-used, suitable for wagons. We have one of our small castles north of Horsham where we can camp for the night. From there, you can send your vedettes to Leigh Hill; they can see for many leagues in case the Duke's forces are moving towards us. The road north from Horsham is well used, and the army can pick up speed and head west around the bottom of the Downs towards Cranleigh and Chiddingfold. That will lead you to the gap at Hindhead, and you can assemble your men in the valley on the far side on the lower slopes of Headley Down. Taking this route will no doubt surprise the Duke as he'll expect you to take the southern route via Midhurst and Petersfield.'

Henry and his assembled nobles followed his proposed route with intense interest.

'Give him a quill. Mark what you have told us on the map, and I agree, we will camp north of Horsham tonight. How long will it take us from Horsham to the gap at Hindhead, De Braose?'

'It will be a full day's march, Sire; you should probably be there to set up camp by early evening.'

'We will have a good night's sleep there and move through the pass the next day to face my brother's army. Do we know his exact position yet, Mortain?'

'A rider has this moment come in from Fitz Hamon. Good news, Sire—Duke Robert has chivalrously refused to attack the Queen at Winchester. Instead, he has moved his army to Warnford and seems to be settled on the plain there.'

Henry nodded. His brother's chivalry gave him pause for thought, for he had heard it said that the crusades had changed many knights. They became more pious. Some even took the cloth to enter a monastery. Not that he thought for a second that Robert would do that, but his experience in the Holy Sepulcher in Jerusalem might make him more amenable to negotiation. Henry was very aware that he needed Robert to negotiate, as many of the Norman nobles with his brother, demanded his death for breaking his oath and taking the crown.

'Do we have any actual numbers to put to this considerable force yet? Is Malvais right with the estimates of what he saw in Rouen?' asked Henry of the nobles around the table, many of whom looked away or shuffled their feet and stared at the ground.

Robert Beaumont, recently arrived, had more courage, and he nodded. 'I would say he has at least three times the size of our force, but it is not so much the numbers, Sire, it is the quality. Roberts's men are predominantly Norman nobles with dozens of their trained knights and retinues. I rode ahead, Sire, to be at your side, but my forces from Pevensey are close behind, several hundred of them marching to join us and swell our numbers.'

There was silence around the table, and all eyes went to Henry's face. Having heard the odds, some even wondered whether he would stay and fight or run.

'Well, we are here to defend and keep the crown, and defend it we will. Even against such odds. I hope it may not come to that; we need to negotiate. However, let us ensure that this camp of his at Warnford is not just a ploy and that he has not sent another force to the south or the north to outflank us. My brother is a skilled warrior and strategist with several triumphs under his belt; he's not one to leave things to chance. Let us pick up the pace and make the castle at Horsham by this evening.'

They began to disperse while Henry thanked Philip de Braose and waved Conn over.

'Malvais, I want Philip and a few of his men to ride with

you in the vanguard. He will guide us through these lands by the most accessible routes, as he knows them well.'

Conn bowed and smiled at Philip. He was an open-faced, earnest young man, pleased to be chosen and singled out by the King.

'I have heard much of you, Malvais, and have enviously watched your men train. I'm honoured to be able to ride with you.'

Conn inclined his head and smiled. He was sure that the Lord of Bramber was several years older than him, probably in his late twenties or early thirties, but Conn had to admit that he felt older than him. Rohese had said to him in Oxford that events leave their mark on people, and he thought she was probably right.

With that thought, he glanced around the large group that was mounting up, and there she was; she seemed to be in some altercation with her husband. He sent Philip to rally his men and waited until Robert de Courcy trotted off to join the King. He walked over to where she was tightening her girth and tying on a saddlebag, and put a hand on her shoulder. She whirled around to shout at him, but then she smiled when she realised it was him.

'I'm sorry, I thought Robert had come back for another argument. He wants me to ride back to Westminster to be with our son. He thinks my place is not to be here in the King's camp. I pointed out that two of Henry's favourite mistresses are riding in his train, but he had no answer to that without bad-mouthing the King, so he rode away.'

'Here, let me give you a lift up,' he said, holding her foot and throwing her up into the saddle. He placed her foot into the large stirrup cup but kept hold of her ankle and began to caress it, moving under her gown to do the same to her calf.

'What are you doing?' she hissed in alarm, glancing around, but he heard her voice break into a giggle, and he continued the stroking with a mischievous grin.

'I'm obeying orders from our mutual master and flirting with you. I do want to stroke so much more, though,' he murmured as he reluctantly removed his hand and straightened her heavy riding gown.

'Chatillon is arriving at Portsmouth soon. He is moving somewhere close to Robert's camp, I believe,' she whispered as he bowed, kissed her hand and turned away.

She watched him stride away through the crowd of men and horses. Her eyes moved over his body from his broad shoulders to his long, muscled legs. For a few moments, she closed her eyes and imagined what it would be like to wrap her legs around his naked body, and then she felt her cheeks flush. She was a respectable married woman and a lady of the King's court, and she thought of her rule: no strings, no involvement with any of her informers or lords in the court—too much could be given away in the throes of passion. She shortened her reins and kicked her horse to join the wide cavalcade moving north.

Owen and his Welsh mercenaries also mounted and rode out. He narrowed his eyes and reined in as one of the first sights he saw was Conn Fitz Malvais cantering to the front with Philip de Braose, one of the hated Marcher lords who patrolled the borders and built Norman castles on what he considered to be Welsh land. The Welshman was already unhappy with what he was hearing about the possible size of the Norman Duke's army. His men were always ready for a battle or skirmish, but not where the odds were overwhelming.

CHAPTER SIXTEEN

However, he knew that men were prone to exaggeration in these circumstances, so he would wait and let his own eyes judge the odds once they had sight of the enemy.

Chatillon arrived at Portsmouth with Edvard and several of his men the following day. As expected, horses waited for them as they stepped off the boat. Edvard had arranged for them to stay at the Bishop's palace at Waltham that night, as they expected to travel to Winchester the following day. Early reports had kept Chatillon informed that Duke Robert's forces had landed successfully and set off north for Winchester. Chatillon had stayed at Waltham previously; by no stretch of the imagination would he have called it a palace. It was a large, timber-built, rambling residence, but fortunately, it had several things in its favour: large spacious rooms, a full household of staff and a good cook.

It belonged to Lord William Giffard, but he was rarely in residence, as he had also been the King's Lord Chancellor since Henry's accession to the throne. Chatillon was happy to have the Bishop's residence to themselves, as he should not be in England. As the Senior Papal Envoy, Piers was still in a difficult position: Pope Paschal had not come out in favour of one claimant or the other to the throne of England. So, he was here as Duke Robert's friend and advisor, which meant keeping a low profile and not wearing his papal regalia.

He felt he had done as much as possible to help the Duke by removing Sir Hugh and bribing the English pilots and crews to change sides. Now, it was up to Robert to take the crown back; he certainly had the forces and support to do so. However, as he read the messages waiting for him, he became more alarmed and frustrated. There were several from Rohese de Courcy. Sir Hugh was indeed dead, and Henry's army was moving northwest. Unfortunately, other messages informed him that Duke Robert had decided not to take Winchester, and was heading to Warnford to establish his camp there.

'Madness! Why on earth did he not attack Winchester? The Treasury, full of English silver, was there for the taking. Surely Mortain, Belleme and the other nobles around him must have encouraged him to do so!' he exclaimed in exasperation to Edvard, who was equally puzzled and shook his head in sympathy.

'I have spent most of my life at your side, Sire, and therefore have, perchance, had a great deal of leisure to watch Duke Robert from the days when he was simply Robert Curthose, and we were trying to direct him onto the right path. He has never liked making difficult decisions, so you placed Morvan de Malvais at his side. Morvan was a strategist and told him what to do in every battle they fought. The Duke is ruled by his emotions—with his heart rather than his head. On the crusades, he developed into a natural leader and a hero because he had no choice; Pope Urban had appointed him. The alternatives in the Levant were stark: fight against the enemy, heat and dust or be starved of food and precious water. Now, he has to make decisions against his brother, and there are no easy ones.'

Chatillon raised his eyes to Edvard and inclined his head in agreement before staring into the fire and taking a long draught of wine. Edvard was astute and had always been a deep thinker. He was invaluable because he watched, listened and absorbed details about people that others would miss. He provided information and insight that Chatillon had always found useful. This time, although he agreed with some of what his friend had said, this move of Robert's still did not make any sense, not when he had some of the most powerful nobles in England advising him.

'I wonder, is Robert so confident of his victory that he feels no need to take Winchester and the Treasury now? Is he moving first to a confrontation with his brother, the man he curses as an oathbreaker because he knows he can defeat him and take the crown?' queried Chatillon.

'It's more than that, Sire; the Bishop's steward here tells me that Queen Matilda is holding Winchester, and rumour has it that she is with child.'

Chatillon raised his eyes immediately to Edvard's face at this news and sitting forward, he gave a wry smile.

'And there we have the answer, Edvard. The knights and lords recruited by my uncle, Pope Urban, were constantly reminded that it was their knightly values and virtues that would carry them to Jerusalem with faith, honour, chivalry and bravery. Robert is showing that, as the saviour of Jerusalem, he does not have to frighten or threaten the Queen into submission. I only pray that he never regrets this move,' he said, sitting back and closing his eyes.

Edvard filled up their goblets again. He could feel his friend's irritation and annoyance at the Duke's foolishness.

'Robert still has a far larger force than his brother. If it comes to battle, there is little doubt that he will win.'

'Let us hope that the threat of that will make Henry hand back the crown and ask Robert's forgiveness. If that happens, they both may come out of this alive. Now, Edvard, how far is this Warnford?'

'It sits on the River Meon, at the crossroads on the Whickham road. I would say an hour at the most from here.'

'Good, a leisurely start. Send a message to Robert that I congratulate him on his unopposed landing and that I'll be with him at about noon. However, we'll continue to stay here until we know Robert's plans. I have never been fond of life in tents, and I do not want my presence in his camp to be too obvious or to send the wrong impression.'

Edvard stood to send the message with a wry smile. Piers De Chatillon was never inconspicuous, but he would do his best to make him so. Then, a thought occurred to him.

'I am sure our friend, Flambard, will be elated to see us, Sire. He believes we are still in Normandy and that he has the freedom here to spin his webs. Do you think he was behind the decision not to take Winchester?'

'I think I have an inkling of Flambard's plans, as we know he has been stripped of his lands and titles. He must yearn to get those back at any price, but we must ensure that the price is too high for him.'

Chapter Seventeen

The weather was fair for both armies, which was fortunate as the smallest amount of rain would turn the ground troublesome, clinging mud under so many feet, hooves and carts. Not that the hard-baked ground didn't provide as many problems, with hard ruts that could break the wheels and axles of the heavy wagons.

The journey through St. Leonard's Forest had been without incident, and they had set up camp by the motte and bailey castle, slightly north of Horsham. Sir Philip had sent ahead, and at least a dozen pigs had been slaughtered, so the smell of pork roasting over fire pits greeted them as they rode into the meadows. Spirits were better that evening with Sir Philip and his retainer's generous supply of food and drink.

King Henry was woken by the usual early morning camp sounds of skillets and pots being filled with oats and chunks of bacon; to provide something to stick to the ribs to prepare them for the long day's march ahead. The camp dogs began to give voice with the smell of food and the emergence of people from their blankets and tents. He had brought his own pack of hunting dogs with him, and there were always dozens of other dogs with a marching army, scavenging the cold campfires for bones and scraps.

He lay on his back, his hands behind his head, as the pavilion gradually lightened in the early morning light. He wracked his brains for a way forward with his brother. There was now no doubt that Robert had thousands of men at Warnford and vastly outnumbered him. His army would be obliterated if it came to battle, and he may well be killed—King of England for less than a year, but at least he had lasted longer than Harold Godwinson, another oathbreaker, he thought with a wry smile.

He sighed. If he was going to die, he might as well take as many of life's pleasures as he could in the short time left. He turned and ran his fingers along the naked back of his mistress and then threw a leg over her soft, warm body to lean in, lift her hair and softly bite the back of her neck. He felt her stretch beneath him; this was a well-known morning ritual between them. Ansfride Anskil had been one of his long-term mistresses since she was sixteen and had given him three children, Julianne, Fulk Fitzroy and Richard. She was of noble Saxon stock, very pretty with thick corn-coloured blonde hair. More importantly, she knew exactly how to please him as she willingly opened her legs to allow him to take her from behind. Afterwards, they lay for a while in companionable silence. Henry was a considerate lover who recognised his mistresses and supported his many illegitimate children, but he also often sought her advice. Now, she raised herself on her elbow and stroked the hair from his eyes.

'You are preoccupied, my lord. Is that because you believe it will come to a battle?'

Henry shrugged. 'It depends on my brother's purpose and willingness to negotiate. He and William Rufus have betrayed me in the past, so there is little trust between us.'

CHAPTER SEVENTEEN

She kissed his brow and stroked his cheek. 'Use the Archbishop of Canterbury, Sire. If anyone can find the arguments to influence your brother, surely it is Anselm, the most important prelate in Europe after the Pope. Robert must listen to his views.'

Henry held her face with both hands and kissed her soundly.

'You are right, Ansfride, and if I can persuade Robert to the table, I will do just that. Now, pleasant though it was, we've been abed too long.'

So saying, he shouted for his squire to bring them food and pulled on his braies and chausses. He was still bare-chested as he sat and devoured the cheese, fruit and bread that had been brought, when Henry Beaumont, Earl of Warwick, arrived with Sir Richard Redvers close on his heels.

'Sire, the vedettes have returned. Robert's forces are still at Warnford and they say that he looks settled there as if he is just waiting for us.'

'What is the terrain like? Is it better for his forces? Is he in a defensive position?' asked Henry.

'No, Sire, there are many rivers and streams in that valley bottom, and to the south, there are water meadows—totally unsuited to battle.'

Henry stood and paced back and forth while neither of the others gave a second glance to the naked shoulders of the King's mistress as she sat in bed. Henry's mistresses were often at court, and the Queen, although unhappy about that, had quickly learned to look the other way.

'There is no way your brother would choose to fight there. He and his entourage of nobles are all experienced in warfare. He is taking advantage of the plentiful grazing and water before he moves forward to confront us, Sire,' added

Beaumont.

Henry stopped and agreed. 'We will keep to the plan that Philip de Braose put forward. We will proceed through the Hindhead Gap and position ourselves somewhere on the west-facing slopes of Headley Down. That will give us an advantage of height with our cavalry on both wings to charge down and attack the enemy.'

'It seems an odd word to use against those who were once friends and family, but let us hope it does not come to that, Sire. Reports say that over half of Robert's forces are mounted—that is over a thousand men,' said Henry Beaumont, his voice dropping to almost a whisper at the end of the sentence.

'I hope that is not fear I see in your eyes, my Earl of Warwick!' exclaimed Henry with a bitter laugh.

'No, Sire, just realistic apprehension. As you know, my brother, Robert, caught up with us last night with several hundred mounted men that he took down to patrol the coast, and both he and I will be at the front of one of those wings, leading the charge down the hill for you.'

Henry smiled. He knew he was right to be apprehensive. Any man would against these odds.

'We will have Malvais, his Horse Warriors and the cavalry he has trained on the other wing; how can we possibly lose? Now, let us make a move. We need to be close to the Hindhead Gap when we make camp tonight.'

They bowed and left while Henry pulled on his tunic and, reaching out a hand, pulled Ansfride to her feet. His eyes travelled over her buxom, naked body, and he sighed.

'It would be so easy to take you back beneath the covers, but we must go,' he said, pulling her into his arms for a final kiss.

As he emerged into the bright, early morning light, he found

CHAPTER SEVENTEEN

several of his nobles outside, including Malvais and Sir Philip.

'Ah, Sir Philip, we are following your advice to ride northwest towards Chiddingfold. Is there a high point on the far side of the pass, where we can see across the Downs?'

'Yes, Sire. As you travel through the gap, Highcombe Edge is to the north. Although it is heavily forested on the lower slopes, when you reach the highest slopes, it is mere scrub, and you have a view clear across the Downs and plains to the west.'

Henry inclined his head in thanks and turned to Malvais. 'The intention is to set up camp at the entrance to the pass. We should arrive in the early evening, ready to start feeding our army through the next day. There will not be enough light then, but tomorrow morning, as dawn breaks, send up two of your men to watch for any movement of Robert's forces. I am reluctant to send more vedettes through the gap, as I don't want to give away our plans. I've sent a few hundred men south, so his scouts will think we are coming via Liphook. That will give us the valuable time we need to move into position and deploy our forces on the slopes of Headley Down.'

Conn was impressed; it looked like Henry was becoming a strategist. He bowed and assured King Henry he would send his men out the next morning. As he turned away, he saw Rohese talking to Henry's mistress, Ansfride, and strolled over. Both women bowed their heads as he approached, and he noticed how their eyes ranged over him. He smiled.

'I hope I am not interrupting?' he asked.

'No, my lord, we have already exchanged the exciting salacious court gossip and are now onto more mundane topics. The King wants me to return to Westminster to be closer to the children. He does not say the words, but he fears for our welfare if he is defeated or killed,' answered Ansfride.

Conn could see in her face that she really feared for Henry and truly loved him.

'I am sure it will not come to that, my lady, for we are still a force to be reckoned with, and it is certainly not unheard of in history for a smaller force to use strategic cunning to defeat a much larger one.' She murmured her thanks for his encouraging words and left them.

'She is right to be concerned, but Henry always takes care of his mistresses and bastards. She has a house in her name in London, and all the children are provided for. The eldest, Juliane, has an advantageous marriage already planned for her,' said Rohese, as Conn purposefully stepped closer.

'Any news of Chatillon? Is he in Robert's camp,' he said, lowering his face to hers and his voice to a whisper. From a distance, it looked like the flirtation it was meant to be.

'Not really. He's being very circumspect and is staying at the Bishop's palace in Waltham,' she whispered. Conn quickly shared Henry's planned route with her, but he suddenly felt uneasy.

He turned to find Owen and a few of his men nearby watching him. He immediately raised Rohese's fingers to his lips and kissed each one, gently biting the last one. At first, her eyes widened; it was beginning to excite her. But she realised he had gone very quiet, and the bite was a signal. She lowered her lids and cast a glance around them.

'You seem to have made another enemy, my lord,' she said while letting her hand linger in his and smiling up into his face.

'One of his men murdered one of mine. Do you know who

he is?'

'Yes, he is very dangerous. Be careful.'

'Can it be that you already care about me, Rohese?' he whispered teasingly, and she laughed.

At that moment, another unhappy voice brought them out of their reverie.

'Rohese!'

Conn turned to find her husband, standing hands on hips, glaring at them both.

'We are leaving! Unhand my wife, Malvais,' he shouted before taking Rohese by the wrist when she did not immediately move, and pulling her away.

Owen had watched all this with interest. He sent his men to mount up and followed the couple through the bustling camp. When they reached the horses, he saw Robert de Courcy castigating her for her behaviour, but she gave as good as she got. Mounting, she rode away without him as her husband angrily ran his hands through his hair.

'My lord, can you tell me where I can find Lord Robert Beaumont?' asked Owen.

De Courcy was still glaring after Rohese, but he brought his attention back to the Welshman.

'Yes, he went with his brother and their men to water their horses at the stream.'

To De Courcy's surprise, the Welshman placed a hand on his arm. He looked down at it in amazement but knew of Owen's well-earned reputation, so he didn't shake it off like he would with any other upstart.

'Apparently, he is a dangerous man around women, that Conn Fitz Malvais. I heard that the true reason he was forced to leave Anatolia was for swiving the wife of a great tribal chief. I would watch him with your pretty wife if I were you, Sire.'

Astounded at the man's audacity, De Courcy controlled his features and inclined his head in thanks. He walked away, burning with a wave of even deeper anger that someone like Owen had witnessed his wife's dalliance with the Horse Warrior and thought to give him advice.

Owen, meanwhile, had found the two Beaumont brothers, and he bowed to both as he thought they deserved his respect despite being Norman.

'My lord, do you have any orders for me? We have not been told as yet where we are headed,' he asked, addressing Robert Beaumont, who had recruited them for this campaign.

Robert turned to his brother. 'Yes, update us both, Henry. What are the King's plans now?'

'At present, we ride for the Hindhead Gap and camp there tonight. We wait for news of Duke Roberts's movements, but once through, we expect to deploy our forces ready for battle. The King is sending two Horse Warriors to the highest ridge to survey the downs ahead of us to ensure the Duke is not pulling a flanking manoeuvre. Now I must go. Move your men nearer to the front, brother, or you will eat dust clouds all day.'

'We could do with a quick shower to lay the dust, or it will rise above our heads, and the Duke will be able to see us coming four leagues away,' Robert said with a laugh.

However, Owen was not finished yet. 'I have heard that we are severely outnumbered, Sire, but you know what camp rumours are like, and I do not believe everything I hear.'

'Unfortunately, it is true, Owen. I estimate it is about three to one in his favour, but the King does not believe it will come to a battle, as it would be a slaughter. I believe they will negotiate—they're brothers, after all,' answered Henry Beaumont.

Owen laughed harshly. 'I assure you, my lord, that *sometimes* counts for nothing. Both of the Duke's brothers have betrayed him; he may not be talked around so easily. Also, my experience with my half-brother taught me the same—there is no liking or trust there either. Where would you like me to position my forces?'

'I want you on the eastern flank with my cavalry, Owen; we have Malvais on the west.'

'I will be there as long as the promised payment arrives today. My men are brave but simple souls. They ask for very little—decent food, wine, women and payment in silver in their pouches before they ride into battle.'

Robert nodded. 'I will see to it; you will have it before sundown.'

The Welshman bowed and was gone, leaving Robert Beaumont to stare after him. He was pleased they had answered his call, but Owen was right—money talked. They needed the Welsh mercenaries; they were fearsome and brutal in battle, and the King would need every bit of help he could get without Sir Hugh and his troops.

Robert Beaumont would have been shocked and angry if he had heard Owen's words to his men when they halted at noon.

'This is going to be a battle that cannot be won. We will leave at dawn to go through the Hindhead Gap, but then we will go north. This is not our war; let them fight it out between themselves. Our silver arrives tonight, and we will put it in our pouches and return to Wales.'

His men gave a resounding cheer at the news, with much banging of swords and shields, so the noise echoed through that part of the column.

'Is it not good to hear so much enthusiasm from our troops—so much courage?' commented Philip de Braose to Conn.

They had halted to rest and water the horses, but now they sat on a slight rise looking back at the huge cavalcade of Henry's forces, spreading for at least a league behind them.

'If it was anyone but that group of mercenaries, I would agree. But I do not trust them one jot, and for a reason I cannot give you. I do not think their cheering bodes well for us,' murmured Conn.

'You should have killed him!' spat Georgio, glaring back at the large group of Welsh mercenaries in their black leather doublets.

Philip looked from one to the other in surprise, hearing the anger and hatred in Georgio's voice. 'You have had trouble with Owen ap Cynan and his men? Who indeed has not? We have lands in Wales, and he and his family regularly raid our lands to steal our sheep and cattle.'

'It will be more difficult for you with the death of Sir Hugh, no doubt, but our vendetta with Owen is more personal. His man killed one of our men, and in turn, he died for it. I assure you there is mutual antipathy between us. Meanwhile, we will need to watch our backs in battle—as I said, I don't trust them. We will have our day with him, I swear, Georgio.'

Chapter Eighteen

July 1101 – Warnford

Chatillon both heard and smelt the camp long before it came into view. Thousands of men and horses leave their own particular taint upon the breeze, and it was never a pleasant one. It took them some time to wend their way through the hundreds of tents and campfires on the outskirts. They were greeted by several knights who recognised Chatillon despite him discarding the sweeping papal regalia of purple tunic, cloak and badges. He was now dressed as befitted the wealthy French lord that he was, all in black, of course, with an Italian decorated, laced, leather doublet and his sword at his side. Some tended to forget that he was one of the finest swordsmen in France, until they were unlucky enough to be pitted against him and found their weapon whisked from their hand and his blade at their throat.

'The troops appear in good spirits, Sire,' said Edvard, listening to the banter and laughter as they picked their way through the thousands of men camped on both sides of the river.

'They should be, Edvard. This army must be twice or even

three times the size of Henry's force, and they have just pulled off the successful manoeuvre of landing on the south coast, where they were not expected to be or challenged. They have reached as far as this ford, totally unopposed. That does tend to lift the mood.'

Finally, they emerged onto a wide grassy lane that led directly to large pavilions and dozens of brightly coloured banners waving in the slight breeze. Looking at their insignia and crests, Edvard surmised that most of the English and Norman nobility seemed to be here with Duke Robert. Again, there were high spirits and laughter outside the tents of the nobles as they relaxed in the sunshine. Several senior lords shouted a greeting or raised a fist to Chatillon as they pulled their horses up outside Robert's headquarters. Edvard waved a few squires to come over and take the horses as they dismounted. Robert de Belleme was the first to rise from his seat and limp over to them.

'Thank God you are here! I did wonder if you would come at all, Chatillon. I suppose you know by now that he refused to take Winchester,' he said in a low voice.

'Yes. Not a good decision, but not a surprising one for a returning crusader, and who knows, it may act in his favour with the people of England. After all, a siege of Winchester with only the Queen in residence could have backfired if she had been injured or miscarried. The last thing we need is for public opinion to move to Henry's side. He is the despised Oathbreaker here, and that message needs reinforcing. Where is Robert?'

'In the pavilion with Mortain and the ever-present Flambard.'

'Well, let us both go and see what devious strategies our

friend is dripping into the Duke's ear, shall we?'

Before lifting the tent doorway, Piers waved Edvard forward.

'Go in and announce us, Edvard,' he said, and Belleme, getting the jest immediately, laughed.

Edvard smiled and swept the heavy striped canvas to one side. His booming voice echoed over the tents. 'Lord Piers De Chatillon and the Earl of Shrewsbury, Sire.'

The pavilion was large and spacious, with two further small rooms used as a bedroom and a store for the Duke's armour and weapons. Three men looked up from the table at this announcement. Duke Robert's and Count William of Mortain's faces lit with pleasure, while Flambard's face blanched in dismay. He had not expected for a moment that Chatillon would cross the Channel, so he believed he was free from interference in England. This arrival could throw his carefully thought-out plans into disarray.

'Piers, I'm delighted you have come. I know that you promised, but I understand your difficult position as Papal Envoy,' said Robert, while grasping arms in greeting with Chatillon.

'I'm here as your friend, Robert, and, of course, to share my worldly wisdom, advice, and the information I have already gathered from the dozen informers I have in Henry's camp.'

Robert threw back his head and laughed, for he knew it was probably true.

Piers knew that Robert would expect criticism from him for his failure to take Winchester, so he did the opposite—he knew how to handle the Duke after years at his side.

'A wise decision not to take Winchester yet, my Lord Duke, for that could have slowed your momentum and true purpose, especially if it had involved a prolonged siege. Now, the city is still there for the taking, and you can arrange safe passage for the Queen, and seize the Treasury at your leisure.'

Robert's face lit with satisfaction. 'I knew you would understand, Piers. Matilda is my goddaughter; I would not put her at risk.'

Piers merely nodded and moved to the table to look at the map. Mortain had drawn several significant lines on it, and taking a quill, Chatillon crossed off all the smaller lines at the bottom, which raised eyebrows from the Duke and the Count. Flambard had stepped back from the table and stood, looking as unobtrusive as possible, at the side while trying to see and hear what they were doing.

'Ignore the troops down here, Robert; this is a clumsy feint of a few hundred men to try to get you to split your forces. Henry's army will come through the Hindhead Gap here, and at the moment, they intend to settle themselves in a wide arc across the Downs, probably here, which gives them the advantage of height. What are your plans, Sire? I presume you mean to move your forces to the east.'

'Flambard here is suggesting we negotiate, as he tells me he has information that Henry will accede to my demands without a fight.'

'Has he indeed?' exclaimed Chatillon, turning a withering glance on Flambard, who dropped his eyes to his feet.

'And why on earth would he do that, Robert? At the moment, I have every indication that Henry wishes to defend the crown. He believes it is his by right, and he seems unafraid of the disparity in your forces. However, Henry was expecting a thousand men to arrive with the Earl of Chester. He hoped they may still arrive and that one of his commanders would bring them south if Hugh were too ill, but I now know that this will not happen. I assume the estimable and well-informed Flambard has told you that news.'

Flambard felt the accusing eyes of Mortain, the Duke, and Robert de Belleme suddenly upon him. Of course, he knew of Sir Hugh's death from his man, Bernard, but he had not wanted to share it with Duke Robert, or explain how he knew. It highlighted another large weakness in the King's forces. Flambard wished to bring both sides to the table to earn King Henry's and Archbishop Anselm's gratitude for his role as peacemaker and negotiator. He did not want Robert to see it as an opportunity to attack earlier than planned, as he needed time to push for negotiations.

'I have only just become aware of this myself, Sire. I wished to check the veracity of it before I told you,' he said in a rush of words.

Chatillon smiled, shook his head at Flambard's obvious duplicity and continued.

'Sir Hugh is dead, God rest his soul. Not a pleasant man, and I will not mourn his passing. However, his troops are still leaderless outside of Oxford as his widow, Ermentrude, is being advised by a Benedictine abbot with his own agenda, which does not include war. These are trained troops, used to fighting on the Welsh borders, and would no doubt have truly bolstered Henry's rag-tag army of peasants,' explained Chatillon.

Mortain shouted and punched a fist into his palm in triumph at this.

'I was always confident of us winning, even before this news, but now I am doubly certain that we will wipe them from the face of these downs, Henry,' he proclaimed.

Duke Robert smiled at his cousin's enthusiasm—Mortain had always been a firebrand—but Chatillon also saw the flicker of concern in his friend's eyes and tried a softer tack.

'I think we need to remember, Mortain, that this is a civil war between brothers, and the troops on either side are English and Norman. I am sure we can avoid slaughtering them, as at least half of Henry's men are the fyrd, called up to fight with their pitchforks. They will be needed on the land to harvest the crops in a few months if we are not to let the people in southern England starve. I believe a token battle to show the strength and power of Duke Robert's army may be needed, but with minimum casualties,' commented Chatillon.

They could all see the sense of this, and, for the first time, Flambard felt a small flicker of hope that his plans could still succeed.

'However, we need to show our resolution now, Robert. He will no doubt know what he is facing, so let him see your determination to take back your crown,' said Belleme forcefully.

'What do you suggest?' asked the Duke.

'A clear message from you to your brother—one that leaves no room for doubt. Something to the point, such as... *Fight or abdicate!*' he exclaimed.

There was silence in the pavilion for some time as they all considered this suggestion.

'Yes, that would be succinct and show your purpose and resolution, Robert,' said Chatillon.

Flambard, seeing his chance at that moment, stepped forward.

'I am happy to take that message to your brother, my Lord Duke.'

That was too much for Chatillon, and he gave a shout of laughter that both Edvard and Belleme joined in with.

'You never tire of your machinations and plotting, do you, Flambard? We can all see what a slap in the face that would be for Henry. The man he imprisoned and was about to execute, who then fooled him by escaping and sailing to Normandy to give his brother all the secrets of England's defence, riding into his camp with a message. Can it be that you are trying to worm your way back into Henry's good book, Flambard? I presume you know by now, Robert, that not only has Flambard lost his lands and title in Durham, but the threat of being defrocked by an ecclesiastical court now hangs over his head,' explained Chatillon.

Flambard's face turned a red, angry hue, and Edvard saw him clench his fists as the truth was laid bare.

'You do me great wrong, as usual, Chatillon. I've done my best to assist the Duke, and I want to see the crown returned to the rightful brother. But I'll not stay here to be mocked. You know where I am when you need me, Sire,' he said, bowing and leaving the pavilion before saying, in anger, something he would regret.

'Perhaps he *has* changed, Piers. I think his recent stint in the Tower of London has left its mark, and I must admit, he's had his uses since he arrived,' suggested Robert, who usually tried to see the best in people.

'A man like Flambard never changes, Robert; he always has his own agenda. It suited him to come to you in Rouen, but I have caught him with his fingers in several pies where they had no right to be. All I ask is that you be wary of his suggestions, Sire. Weigh them up carefully and then run them past the experienced advisors you have here, such as Belleme and Mortain—warriors like yourself who have fought at your side for years. Men who truly have your best interests at heart. As do at least a dozen others of your supporters, such as William de Warrene and Henry of Eu.

'Now I must go. I cannot be seen to spend too much time here with you, Robert, for obvious reasons. We are staying not too far away at Bishop's Waltham. Let Edvard know if you need anything, and do not sit here at Warnford for too long, my friend. With your own recent experiences, you know better than most that you need a shorter march to the battlefield so your men arrive fresh and ready to fight.'

'We were already looking for a possible site on the map when you arrived, Chatillon, somewhere with large meadows and fewer trees. We took the advice of the local lords, and I think we have settled on the area around Alton, which sits on the River Wey. It is also on the London Road, for Henry has not, as we thought, invested and reinforced the city. Instead, he marched past it,' explained Mortain.

'Alton sounds a wise move, Mortain; less than half a day's march from here and only a few leagues from Headley Down if you do decide to confront him there, which I wouldn't advise as you are then marching to his tune. It would be far better to draw him down into the valley at Alton, where there will be better ground. Then, you will have the time to position your forces. Perhaps Belleme's short message may bring him forth sooner than we think. Time will tell.'

With that, he bade them adieu and swept out, leaving them to consider his words and pore over the map.

Chapter Nineteen

July 1101 – The Hindhead Gap

Conn rode out deep in reflective thought as he led the vanguard column towards the Hindhead Gap. He would be the first to admit that he was not usually one to engage in casual conversation. He was never one to share his feelings or innermost thoughts. Years in the hands of the brutal warrior monks had caused Conn to retreat behind several protective layers, and few people even penetrated the outer one. The only person he opened up to was Georgio, and that was rare enough. They had shared so many trials and tribulations, from their brutal childhood to fighting side by side in Spain with El Cid and in Anatolia. What Georgio had once shouted at him in anger in Constantinople was true... like it or not. *They were like brothers, and each could feel the mood change in the other.* With that in mind, he dropped back slightly to let Philip take the lead so he could ride alongside his friend.

Conn was worried about Georgio. He was usually a talker, although not a babbler by any stretch of the imagination. Still, he would often use Conn as a sounding board to talk about issues with the men, events that had happened, or suspicions he had. He also brought a host of interesting and amusing tidbits from the camp or barracks. He had a bright, upbeat personality and was well-liked and respected by everyone. Now, however, Georgio was unnaturally quiet. He had been like this since Conn returned from Oxford. Conn could only assume that Georgio had been far more affected by the death of Andreas than he was letting on.

He pulled Diablo alongside Georgio's horse, as close as he dared, and offered some information. 'Chatillon has arrived in Portsmouth with Edvard and their men, and they are riding up to Robert's camp, though keeping a low profile.'

He received only a grunt and nod in response, so he tried again.

'Chatillon also sent us a joyful piece of news. Edvard's wife, Mishnah, is with child! Who would ever have thought a few years ago that this would happen or even that he would marry? A defrocked monk, employed as an assassin and bodyguard, marries a beautiful but mistreated concubine, and now, he is a husband and soon-to-be father.'

This elicited some response from his friend. 'Edvard is so much more than that. He has been with Chatillon since they were in their early twenties. They are good friends, and they would be lost without each other. Edvard, as you know, also manages most of Chatillon's estates and properties all over Europe. I spent much time with him when you were in England last year. I'm pleased for him; he's an honourable and estimable man. He will be a wonderful father, and he deserves some luck and a life of his own, not only the man constantly following in Chatillon's shadow,' murmured Georgio, without raising his eyes from the forests ahead.

Conn was surprised. It was rare for Georgio to criticise

Chatillon or comment on people at the chateau, which he considered his second home.

'And what of you, Georgio? You are another honourable, estimable and brave man—do you not deserve some luck in your life?'

This was a surprising enough comment from Conn to bring Georgio's eyes to his friend's face. He saw the concern and sighed.

'I consider myself very lucky, Conn, for God brought you into my life to save me. Then, your family adopted me and showered me with the love I had never had. Your father and uncle trained me as a Horse Warrior, and now I travel the world at my friend's side.'

'If that is the case, are you going to tell me what is troubling you?' said Conn softly.

Again, Georgio just stared ahead for some time before answering.

'I have an anger inside me; an anger I have not felt since we were children when I found that my parents had sold me to the warrior monks. However, I cannot seem to diminish or remove this anger. It controls my actions, and at the moment, I feel that it drives me rather than me unleashing it.'

'Andreas,' whispered Conn.

Georgio nodded, and Conn reached over and put a hand on his friend's shoulder.

'We both know that the death of friends, comrades, and family leaves a deep wound—me better than most. Chatillon told me recently that I have to find ways to heal that wound, and I'm doing that by keeping my mind engaged and throwing myself into his assignments. Sometimes, the wound still bleeds, and it isn't easy to staunch it. That's when I may get rip-roaring drunk night after night, as I did in Constantinople, because it dulls the pain for a while. Your wound is about the injustice and pointlessness of his death at such a young age, but you have to find some way to divert or release that anger. We all sign up to be sell-swords, knowing how dangerous it is and that we may lose our lives. Andreas loved his time with us, but he also signed up knowing he was a mercenary with all that entails.'

'I'm driven by the desire to stab and stab until I carve out his black heart and that of that snake, Bernard. It occupies my waking thoughts and much of my night, Conn.'

Conn took a deep breath; this was worse than he thought. Undoubtedly, Georgio meant Owen, who was riding not far behind them.

'I know it is difficult, but you have to put this in perspective, as De Clare did when he spoke about it to me. This unfortunate death was not personal. Black Brynn was paid to follow and spy on us, not to kill or remove us. Unfortunately, Andreas chose to attack him, and he paid the price for that. I have watched you develop as a leader, Georgio; the men listen to you and respect you as a warrior. But, if you were in my place, you would say the same thing to one of your men if he had similar thoughts. You must move on from this, my friend.'

His friend did not reply, and Conn decided that he had to remove Georgio from the sphere of the Welsh mercenaries.

'I want you and Gracchus to leave early tomorrow morning. You must ride up to Highcombe Edge. Philip de Braose will give you instructions tonight. Stay up there for a day or so and see what movement you can see on either side of the downs. You shouldn't have any problems with any of Robert's patrols up there. Henry does not want Robert's men outflanking us,

CHAPTER NINETEEN

coming along the far side of the downs from where they can appear behind us. He thinks Robert may send out cohorts early to do just that. Now come up to the front with me, and you can listen to Philip's constant chatter,' he said, smiling and hoping he had given Georgio something else to consider.

The first clouds appeared late that afternoon, and a summer storm set in that kept up a steady drizzle until late evening. Men who had happily slept in the open, now huddled in small tents or under wagons in an attempt to stay dry, and the rain dripped relentlessly from the trees above them. With the rain came a low mist that crept between the trees under now-darkening skies.

Under the cover of this darkness, a cloaked figure stepped quietly through the trees into the camp of the Welsh mercenaries. Seeing the shape emerge and hesitate at first, Owen's hand went to the hilt of his dagger, but as the man approached the fire, he gave a low whistle of astonishment. The light from the fire lit the smooth, bland features of Flambard's servant, Bernard.

'You are taking your life in your hands appearing here. How did you get past the pickets and patrols without being stopped?'

Bernard held up a leather pouch with the King's monogram on it.

'I am a royal messenger, and they recognised me as a regular in the camp,' he explained in his usual soft voice.

'There are others, not so far away from us, who will slit your throat if they recognise your face,' Owen said with a low laugh.

'I am glad you find the thought of my death amusing, Owen when I risked my life to bring you a pouch of silver,' he said with a glare, and Owen assumed a serious expression.

'I will be brief, and then I will be gone, for you are right—I dare not linger. We need confirmation of the King's plans. Piers De Chatillon seems to have a dozen spies and the Horse Warriors in this camp. My master does not like surprises or being wrong-footed, so what can you tell me?'

Owen outlined the plans the Beaumont brothers had told him. Bernard nodded satisfactorily and handed a heavy pouch to the Welsh mercenary.

'This is your reward for that information, but also, Flambard wants you to return to Wales, as he does not want you or your men in the battle that will take place. You will leave another hole in Henry's flank and take away experienced fighters, hopefully bringing him to the negotiating table sooner.'

Owen fought to keep the laughter and pleasure off his face. He had already decided to flee, and now, he was being paid to do so.

'We will have no difficulty with that order. There was little hope of the King winning against such high odds, and now we have opportunities in Wales. With Sir Hugh gone, we can go home and take back our lands.'

Bernard raised an eyebrow. That was not quite the outcome that Flambard would wish for, but his job was done, he thought, as he accepted a cup of wine from the Welshman.

'So, this Chatillon. I know who and what he is, and that it is said that he is richer than the King of France, but which side is he on, Bernard, if he is helping the Duke? I heard a tale that he was with Henry in the forest when William Rufus was killed.'

'Your guess is as good as mine, Owen. He rides a clever path down the centre, influencing both sides. However, I do not doubt that the Horse Warriors carry out his orders, for all of their sudden allegiance to King Henry. I'd lay silver that they are on Chatillon's payroll,' answered Bernard.

'Ah, so they are open targets as spies and traitors, are they? I have scores to settle there. As you know, they killed my cousin, Brynn,' he responded with a scowl.

'Yes, I'd say most of them can be killed if that is what you wish—but not their leader, Malvais, for I know my master has a plan for him. Chatillon has always been close to them. Flambard tells me that he saved their lives when they were mere boys, so they owe him a debt, but he treats Malvais and Georgio di Milan as sons.'

'You should go, Bernard, with so many eyes on us. Your discovery here would not bode well for my men and me since you became such a persona non grata in the camp. Tell Flambard we will follow his orders to the letter and to let us know if he ever needs use of us again,' he added. Bernard nodded, put up his hood, clutched his cloak, and disappeared into the mist.

Owen sat and stared into the flames. He had met Flambard and knew of his reputation. Another man like Chatillon, who worked predominantly in the shadows. He did not doubt that Flambard would rise again and could be useful. Meanwhile, he mulled over and wondered how to use this information about the Horse Warriors to his advantage.

At the far end of the camp, a confrontation of a different sort was underway. Rohese and Henry's other mistress, Edith Forne, with the help of their manservants, were helping some of the soldiers' families and camp women who were wet and shivering in the sudden deluge and with no shelter. They were ensuring shelters were rigged and food was provided when her husband and his squire appeared and, taking her by the arm, pulled her away.

'Do you never think of me, my name and my reputation when you decide to do these things? When Gregory told me what you intended, I was beyond speech for several moments.'

Rohese pulled her arm free and glared at the smug-looking squire.

'Someone has to help these families in times like these, and Edith came to me to see what I could do.'

'Most of these women are whores, trailing the camp to bleed the men dry of their pay. And when you think on it, Edith Forne is just a better-class whore,' he hissed.

Rohese looked at him in astonishment. 'And as the King's Royal Steward, do you share your view of her with Henry, my lord? No! You do not dare, or you would quickly lose your position. You do know that Edith is the daughter of Forn Sigulfson, the lord of the huge Greystoke lands in the North West. He would take your head from your shoulders if he heard you describing his daughter as such. She is beautiful, intelligent and has a charitable Christian soul—unlike you, my lord husband.'

He stood, arms folded, and glared at her. 'I sometimes wonder why you married me, Rohese. Was it purely to try and save your traitorous family from disgrace and imprisonment?'

'Every week I wonder why I married you, my lord, when you are so small-minded. What happened to the light-hearted young man I married?'

'I grew up and assumed responsibility, Rohese, for my position at the King's side, for my wife and family. A responsibility you seem to shrug off in preference to spending your time with a Horse Warrior. I hear you even danced with him in Oxford.'

'Jealousy as a mantle does not suit you, my lord, and it would make you an object of ridicule when all those about us in the court have mistresses and lovers. I have not betrayed you, but your unpleasant, suspicious, overbearing behaviour toward me may drive me to find some happiness elsewhere.'

He swore long and loudly at her, which everyone heard, before he leaned close to her face. 'As you prefer the company here, you can spend the night with them. I will not have you back in my pavilion while you so blatantly defy me,' he said and strode off with his squire, leaving her standing in the rain.

Edith, who had witnessed all this, put an arm around her shoulders.

'They like to sound off when they think they have been wronged. It will blow over—it always does. You have a bed in my pavilion tonight if you wish.'

Rohese smiled weakly and thanked her as they returned to finish their work with the families huddled under the wagons at the column's rear. When they had finished, Rohese did not go back with her immediately. Despite the rain, she wanted to walk and try to forget the loveless, bleak marriage that was her future. The rain now seemed relentless, and she realised she was cold. It felt more like autumn than summer. She saw a fire between the trees and approached. She had not realised that her walk had taken her to the front of the column until she recognised the figures around the fire. She did not approach but stood, watched, and listened to the banter and laughter under the canvas awning they had erected.

Georgio was the first to see the figure in the trees. Someone was watching them, but then he recognised the wet, bedraggled figure and stood up.

'My lady, come sit by the fire. You are soaked through.'

Conn had also stood, and his eyes went to her face in surprise, for it must be an urgent message or news if she had risked coming here to their camp, especially in this downpour.

'Darius, bring a few blankets here,' he shouted, taking her arm to guide her to the fire. She clung to him until he gently led her to the log they were sitting on. Taking her dripping cloak, he hung it on a branch and rubbed her arms, face and dripping hair with the dry blankets. The others all moved to the fire's far side or curled up in their blanket rolls to leave them to it.

Despite the question hovering on his lips to ask what had happened, Conn stayed quiet until she spoke.

'Do not ask me why I'm here, for I'm unable to tell you. I just needed to walk and get away from him,' she whispered.

Seeing the look in her eyes, he decided not to ask her what had caused her obvious distress. He took her hands and led her into his tent. He pulled her, unresisting, down onto the bed, and pulled the covers over them both. She curled around him with her head under his chin and let out a deep sigh. He kissed her forehead, pulled her even closer and felt her drift off to sleep. This was a novelty for him as he realised he had never been with a woman who just wanted to sleep in his arms. Smiling, he closed his eyes.

It was still dark when he woke, and he felt her beginning to stir. The rain had stopped, and he brushed the long, curling hair from her face. Her hands had crept under the linen shirt he wore, and now, they reached up to run over the muscles in his back. His mouth dropped to kiss her gently, and he felt her body rise and respond to him, so his hands moved to cup

CHAPTER NINETEEN

her breasts. She moaned gently.

'Are you sure?' he whispered and felt her nod, so he loosened her dress and pulled it over her head. His hands began to move over her body, and she felt flickers of excitement and quivers that she had never felt before. She felt her body move to mould with his. She could feel his impatient manhood pushing against her stomach, so she slid her hand down and untied his braies. In moments, he was on top of her—his mouth was on her breasts, and he was between her legs, gently entering her. She cried out in guilty rapture at the feel of him deep inside her, and she began to move with him. She could hear his breath coming in short gasps and was aware she was doing the same as they both neared a peak that made her cry out in pure joy. She had never experienced this before; lovemaking with her husband had always been perfunctory and over so fast that it had always left her unsatisfied and unhappy as her husband snored beside her. To her surprise, Conn pulled out just before he climaxed. A *true gentleman*, she thought, as she lay warm and content, wrapped in his arms with her body still tingling from his lovemaking. Then she realised that she had no regrets; she deserved this and needed it.

The slightest hint of light began to appear, and he held her face between his hands and kissed her.

'You must go. You should not be seen leaving my tent, or even our camp, for more reasons than one,' he warned her.

'Thank you,' she whispered, touching his cheek.

She quickly pulled on her overgown, wrapping herself in her still-damp cloak. She pulled up the hood and slipped away through the trees. Conn stood for a while watching until she disappeared. He returned to the tent and lay down, his hands behind his head. He thought through what had happened. He had remained celibate since his experience with Rhea, the general's daughter in Nicomedia. She had tried to trap him with a child that was not his, and that had taught him a salutary lesson. This, however, felt so different; an exciting affair with a married woman was easier and safer, and she was very lovely. He wondered if she would return on another night. It would not be easy in the camp, but he hoped she would.

"No strings, no attachments, no complications."

Her sharp words, when warning him off in Oxford, suddenly came to him, and he laughed.

Chapter Twenty

July 1101 – Hindhead Gap

Conn stood beside Georgio and Gracchus as they tied on their saddlebags and blanket rolls. Darius came running up with packs of food and a sack of wine, which Gracchus gratefully received.

'They are only away for a night, two at the most, Darius,' said Conn, shaking his head.

'Yes, but hunting may be impossible if last night's rain returns.'

Georgio smiled and thanked his squire. 'Try not to be a hero, Darius, if it comes to battle before we return.'

He had been with them for less than a year, this boy from the streets of Constantinople, but Georgio felt as if he had always been there.

Conn was pleased to see an improvement in Georgio. He seemed lighter as if their talk had done some good, and he had happily quizzed and joked with him about Rohese's visit to his tent.

'There may be small groups of enemy scouts; if so, avoid them. You are on that ridge for reconnaissance only, and we all know how Gracchus likes a good scrap, no matter the odds,' he said laughing, while Gracchus assumed an expression of sainthood as if he was never to blame.

'Ride along the ridge, as Philip de Braose described, and head west for the northern side of the Downs to ensure no surprises await us on the far side. By that time, Henry's army should be through the long pass. I have been told it will take at least a day to get us all through; it is a long valley with steep sides in places. I imagine you will ride down and join us there, for I presume he will set out his camp on Headley Down. Duke Robert is not rushing towards us, so time is on our side. Godspeed, boys, and be vigilant,' he added as the two Horse Warriors mounted and raised a fist in farewell. They trotted out of the camp in the early morning light, looking forward to the break away from the camp-site and slow-moving column.

Owen and his men were up ahead, already mounted and hidden in a thick copse of trees, ready to move out. When the two Horse Warriors appeared in the dim light, Owen tutted in annoyance. He raised a hand, palm open, to his men to indicate that they should stay quiet and wait. He did not want the two Horse Warriors or anyone else to witness their departure from Henry's army. A local had told him there was only one good, safe path up the steep sides of the pass to get them onto the ridge. No doubt, the two men would be taking the same route, so he needed to give them time to get ahead, but every minute they had to wait risked discovery.

When they drew level, he recognised Georgio, and his eyes narrowed and followed them as they rode into the narrow pass ahead. He waited until they were out of sight and waved his men forward at a walk. Fortunately, last night's rain had produced a helpful ground mist, which muffled the sound of their hooves on the increasingly rocky path as they followed on. Owen knew he could not rely on this mist as it would dissipate when the sun rose, so he would ensure they stayed well back.

It was a hard climb to the top of the Hindhead Pass, a combination of a rocky path, often covered in scree, and low scrub with tangled roots that the horses found challenging to get over or through. Many were thorn bushes, and there was so much shying away and stumbling that Gracchus and Georgio had to dismount and lead their horses up the steepest part. It was a relief to reach the top, where there were more distinct but still narrow trails used by goat herders or wildlife. It was clear here on the top of the hill, and, to the west, Hindcombe Edge stretched out in front of them, although the valleys were still shrouded in mist. They pushed on for several hours and then stopped to break their fast as they realised they would have to descend and then climb the opposite slope to reach the highest point.

They gazed across the valleys to the south and west as the mist evaporated. The Weald was a densely wooded area on the south-facing slopes and valleys, and the greenery stretched for leagues around.

'I imagine the hunting is very good around here; those woods must be full of deer and boar,' said Georgio.

Gracchus nodded as he took a chunk from the round of bread that Darius had packed for them.

'I was thinking more about the King. His idea of placing his troops on the lower slopes of the Downs is fine in principle, but after what we've toiled through, I think his men and horses will find it difficult in the scrubland, while the valley bottoms are full of trees. If I were him, I would move west to find meadowland.'

Georgio smiled; Gracchus often surprised him. He was a big, bearded, burly man who had been the first to openly challenge Conn for the leadership of the newly formed Horse Warriors in Constantinople. But people often only saw the strength and brawn of him without seeing the quick mind that accompanied it. Georgio knew Gracchus could read and write in Greek and Latin, which is why Conn had made him his captain.

'Where are you from Gracchus? Are you from the city of Constantinople? You seemed to know it very well,' asked Georgio.

'No, my family are all from Yerakini, on the coast in southern Thessaloniki. My father was a well-to-do fisherman with my uncle. They owned a small fleet of a dozen fishing boats. The brothers decided their eldest sons would not become fishermen. They wanted something better for us, so we were sent to the monks to learn to read, write and cypher. My cousin, Dimitri, stayed there; he became a monk and rose in the monastery ranks. They say he will make abbot one day. I never felt destined for the Church as I'd always loved the outdoors and horses. One day, the army of the great John Doukas, the Emperor's Mega Doux, arrived. They were fighting pirates at that stage, and their ships came into Yerakini. But I loved his cavalry: the uniforms, the horses, the curved blades. In every bit of free time, I learned to ride. Once I was old enough, I left the monastery for Constantinople, went to the barracks and begged them to take me in. I was a groom for a few years, but I got to exercise the horses, and gradually, I began to fill out and became a cavalryman and then a serjeant.'

CHAPTER TWENTY

Georgio looked at the big man in amazement. 'All of us have such different stories, but now here you are, on an English hill, about to fight for an English king you had never heard of before.'

Gracchus grinned. 'Ah, but it was worth it to see this,' he proclaimed, sweeping an arm over the verdant countryside stretching for leagues in front of them.

'I had heard much of these green lands of the Western Islands. Now I am here, and this is so different from my arid homeland, where a blade of grass rarely survives the early summer months.'

Georgio smiled at his enthusiasm. 'Come. We must push on to reach the ridge Philip described. We can just see it ahead of us.'

They had barely mounted when Gracchus quickly turned and stared behind them.

'What is it?'

'The sound of scree moving,' he said, drawing his sword, and Georgio did the same.

With a loud grunt, one of the many pigs that rooted in the woods appeared, followed by two dozen more. The two men stared as the animals spread out in the scrub, when suddenly, a drover and his dogs appeared, his family behind him. They looked at the two Horse Warriors with interest, especially the enormous War Destriers. They doffed their caps while Gracchus smiled at the two young boys driving the pigs with long switches. He took three apples from his pack and began to juggle them. The boys stopped and watched, open-mouthed, but then deftly caught the apples as Gracchus threw one to each boy and crunched on the third, splitting it in two and asking the boys to give a half to each horse. The drover and his wife, a small, dark, weathered but still pretty young woman, smiled before moving off, the boys waving as they glanced back at the two warriors.

'Off to market, no doubt. Philip told us these were mainly drover trails. Let us ride on.'

A few hours later, they reached Hindcombe Edge and scanned the land around for any sign of Robert's forces or even patrols. Nothing could be seen, and there was no movement anywhere apart from the drover and his pigs going down a slope to the north.

'It makes me wonder what Duke Robert is doing. Is he sitting and waiting for Henry to come to him?' said Georgio, scanning in every direction.

They positioned themselves in the best spot and watched and waited for several hours. The sun began to sink, and they descended to a wooded glade beside a stream that Gracchus pointed out below them to set up camp. There were several rocks that Georgio kicked into a rough circle, then lit a fire in the middle while Gracchus saw to the horses. Then, the big Greek warrior took his bow and disappeared into the woods, returning later with two plump pigeons he expertly plucked and hung to roast over the fire.

'Our friends, the drover and his family, are camped not too far over there. I was very tempted to quietly lift one of the smaller pigs. I tell you, I could almost taste the pork crackling as I watched them rooting in the forest and coming closer, but then my conscience got the better of me,' he said, as Georgio laughed and waved a pigeon leg at him, happy with what they had.

With the wine provided by Darius, and the roast pigeons, Gracchus commented that they had feasted like kings. They sat with their backs to large boulders, the heat of the fire on their faces. It had been a long day, and Georgio felt his eyes closing as the sound of gentle snores from Gracchus lulled him to sleep.

It was a different noise—a laugh—that caused him to snap awake suddenly, and he found himself looking into the face of Owen ap Cynan, who squatted on the opposite side of the fire. The white faces of his men shone from the trees behind him, and Georgio's hand crept slowly towards his dagger as he thought of kicking the embers of the fire into the Welshman's face, which might give them a chance. Owen laughed again, loudly this time, as if he could read his thoughts. This laugh woke Gracchus.

'I wouldn't move a muscle if I were you,' said Owen, indicating three or four men with swords drawn behind them.

Georgio's anger and intention of killing this man still burned bright, but Owen now had them at a disadvantage.

Georgio went cold as he remembered his last words to the Welshman, and he did not doubt that Owen meant to kill them.

Chapter Twenty-One

30th July 1101 – Hindhead Gap

It was, as expected, a slow process getting Henry's camp through the pass. It took most of the morning for horses, men, camp followers, dozens of wagons and carts, and herds of sheep and goats. This was the main track from east to west, and it was well used and travelled. It was a good cart's width, but regular rock falls meant it often had to be cleared, and it was still very rocky in places, which could break wheels and axles. The previous night's downpour had not helped, as there were several areas where springs came down from the heights onto the track, and the heavy rain had turned these areas into bogs churned up by troops and horses, causing problems for the carts. Eventually, they were out into the wide valley beyond and could spread out from a narrow column, increasing their speed.

Conn cast a practised eye over the valley and slopes of the Downs and turned to Philip de Braose at his side.

'This is no place to meet the enemy—the slopes have far too many knee-high scrub bushes, and the valley's quite heavily wooded.'

CHAPTER TWENTY-ONE

He reigned in and waited for King Henry and the Beaumont brothers to catch up, and he shared his concerns. Henry glanced keenly at what Conn pointed out, and he agreed.

'What is at the end of the valley, Philip?'

'It widens out into a plain, what we call a common, with another smaller ridge of hills to the west, Sire.'

Henry looked thoughtful and turned to the Earl of Warwick to ask his opinion.

'That sounds a far better prospect to meet your brother. It would be a nightmare to fight in a place like this; they could come from any direction, and we would not see them.'

Henry nodded. 'We'll push ahead and ride onto this plain. You never know, we may find my brother, Robert, already waiting for us there.'

They shortened their reins, ready to ride on, when a shout was heard in the distance. Two vedettes were coming in fast towards them, and between them, there were two riders: one holding the standard of the Duke of Normandy; the other, the Norman noble, Count Henry of Eu. They pulled up in front of the King.

'I have a message for Henry Beauclerc, the Oathbreaker, from the rightful king, Robert of Normandy,' he announced.

Henry narrowed his eyes at the Count. 'It is a good thing that you are under the protection of parley, Henry of Eu, but I promise I will not forget your words,' he said, waving Robert Beaumont forward to take the proffered message.

'Not a word I spoke was a lie, my lord, as every man here could attest if they also searched their conscience.' His smile infuriated Robert Beaumont, known for his quick temper, and his hand went to his sword hilt. King Henry held up a hand to stop him.

'We are not ruffians, Robert, to take the life of messengers just because they are insolent. Are you waiting for a reply, Count Henry? If so, we can offer you refreshments. I remember you once called me a friend, and we hunted together.'

'No, my lord. Your actions will be the answer, and your friendship was forfeited when you betrayed Duke Robert,' he exclaimed. With that, he turned and rode away, the standard bearer following.

Henry Beaumont broke the silence that ensued with the messenger's departure.

'Perhaps, when it comes to it, your brother has decided he does not want an internecine war, and he offers negotiations.'

Henry broke the seal and unrolled the vellum sheet, then gave a great laugh after reading what was written. 'I do not think that is the case, my Earl of Warwick, for he gives me two choices.'

He held up the sheet so the group could see three large words written on it with a sentence below.

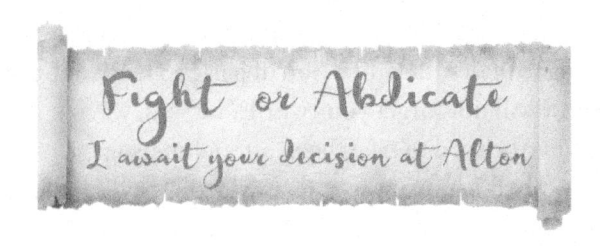

Fight or Abdicate
I await your decision at Alton

'He is still clearly very angry, Sire,' said Conn, whilst looking

CHAPTER TWENTY-ONE

at the faces of those around him. They were shocked by the stark nature of the message.

'Yet, he turned away from Winchester so as not to attack the Queen. A chivalrous gesture indeed,' said King Henry in a thoughtful tone.

Henry Beaumont, the elder and more level-headed of the two brothers, moved his horse closer to the King and leaned in.

'What will you do, Sire?' he asked in a low, hardly discernible tone.

'For now, Warwick, we will push on, set up camp and consider our options. Robert, you can ride over the low hills Philip describes and look at my brother's position at Alton without antagonising his patrols. Where shall we camp, Sir Philip?'

'I suggest we make for Oakhanger, a small village with a stream surrounded by common and heathland, ideal for the camp. Deer are plentiful to the south, while the common abounds with rabbits. Also, it is no more than half a day's march from here.'

The wide column began moving again, with rumours abounding about the messenger and what news he brought. Meanwhile, Conn sat at the side momentarily, scanning the hills and ridges to the north for any sign of Georgio and Gracchus—not that he really expected to see them yet. He imagined they would find the King's camp easily enough at Oakhanger, as the trail of destruction left by Henry's army was plain to see and easy to follow. They were two experienced warriors, and he was sure they would be safe and well and would no doubt gallop into camp tomorrow.

Georgio's plight was, in fact, dire: he was bleeding from several wounds; his left eye was swollen and crusted shut with blood; and he could hardly catch his breath for the pain from his ribs on his left side. His hands were tied in front of him, and a tight rope was around his throat, which was attached to Owen's saddle. They were beginning to descend the far end of Highcombe Edge, and fortunately, Owen's horse slowed as the ground underfoot was treacherous and rocky, with sliding scree in places. Georgio concentrated on keeping to his feet despite the pain of his bruised and battered body. If he fell, he did not doubt that Owen would laugh and drag him along behind the horse, which could well finish him off.

They paused at a stream at the bottom of the steep slope to water the horses, and Georgio dropped to his knees and put his bruised face into the water to gulp it down. Owen's serjeant, or second in command, Rhys, grabbed the rope around his neck and pulled him back up. Georgio choked and coughed and then swayed, lightheaded, on his feet. Rhys looked him up and down with a critical eye and went to where Owen was sitting in the grass. The rain had cleared, and the sun was high in the blue sky. Owen shaded his eyes and looked up at Rhys.

'What is it?' he asked.

'Two things. We need to move faster, as our friend, Robert Beaumont, will take our desertion as a personal affront and will no doubt send men after us. I'd like several leagues between us when he does. We have seen Beaumont's temper;

he is a powerful man with a long reach. Secondly, the Horse Warrior—what do you want him for? If you keep him running behind your horse, it will not be long before you are pulling a corpse, for he is badly beaten.'

Owen got to his feet. He recognised the truth in those words and liked that Rhys was a sensible and estimable man; he kept them all on the right track.

'Put him on one of the pack horses but tie his feet under its belly. Beaten or not, I don't trust him an inch. I intend to keep him but have not decided what to do with him yet. Now, let us go; I want to cross into Surrey and reach Frimley before dark. The abbot there owes me a favour and will give us food and a bed.'

Bouncing along on one of Owen's spavined, bony nags was almost as painful as running behind his horse, as Georgio was sure they had cracked more than one of his ribs. His hands gripped the horn at the front of the saddle as they cantered across heathland and meadows before reaching the road north. The sun was beginning to set as they cantered through the gates and into the yard of a large stone building. Rhys loosened the ropes on his feet and then pulled him off the horse. He cried out in pain as he hit the ground and collapsed to his knees. Two of the mercenaries picked him up, gagged him and pulled him into a stable, where he was tied to the post of an empty stall and left there.

He hung in the ropes with exhaustion while trying to push the filthy cloth out of his mouth, to no avail. He thought over the previous night's events and how easily they had been taken. They had been too careless on the Downs; anywhere else, they would have taken turns to be on watch. Conn would never let him forget this, that's if he ever saw him again.

Georgio could not understand why he was still alive; why had Owen not killed him, as they had Gracchus? They had come from behind and disarmed him quickly, pinning him down, but Gracchus, next to him, had come off the ground with a roar and had shaken the two Welsh mercenaries off as if they were children, flinging them into boulders and trees. At that point, another half dozen of Owen's men had piled in, kicking and punching until Gracchus was on his knees, his face streaming with blood. Owen had stepped forward and punched the Greek warrior so hard that Georgio heard the crack as his head hit the boulder behind, and Gracchus lay lifeless at his feet. They then turned on him and gave him such a beating, he thought he was going to die, but Owen had called a halt, pulled him to his feet and laughed in his face.

'What were you going to do to me, Horse Warrior? Well, now's your chance,' he said, letting him go. But although he ached to hit him, he had dropped to his knees and fallen to the ground. He knew no more until he was kicked awake the next morning and roped to Owen's horse. The pain was so bad everywhere that he had vomited at first while an argument went on over his head about their horses, which Rhys won. They left the large War Destriers behind, as they were too distinctive and would be noticed in the villages they went through. Now, he was here and alive, while his friend was dead—another Horse Warrior from Constantinople who had chosen to come with them, another put into his care. If he did survive this, how could he ever face Malvais again he thought, and let out a sob.

Several hours later, the stable door opened, and Rhys appeared. He removed the gag and lifted a tankard of wine to Georgio's lips, which he hungrily gulped down. Then, the gag was replaced, and Rhys, raising the small oil lamp he brought, looked at Georgio's bruised and purple face. A cut above his eye was nasty, and the blood had streaked down his face.

'I do not know, or understand, why he is keeping you alive; I would have cut your throat as you are too much trouble. Maybe he thinks that is too quick for you, for after all, you killed his cousin, and they were close—almost like brothers. He will likely hand you to Brynn's mother and sisters, who will tear you apart with their fingernails,' he said, laughing and leaving Georgio alone in the dark with his thoughts. He prayed that he died on the road to Wales, or managed to escape before they arrived at Brynn's home village.

He was shaken awake at first light and untied from the post. He was apprehensive to see Owen sitting on the edge of the water trough as he was pulled into the yard. His legs nearly gave way twice as they pulled him to stand before Owen.

'Ungag him and dip the cloth into this water to wipe some of the blood from his face. We do not want anyone to notice him as we ride north. Put a cloak or hood on him, Rhys. I think our Italian friend here will be a very useful addition to our band, and I hope he may even prove very lucrative.'

Rhys raised an eyebrow at this. Owen obviously had a plan, but he always kept his plans to himself until he needed to share. He took the gag from Georgio and turned to dip it in the trough, but Georgio, his anger rising at what Owen had said, gathered every speck of saliva in his mouth and spat at Owen's feet.

'Do you think I would ever ride or fight for the likes of you, you murdering scum? Why, you are not fit to clean the boots of a Horse Warrior like Malvais. And now you have proven to be cowards, abandoning the King, who paid you in good faith—deserting him on the eve of battle.'

Georgio knew he should have stayed quiet, but his pride had risen through the waves of pain. Owen stood slowly and smiled while Rhys, a dripping cloth in his hand, shook his head. Owen turned his body away and swiftly returned to deliver a punch to the Horse Warrior that knocked him back through the stable door. Georgio heard his nose crack, and blood gushed down over his doublet. Owen stood over him.

'I promise you, Horse Warrior, you will wish I had let you ride with us, for I intend to put you in the darkest dungeon I can find in Wales,' he growled before turning away and ordering his men to mount up.

Rhys and another man pulled Georgio to his feet and tried to clean his face and clothes of the blood.

'If nothing else, I admire your courage, but it was foolish; Owen takes every insult to heart and never forgets them.'

So saying, he stuffed small rolls of cloth in each of Georgio's nostrils to staunch the blood, then he tightly grasped his nose with his thumb and fingers and tried to straighten it back into position. Georgio cried out in pain as Rhys stood back and admired his handiwork.

'Well, that has spoiled your looks, but it is less crooked. If I were you, I would stay quiet and try to stay alive. Find him a cloak, tie up his feet and let us get moving. I can almost hear the sounds of hooves behind us,' he said, signalling the men to put him on a horse.

Georgio felt a wave of hopelessness as they rode back north, and he prayed that Conn would realise, sooner rather than later, that they were missing or there would be little trail to follow.

Chapter Twenty-Two

Late July 1101 – Alton

Alton was a pleasant little village in east Hampshire, but larger than Robert expected. There was even a busy livestock market and hiring fair taking place when he rode into the village square with his senior nobles. He waved Mortain over and pointed at the local farmers.

'Mortain, you tell me we need more supplies, so see to it. Tell them we will buy all the surplus stock and more if possible.'

Watching this, Belleme laughed. 'The great Duke of Normandy reduced to haggling for sides of lamb—there's a sight I never thought to see again after our days in Antioch.'

Robert smiled; no one could ever forget the siege of Antioch if they had been there. They had nearly starved to death and, towards the end, had been reduced to eating their valuable horses.

He was pleased by the welcome of the locals; every house seemed to empty, and they cheered the brave Duke, the saviour of Jerusalem and the Holy Sepulcher. Many came to hold onto his stirrups and kiss his boots. Even the local priest came out with holy water and blessed him for his new campaign. With some difficulty, they extracted themselves from the melee and rode out to the east to look at the ground where Robert had chosen to bring his brother to battle. They knew Henry's forces were moving forward, and despite the overwhelming odds, he had decided to fight.

The Duke was pleased with what he saw at Alton; large expanses of meadow pastureland rose to heathland and scrub in the distance. They rode over the fields to test the firmness of the ground after the recent rain, to see if there were any boggy patches or marsh that could bring horses to their knees, but none were found.

They sat for a while as Mortain and Belleme decided where to base the foot soldiers and the cavalry. Two large groups of mounted knights were to be held in the woods north and south, ready to race out and smash into the flanks of the enemy when the signal was given. Mortain and Belleme were confident, but Chatillon's words resonated with Robert. These were English and Norman men he was facing, and some had even been on the crusades with him, fighting at his side.

Robert de Belleme knew Duke Robert better than most; he had spent most of his life at his side and supporting him. Now, he watched the conflicting emotions on his friend's face and was worried. Robert's problem was that since his crusade, he seemed to have little ambition. He had almost stepped back and let his wife, Sibylla, rule the day-to-day issues of the duchy. Robert had been fired up by the betrayal of his brother, but now, Belleme could see that the Duke was becoming unsure about a battle that could bring much death. He had prevented Flambard from riding out with them today, telling him firmly that only the inner circle of nobles would ride out to plan the strategy. This was because he had walked in and caught

CHAPTER TWENTY-TWO

Flambard arguing that a pitched battle was unnecessary, a waste of men, and that now was the time to negotiate.

Now, bearing this in mind, he turned to the Duke.

'We will teach your brother a salutary lesson here, Sire. At the beginning of the crusades, you will remember Pope Urban decreed that non-crusaders should protect the possessions of the crusading knights while they were away fulfilling their vow. William Rufus did that for you: he protected the Dukedom of Normandy and ruled it well in your absence, ready for our return. Remember, Sire, that the English crown was also a possession; it was yours, promised to you by William Rufus. Henry signed and agreed to that document, swearing an oath with his hand on holy relics to honour your claim. Yet, he did not protect that crown for you—he stole it from you and deserves what is now coming to him.'

At this point, Belleme pulled his sword from his scabbard and raised it high. The other dozen nobles followed suit until Robert was ringed by shining steel.

'He will feel your wrath and the wrath of all the Anglo-Norman nobles and knights who have flocked to your banner. You are the wronged party, and your cause is just. We all believe in you, my Lord Duke, and, in a short while, you will be our King of England and Normandy, just like your father.'

This was a significant speech by Belleme, the powerful Earl of Shrewsbury, and he had surprised himself with his eloquence and vehemence. Still, he could see that it had an impact on both Robert and the group of senior nobles, who raised their swords and fists in acclamation and shouted the Duke's name over and over. Belleme gave a wry smile as he turned away—let Flambard and his mealy-mouthed persuasion, match that.

Late July 1101 – Oakhanger

The King's forces were much later arriving at Oakhanger than expected as there had been delay after delay on what should have been an easy march across the valley and plain.

Duke Robert was not the only one with conflicting emotions and thoughts about the forthcoming battle. Henry found himself lying awake in the early hours, worrying about the outcome and aftermath of such a battle.

If I am killed, which is eminently possible, what will happen to Matilda and the child she is carrying? She will undoubtedly return to the protection of her brother, King Edgar of Scotland. However, if I, by any chance, win against these impossible odds, Robert is also without a legitimate heir, although his son, William of Tortosa by Agnes de Ribemont, is a knight to be reckoned with. Would William then lay claim to the Dukedom of Normandy? Would he be backed by the nobles who supported Robert, which could lead to further war?

Tossing and turning, he finally gave up in the early hours. He thought of sending for Edith, his mistress, but decided instead to walk around the sleeping camp while the thoughts still raced around his head. He needed an accurate estimate of how many men Robert truly had. Henry Beaumont's account had been indecisive, as the forces were still arriving at Alton. He needed to ride out, see it with his own eyes, and find out what he was up against. He would ride out with his nobles at noon.

He was walking through a copse of trees on the edge of the camp when he heard a noise to his left and he stood stock still. There were two shapes ahead, cutting across in front of him, both cloaked, despite the warm July night. The first thought was that they could be intruders, but then the taller of the two figures turned and pulled the other into his arms. Her hood fell back as he kissed her, and the pale moonlight hit her pretty face as she bade him farewell.

'Rohese,' murmured Henry, and he immediately knew who her lover would be. He had watched Robert de Courcy, seen his dark and angry face as he had stomped in a foul mood around camp. He smiled. He was certainly not one to cast blame—at least three of his mistresses were married and still bore him children. He turned away so that neither of them saw him as he returned to his pavilion. He was able to meet Malvais the next day with a degree of equanimity, while in reality, he felt like slapping him on the shoulder, for no one, himself included, had managed to scale the well-protected walls and gates of Lady Rohese de Courcy.

A few hours later, the King rode out leaving his standard bearer behind. He was accompanied by the Beaumont brothers, Sir Philip de Braose, Malvais, and Richard de Redvers of Devon, all experienced fighters. Philip took them at a gallop across Shorthead Common, which pleased Malvais as Diablo needed a good run. They then crossed over the small range of hills to the west, using the northern pass to drop close to East Wirldham. This was less than a league from Alton, but they saw nothing of Robert's patrols or scouts.

'My brother seems very confident that he needs to have no prior warning of our coming,' he said with a laugh. However, he felt his stomach knotting, for he knew how ruthless Robert could be when determined. Robert had defeated their father at Gerberoi, and then, by constantly raiding the borders of the Vexin, had caused his father's fatal injury at Mantes, which led to King William's death. Robert was a man to be reckoned with, not one to be underestimated.

Sir Philip led them quickly up a small hill to the south and through a copse of trees. The whole pastureland was laid out to the north in front of them. He could see why his brother had chosen it, but then, he moved his horse forward almost out of the trees to gaze at what lay in front of him in the southwest. Henry Beaumont kicked his horse forward and grabbed one of the King's reins to stop him from riding further.

'Do not risk being seen, Sire, or we will all be undone before we even come to battle. You can imagine Robert's boast if he takes you prisoner and has the crown without unsheathing his sword.'

Henry merely nodded. He found it difficult to speak because his mouth had gone dry at what he saw in front of him. The rumours and estimates were right; Robert had brought thousands of men and horses. He stared at the sea of colourful banners and pennants spread across the fields. It seemed endless and surrounded the village. Almost every noble house and family in Normandy and England were there in front of them. They had come to fight for his brother, whom they saw as the rightful king, and to defeat and kill him, the Oathbreaker. His face was almost as pale as the beautiful light grey steed he rode as he turned without a word and, pushing his way through his nobles, galloped back the way they had come.

Conn had seen the King's face blanch, and recognised it for what it was—fear. Henry was afraid, and glancing back at the sight behind them, he thought he had every right to be.

They decided to spend an additional night in Oakhanger, for it seemed as if it was up to them when they wanted to move forward and fight. On his return to camp, Conn immediately

CHAPTER TWENTY-TWO

checked to see if Georgio had returned. Still there was no sign, and he began to feel the first stirrings of concern as he spent the afternoon with the five other Horse Warriors, training the King's cavalry.

He had arranged to meet Rohese again later that evening. They both knew they were taking a risk but thought it was worth it. While hunting rabbits deep in the woods, Conn had chanced upon an ideal place to meet. It was a small but solid hut with a wooden shingle roof; Conn had thought it was probably used by charcoal burners or foresters as there were signs of recent fires inside the circle of stones. As soon as the cooking fires were lit and the usual evening camp tasks and routine began, he slipped away, as he knew her husband would be on hand for duty in the King's pavilion.

It was dry in the hut, and Conn spread his cloak on the ground, unrolled the blanket he had brought and lit a fire from the large pile of dried kindling and logs stacked in the corner. Then he sat in the firelight and waited. His mind automatically went to what he had heard and witnessed today. If it came to battle, which was likely, he realised that they had little chance, and he had seen the same thought on Henry's face. In any normal battle, the Horse Warriors would have minimal casualties, but he did not rate their chances if they were cut off and surrounded by hundreds of Robert's knights. He was so preoccupied with his thoughts that he did not hear Rohese's soft footfall on the mossy ground outside.

She stood outside the open door and put her hood down, watching him for several moments. It had been a warm day, so he wore only the sleeveless leather doublet. His skin was tanned by the many months he had spent in the heat of Byzantium, and his hair just touched his shoulders; she was pleased he had not embraced the short Norman style. The firelight flickered on his strong, handsome, clean-shaven face, and she felt her breath catch in her throat at the thought of this man making love to her. Suddenly, he looked up, met her eyes and smiled as she stepped into the hut to join him.

'It's just as you described—perfect,' she said as she unfastened her cloak, and he pulled her to sit down beside him.

She carried a leather bag over her shoulder and drew two goblets and a small sack of wine. He laughed at the beautifully carved goblets, fine enough to grace the King's table. 'Do you also have a banquet in there?'

'No, but I thought we would have a goblet of wine or two, and you could tell me what is troubling you. I saw your face as you rode in today.'

He sighed, not wanting to share his doubts or frighten her. She would know soon enough, for he did not doubt they would come to battle in a day or so.

'We are vastly outnumbered, and Henry's men are predominantly clerics, priests and peasants. We do not have enough trained knights—a hundred at the most.'

'I heard this too, and I hate to add to your worries, but Robert de Beaumont stormed into his brother's tent as I passed, shouting and complaining about fifty troops deserting.'

Conn shrugged. 'It was inevitable; the fact of the impossible odds we face will circulate like wildfire around the camp, and more will likely run rather than fight. Also, I'm becoming concerned that Georgio and Gracchus have not yet returned. I did not expect them to be away for this long.'

'It has only been a few days, and, from what I have seen of your men, I am sure they can look after themselves. I have watched you train,' she said, and he saw her cheeks flush as she admitted that. He smiled, pulled her closer into his arms, and they stayed like that for a while, her head tucked under his chin, her arms around his waist.

'I'm pleased you came. I know how difficult it is for you to get away.'

'It was easier tonight as a dinner is planned for the senior clergy. Henry is looking for answers and solutions, so Archbishop Anselm, William de Warelwast, and Bishop Maurice of London are there. My husband will oversee the event, dripping charm as usual as he is hoping for an advancement—he has his eye on an additional, lucrative post as the senior cleric of the Treasury. So we have an hour or two at least.'

He kissed her long and deeply, and with his hand caressing her breast, could feel her heart beating and her excitement rising. He released her, and her breathing was ragged as she whispered, 'What is astonishing is that I feel no regrets, no guilt about this liaison with you. I feel as if I deserve this.'

Her hands went boldly to the lace fastenings of his doublet. In no time at all, they were naked and entwined in each other's arms. Conn's lovemaking was not gentle this time. He had a need for her, and she responded, revelling in the feel of him and moving to meet his thrusts until they both cried out. They lay afterwards, gently stroking each other's bodies, until with a sigh, she whispered, 'It is late; I must go.'

He reluctantly released her, and kneeling forward, he reached for his braies, which he had carelessly thrown aside. Then he heard the gasp and gave a wry smile as he turned to look back at her.

'Do you know, I sometimes completely forget what is on my back? I usually keep it covered, but I wished to feel your skin on mine tonight.'

'What is it for?' she whispered, her fingers reaching out to run over the lines of the brightly coloured image which adorned his back.

'It is a long story, but suffice it to say that Georgio and I had no choice when these tattoos were inflicted upon us.'

She leant forward, her naked breasts pressed against his back as her arms came around his neck, and she kissed his shoulder.

'In some ways, it makes you even more special, more exciting. You are so different,' she said, kissing him again.

'Now, you must go!' he handed her the discarded gown and linen shift.

After she had gone, he sat in the firelight for some time, reliving and relishing the intensity of their lovemaking. He closed his eyes and could still feel the softness of her skin under his sword-calloused hands. She was a strong woman, witty, intelligent, and beautiful, and he frowned as he realised how much he was enjoying her company. She was the type of woman who would take anything in her stride—the perfect woman for a warrior. But she was the wife of a senior courtier. She belonged to someone else and had borne him a son. He suddenly felt a stab of irritation at that thought.

He sternly berated himself. 'No strings, no attachments,' he muttered as he rose and stamped out the fire with such ferocity that it was as if it were ten times the size.

Chapter Twenty-Three

Late July 1101 – Churt

Hope came at last to the cottage in Churt, a long, low wooden building with an old thatched roof. Outside, it was surrounded by numerous pens containing a variety of sheep and pigs. Usually, it would be a hive of activity at this time of year, feeding, fattening up and readying animals for the market, collecting animals from other small homesteaders in the area and driving them to nearby markets; for the last few days, the drover's wife had nursed the injured man they had brought home, while the children stood around watching, wide-eyed. The big, bearded man in their parent's box bed thrashed around, sweating and raving, sometimes for hours, in a language they didn't understand. He had numerous injuries, but it was the one on the back of his head that had worried her, for only now, days later, was the swelling subsiding around the wound, and he was beginning to calm.

They had been woken by the sound of many hooves on that fateful night. A large group of men were on the road above them, coming their way, and then there was shouting and roars of rage reverberating around the trees. The drover knew that the camp of the Horse Warriors was not far from their own. Fortunately, they were in a dip, a small valley that ran down to the stream where they often camped, so they could not be seen by the attackers. The drover had stood at first to help, but his wife had put her hand on his arm and shaken her head; there were too many of them. He had kicked the embers of their fire apart and stamped them into the ground so it didn't smoke and give them away, and then they had all huddled together, out of sight against the high bank.

The noise being made died down, but the drover did not sleep. He heard them leave at dawn but still waited a while; men like that did not like witnesses to their actions. He had crept through the trees, and to his surprise, the two big War Destriers were still there, cropping the grass. They had been let loose but were well-trained and hadn't wandered away. He had stood silently in the trees in the dim early morning light and could make out a body on the ground—it looked like the big, genial Horse Warrior who had given his children apples. He could not see the younger man anywhere. He had crept around the boulders and searched for him to no avail, then he had gone back to the body and placed a hand on the man's neck. To his surprise, he could feel a faint pulse. He was such a pasty grey colour, the drover had assumed him dead.

At first, he had presumed that this was a robbery. There were many groups of scavengers and deserters in the forests, but they would never have left the things he saw on the ground: the expensive saddles, saddlebags and certainly not the horses, for they were worth a fortune. A few moments later, his wife and children had arrived, and they turned the big man onto his side. He let out a low groan as they checked him over. He was badly beaten and kicked, and his forearm had been

CHAPTER TWENTY-THREE

snapped, but the wife was worried at the gash and swelling on the back of his head.

'We need to get him on a horse and back to our home,' the drover had announced, but he saw the worry and fear on his wife's face.

'With a head injury like that, he may not survive, and surely he will be missed. They must be knights with the King's army to have weapons and horses like that,' she argued. But he had overruled her—he couldn't just leave a man here to die.

They managed, with the help of their eldest son, to get him onto a horse, and brought him to their home at Churt.

The man had been semi-delirious ever since, but he gradually quietened, and when she applied a fresh poultice to the back of his head, he opened his eyes and blinked at her. She had smiled, but his eyes closed again. This time, however, he drifted off into a deep, undisturbed sleep.

'He must have a much thicker skull than most, for I didn't believe that he would survive that,' she whispered to her husband as she slipped into the pallet bed they had made up on the floor near the fire.

The man woke at noon the next day, and she gently propped him up, gave him watered ale to drink, which he gulped noisily, and then fed him half a bowl of thick pottage before he fell back onto the pillows and slept again until evening.

To her surprise, he called them over in the common language, and her husband sat on the end of the bed.

'You have shouted and raved in a different language for days; you must be from a faraway land.'

'Greece was my home, but we were scouting the Wolds for the King. Where is my captain, Georgio? Is he dead?' he asked, his voice breaking at the thought. The drover shook his head.

'There was only you and the two horses, which I hid behind the house. There was no sign of your friend. However, when we followed the track above, there were signs of forty or more horses. It was a large group that attacked you, and behind their hoof prints, I saw boot marks in the softer mud, wide apart as if someone was running behind them. I believe they must have taken him prisoner. Maybe that was what the attack was all about. Was he important, this captain of yours?'

Gracchus shook his head, which produced dizziness and pain, so he put his hands on either side of his head to hold it still and try to remember what had happened. Suddenly, Owens's face came to him. 'It was the Welsh mercenaries! They took him—but they hated Georgio, so it could only have been for revenge. I don't understand why they were up here on the ridge; they were with the King's army moving through the Hindhead Gap.'

'Well, they've headed north at speed, so it looks like they were deserting the King,' added the drover.

'I must get back. I have to tell Malvais what has happened. He has to go after them before they kill Georgio,' he said, moving as if to get out of bed. However, the room began to spin immediately, and he was hit with a wave of nausea that made him fall back on the bolster as the drover's wife stepped forward and wiped the sweat from his brow.

'That head injury will keep you here for at least another day or so. We have splinted your arm and strapped your broken ribs, but you can't ride for days yet in this state. You are lucky to be alive,' she said.

Gracchus thanked her and closed his eyes, but he was ashamed, and tears began to run from his eyes at the thought of what Georgio was going through in the hands of Owen.

She saw this and sat holding his hand as he muttered through clenched teeth, 'We will find him. I swear we will find him.'

Late July 1101 – The road to Chester

Georgio's days seemed filled with constant pain as his battered body was subjected to long days on horseback, stopping only for the odd hour or so to rest and water the horses. Rhys brought him water and a small amount of food each day, but it was not enough, and he seemed constantly thirsty and hungry. Also, because of the way his feet were strapped under the horse, his thighs and calves were rubbed raw through chafing, and he could hardly stand when they let him down to piss.

The names of the places they passed or stayed in meant nothing to Georgio, although he was relieved when the group crossed a ford on the River Ceiriog and halted for an hour at a small hamlet called Chirk, where they bought bread and cheese at a local inn. While they ate, Owen took Rhys to one side, and Georgio edged closer to them to scoop water from the trough and listen to what he was saying.

'Rhys, I've decided that we should split here rather than further north. I want you to take most of the men and head west along the Dee Valley towards our lands in Gwynedd. Meanwhile, I'll take our hostage and five of our men and ride for Wrexham. I imagine that I will be no more than a week or so behind you.'

Rhys rarely questioned Owen's orders, but he looked unhappy at this as he stared west along the valley. 'Are these not the lands of the Hughes of Gwerclas, family of your enemy Maredudd ap Bleddyn, the prince of Powys, who still bears you grudges? He would, no doubt, be delighted to find us riding his lands without his permission,' he asked with a frown.

'Yes, but you're still taking almost forty men with you. Ride fast; don't tarry on the way, and they'll not bother you nor any armed band of that size,' he said reassuringly, but Rhys didn't look convinced.

Georgio could hear the discontent in his voice as they moved away, Rhys arguing that they should stay together. He heard some mention of an abbey in Chester, but it was obvious that Owen had made his decision.

He only had seconds while the men stood around waving off the main troop, but Georgio pulled off the small amulet, which hung on a leather thong around his neck and flung it near the trough. If Malvais came this way, which was possible, there was a chance in a hundred that he might see it, that was if no one picked it up first. It was a distinctive small ceramic cross that had been given to Georgio by his friend, Diego Rodriguez, the son of El Cid, just before the battle of Consuegra in which young Diego was killed.

They finally stopped that evening at a large homestead north of the market town of Wrexham, which they had avoided. They received a warm welcome, with much back-slapping from the men and smiles from a middle-aged woman. For the first time, Georgio was brought into the house and given a hot meal, which he wolfed down, as did the other men, although his wrists remained tightly tied. The owner of the homestead was a sheep farmer and local bailiff, but he was also a relative of Owen, which became apparent when they retired to their makeshift pallet beds, and the two men sat drinking and talking at the table. Georgio turned to the wall

CHAPTER TWENTY-THREE

and feigned sleep. The swelling around his nose had finally subsided, and he could breathe normally again.

'Who is he? Where you taking him?' the farmer asked of Owen. Before answering, the Welsh leader gave his answer some thought, for no one trusted anyone in these lands, especially not family.

'He is an enemy. He is responsible for the death of our cousin, Black Brynn. I'm taking him to a little-known safe place while I decide what to do with him. He may prove useful as a bargaining tool, and some high-up people may even pay to get him back,' he explained while filling their cups with wine again.

Georgio could almost feel their eyes on him as he kept as still as possible—they had sunk at least a full sack of wine, and he knew emotions could run high at that point.

However, to his relief, they began to talk of other things, such as the good news about Sir Hugh's death and the impact of that on the area. Georgio was exhausted and could not prevent himself from drifting off, so he heard no more until he was shaken awake by the woman the next morning. He groaned with pain as he moved and flinched when he went to sit on the wooden bench at the trestle table. Owen and the others were still sleeping, so she took pity on him and handed him a pot of goose grease while putting her finger to her lips and miming what he should do.

'Spread it on thickly, but be quick,' she whispered, glancing at the sleeping man, as Georgio unfastened his braies and spread it on the raw flesh with relief.

Georgio could have kissed her, and he gave her a smile of thanks that almost melted her heart. She had heard Owen's words last night and could only imagine what the young man had been through. Owen was not a man she liked. He was bitter about the fact that his father never recognised him and this had made him cruel and vindictive, always ready to see insults and quick with his fists against men—and women.

An hour later, Georgio was back on the horse and on the busy road to Chester. There were several delays, and it was early evening when they finally approached the huge gates of another monastery or abbey deep in the city. Georgio had looked around with some interest as they rode through the streets, and it occurred to him that for a black-hearted Welsh mercenary, Owen ap Cynan seemed to have a lot of influence in monasteries and abbeys up and down the country. He wondered why that was. The words, "The Abbot owes me," returned to him. What service or task was Owen carrying out, he wondered, for these so-called Houses of God? He was soon to find out as the huge gates were opened, and they rode into the large abbey and monastery of St. Werburgh.

Several young monks came bustling out to take the horses as they dismounted, and Georgio was untied, pulled down and pushed along in front of them, as a tall, gaunt, but impressive figure strode towards them. He wore the best quality black woollen Benedictine robes, and an expensive large silver crucifix hung at his belt.

'Welcome to St. Werburgh's Abbey, Owen. To what do I owe the pleasure of this visit? Unless you have come to visit the tomb of Sir Hugh to check that he is truly dead—and then spit on it?'

Owen laughed and bowed his head to the Benedictine. It was the first time that Georgio had seen him show respect for anyone, so he surmised that this was someone of importance and influence.

CHAPTER TWENTY-THREE

'Abbot Columbanus, I have truly missed your wit, but you must remember there is still the matter of the forty pieces of silver you owe me for clearing your lands of those troublesome tenants.'

The Abbot glanced nervously around and shot a quick, darkling, warning glance at Owen, who laughed again.

'Do not fear; no one will ever know of our arrangement,' he said in a loud whisper.

'Come inside where we can talk,' the Abbot murmured, ignoring Owen's jibe, and leading the way at a quick pace.

Georgio realised exactly who this Benedictine was, and glancing around, he could see how new the buildings were. Sir Hugh had paid for this large abbey church and attached Benedictine monastery to be built and dedicated to St. Werburgh, a venerated Anglo-Saxon princess and the patron saint of Chester. The Abbot's house was commodious and well-furnished. Columbanus led them through into the large hall and bade them sit while refreshments were served, then, he noticed Georgio's hands tied in front of him and the yellow, purpling bruising still clear on his face, and he raised an eyebrow in surprise. Of more concern to Columbanus was the unusual, quality leather doublet, laced at the sides and imprinted with Breton designs. He had only recently seen the same attire worn by Conn Fitz Malvais.

Owen sat in one of the chairs by the window, patiently waiting, while ale and food for the men, and wine for the Abbot and his guest were brought.

'So, are you here to collect your payment, Owen?' asked Columbanus, but his eyes still went to the beaten Horse Warrior sitting with the others at a long table at the end of the room.

'No, not exactly. I'm here for a favour, and I have certainly done enough of those for you over the years, my dear Abbot. This favour will wipe out the debt you owe me.'

Columbanus stared at the Welsh mercenary, immediately cautious and suspicious; Owen was not the kind of man who would ask for a favour lightly. He took a mouthful of wine, placed the goblet back on the table and steepled his fingers.

'How exactly can I help you, Owen?'

Owen sat forward and lowered his voice. 'I was here in Chester when you first started to design and build this monastery. You were having problems with a local merchant who did not want to sell his land, do you remember? I persuaded him to sell you the land.'

The Abbot nodded, wondering where this was going and how it was relevant.

'There were the remains of an old Saxon church, most of which was demolished as that was where the new monk's refectory was to be built, but you had a problem because attached to the old church were two sunken anchorite cells. Some ancient hag who was supposed to do miracles by curing the sick was in one of them, had been for nigh on twenty years. I remember that you had to keep them and include them in the north-facing wall, leaving them attached to the abbey Church, or there would have been an outcry from the locals. Is she still alive?'

Columbanus was now indeed perplexed. Was there someone Owen needed curing? If so, he was too late. 'No, she died five or six years ago,' he replied.

'So, the anchorite cells—are they still intact?' he asked, and Columbanus nodded.

'Good, as I have brought a prisoner with me. I want to put

him into one of them. I will expect you to make arrangements, to feed him well and keep him alive, but no one here can ever know who he is. I need you to ensure that if anyone comes looking, they will never find him or even suspect he might be here. I may need him keeping here for a year or two.'

The Abbot's eyes went immediately to the man on the bench, who, with his hands still tied, was trying to raise the tankard of ale to his lips.

'Who is he?' he whispered.

'He is a Horse Warrior responsible for killing my cousin, but I've been led to believe that he's also the protégé of a very wealthy man, and he could prove very lucrative to both of us. He could bring us a ransom that would pay for half of the new abbey you want to build on the land Sir Hugh promised you.'

Columbanus sat back. He was not naive; he knew that Owen had been recruited to fight with the King's army, so he realised that the Welsh mercenary must have deserted. This meant he needed to get Owen away from the abbey as soon as possible, just in case the Beaumont brothers came looking for him and suspected he was harbouring him. However, there was another aspect of this 'favour' that worried him.

'This prisoner of yours, is he one of Malvais' Breton Horse Warriors—one of his men?' This threw Owen for a moment, and the Abbot, seeing the surprise on the Welshman's face, smiled as he watched him struggling to form an answer.

'Yes, but you don't need to worry about Malvais, as he's leading the cavalry charge for the King in the forthcoming battle. Duke Robert's army is three times the size of Henry's, and Malvais will not survive the fight. At the moment, he thinks his men were attacked and are both dead, and no one will disabuse him of that.'

Columbanus frowned. He was only partially reassured by that answer.

'You may stay tonight, Owen, but I want you gone from here tomorrow. I will order the cell cleaned tonight, and two servants will help seal it tomorrow. They can all be trusted, and we'll find him the robe of an anchorite and place him there tomorrow. However, you will keep me informed if things change and anyone starts looking or asking questions. Also, the ransom, if it is paid, can never be traced back to me, Owen.'

Owen nodded, pleased with the way things had fallen into place. The next morning, they were woken early, sat in the refectory to break their fast, and then Columbanus led Owen, two monks and Georgio to a long, narrow, stone corridor which led to the back of the abbey. At the end was a heavily barred door which stood open, and it led to a small walled yard and steps down to a wall that looked as if it had partly collapsed. Two monks in brown robes stood waiting with buckets full of some thick substance.

Georgio was pushed ahead over the rubble and large stones into a small cell. A palliasse lay on the floor in one corner with a folded blanket, a large jug of water and a leather cup stood beside it, while in the other corner was a bucket for waste. Just above head height was a long, thin, barred window and another small opening with a ledge where, in the past, gifts of food would have been given to the anchorite from grateful locals. On the floor was a narrow sluice to pour or empty the waste away. He stood and waited, thinking it was odd that there was no door; it must have been pulled out or taken from the opening and would now be replaced.

'Strip him,' ordered Columbanus.

CHAPTER TWENTY-THREE

Owen cut the ropes on Georgio's wrists, where they had rubbed the skin red raw. They pulled off his leather boots, took his leather doublet and pulled off the thin linen shirt that was covered in his blood. Then he unfastened and dropped his filthy braies himself, stepping barefooted out of them to stand naked in the cell.

'Dear God, I wonder that he is still alive with those injuries. Did you try to beat him to death first?' he asked, looking at the young man's body covered in bruises, with worrying swelling around his broken ribs.

'It is a miracle one of those broken ribs hasn't pierced a lung if you've bounced him on horseback for days. Get Brother Gerard, our physician, down here immediately,' he ordered one of the monks.

Owen shrugged as Columbanus walked around the prisoner, but then the Abbot gasped, his face blanched, and he stepped back in alarm.

'What in God's name have you brought to my door, Owen? I would never have agreed if I had known of this,' he said, pointing at Georgio, his voice rising in anger.

Owen, wide-eyed, looked puzzled, as Columbanus gripped Georgio by the shoulders and turned him to show the Welsh mercenary what he was staring at. Owens's mouth dropped open at the startling full-length tattoo on the Horse Warrior's back. A long blue steel sword was turned into a cross, flames flickering up the blade from its point.

'What does it mean?' he whispered, also awed by the sight of the tattoo.

'This man was one of the chosen seven. Cardinal Dauferio, who became Pope Victor, established seven cells across Europe, each one with seven boys, who were controlled and run by ruthless warrior monks. Seven extraordinary boys were chosen to become their leaders, true warriors of Christ. They were trained in every skill, taught for hours by the best scholars in every area of knowledge, and could speak several languages. They were trained to become exceptional in the use of every weapon. When they reached their ninth birthday, they were taken out and taught how to kill and murder. At fifteen, they were to be set loose on the enemies of the Church. Each has the same tattoo, with the seven drops of blood dripping from the crown of thorns on the cross-piece of the sword. No one must ever know about this, Owen. You must forget you have ever seen this and never speak of it. I dread to think of the repercussions if the Holy See finds out we have one of The Seven imprisoned here.'

Owen was just as shocked as the Abbot and stepped back as Brother Gerard arrived and tutted repeatedly when he saw Georgio's condition. He immediately set about ministering to him. While this happened, Owen found that he had to step out for air. He was a converted Christian; he had, with many others in his tribe, reluctantly left the old religion and gods behind in the face of this powerful new Christian god and his martyred son. Now, he wondered if, in some way, he might suffer divine vengeance. Being the pragmatist he was, he shrugged it off. It was done now, and he was not one to repent or regret his actions, especially if those actions brought him a large ransom.

Georgio stood and suffered having the deep cut above his eye stitched and his ribs strapped up. He was given theriac and wine to drink and then handed a rough, hooded anchorite robe, tied at the waist with a piece of rope with a plain wooden crucifix attached. During all this, Georgio's eyes had never left

CHAPTER TWENTY-THREE

the face of Columbanus, who leaned against the wall watching everything. Now, as the physician left, Georgio turned on him.

'You knew about us!' he exclaimed.

Columbanus nodded. 'I was a young acolyte of Dauferio and completely under his sway in France. He had this vision, and at the time, I could only see the glory in what he was doing and creating. You were to be trained to be the best in the world. As a young man, I could see this army of shining warriors of Christ.'

'We were trained and will probably never lose the skills and knowledge, but fortunately, we were rescued; Dauferio was killed, and we were all set free. However, we are all damaged by what they did to us.'

Columbanus nodded again. 'Only afterwards did the truth of what he was doing come out, and I did penance for my involvement in finding the boys for him in France. You are Owen's prisoner, not here of my own volition, and I am now returning to my home in Eynsham, but I promise I will ensure that you are looked after and well-fed.'

To Georgio's surprise, he fell to his knees and beckoned the other two monks, who came and knelt beside him as he held up the silver crucifix.

'You are now entering an anchorite cell, and we must say the prayers to signify the anchorite's death to the world and your rebirth to a life of spiritual communion with God.'

They prayed for several minutes, the two monks giving the responses to the Abbot while Georgio stood, bewildered by what he was watching. Finally, they rose, and Columbanus turned to him.

'I may not see you again, so I give you God's blessing to help you survive your ordeal and life in this anchorite cell.'

He climbed out over the stones and rubble when suddenly, a frightening thought occurred to the Abbot. He turned, a tall black figure silhouetted in the light.

'Tell me, was Malvais one of the seven in your cell? Does he also bear the tattoo?'

Georgio nodded, and the Benedictine had to put out a hand for support on the broken, crumbling wall before stepping into the yard and tightly gripping the arm of a nearby monk.

'Go and pack my things and ready my horse; I'm leaving today!' he exclaimed before turning to Owen. 'You have no idea what you have brought down on us, Owen ap Cynan, no idea at all. If Malvais is also one of the seven, he will hunt you down to find this man until death takes him.'

Georgio stared at the light streaming through the gap in the wall, thinking of all he had seen and heard. It seemed impossible that the name of Dauferio was back in his life; he had been pleased when he heard that Chatillon had poisoned the Pope, for he deserved to die for his actions, so many had died in his name.

Suddenly, the light dimmed, and the two monks in brown robes appeared and began their work. They were rebuilding the wall that had collapsed; it was only when it reached chest height that Georgio realised there would be no door. They were bricking him in. He was being entombed.

They left a square opening at the top, barely more than a handbreadth wide, for food to be passed through. As he stared at it, he heard them discussing building a second wall to reinforce the outside.

He sat on the straw-stuffed palliasse on the floor and wrapped the rough blanket around his shoulders. The cell was north-facing, it was July, and it was already cold—he could not imagine what it would be like in the winter.

Then a thought struck him: no one knew he was there, apart from a corrupt Benedictine abbot and Owen, a Welsh mercenary who hated him. How on earth would Malvais ever find him?

Now, at his lowest ebb, his many wounds sore and his broken ribs aching, Georgio finally put his head in his hands and let the tears flow. There was no one to see them and deride him for his despair.

Chapter Twenty-Four

Late July 1101 – Alton

It had taken all day for Henry's forces to arrive and begin setting up camp on the far side of the meadows from Alton. The sea of banners that covered Robert's huge camp was clear to see for everyone now, and produced an awe-stricken silence as men stood and stared at the huge force which would soon be arrayed in front of them. However, the tents and pavilions were soon raised, and their own flags and banners were displayed.

De Clare decided to find Malvais and arrived at the Horse Warrior's camp just as the estimable Darius arrived with a recently killed, plump goose, which he swore was bought from a farmer's wife. Within minutes, the men had quartered and sectioned the large bird, and its innards, seen as a delicacy, were sizzling on a flat stone in the embers of the fire. Conn had risked sending Darius into the village for information rather than food, but it was a bonus. However, although the squire had questioned several troops, no one had seen two Horse Warriors riding large War Destriers, and to their knowledge, none had been captured. A downcast Darius

CHAPTER TWENTY-FOUR

stood in front of Conn outside their pavilion.

'They seem to have just disappeared. Their horses are so distinctive, surely they would have been noticed,' he said.

Tight-lipped, Conn nodded and sent him to help with the food while he poured De Clare some wine.

'They should have returned two days ago. This is highly unusual. If they had been in trouble or injured, they would know what to do, as they are both experienced fighters, and somehow, they would have got a message to us. The problem is we are on the eve of battle; I cannot take my men and search for them. We are leading the charge tomorrow, and the King's cavalry are under our command on the right wing.'

De Clare could see the worry in the younger warrior's face. Conn was the son of his dearest friend, Morvan de Malvais, and he knew that the family had adopted Georgio and thought of him as another son. He had to do what he could to help, for Conn was right—for them to go missing after a simple patrol was odd.

'No, you cannot abandon your post, and neither can I, but I've a very astute serjeant—he can take three of his men and ride out at first light. I know the route they took. If anything is amiss, he'll find them.'

'You can do that?' asked Conn in surprise.

De Clare laughed and emptied his goblet, holding it out to be refilled as he lowered his voice to a whisper.

'We all know the odds now; we can see the size of the force in front of us. Do you expect a few less of my men will make a difference? I suppose you heard that your friend Owen and his men disappeared—the odds were too much for *them*. Robert Beaumont has sworn to hunt him down after this and have his head put on a spike.'

They were finishing the last of the goose, and the sun was sinking when Lady Rohese de Courcy appeared. She stopped short, in alarm, when she saw De Clare with Conn, but he held up his hands and stood to leave while Conn indicated she should go into the pavilion. De Clare hid it well, but he was shocked that she would risk coming to the pavilion of her lover while it was still light.

'You are playing with fire,' he whispered to Conn as he slapped him on the shoulder and left.

King Henry had dismissed all of his nobles. Now, on the eve of battle, he found he wanted to be alone—he needed to think. However, that was not to be, as Robert Fitz Hamon arrived fresh from Winchester. Henry gave in with good grace and waved him to a chair.

'How is the Queen?' was Henry's first question. It was true that she was with child, but it was in the dangerous first four months when women could slip a child easily, especially if shocked or worried.

'She is well, strong and courageous, but she worries about you, Sire. She has sent you a missive,' he said, handing Henry a small sheet of folded vellum.

The King unfolded and scanned its contents and smiled. As expected, she sent her love, which he did not doubt despite his numerous mistresses. She also told him to try to negotiate and not to risk a battle. He was to try and placate his brother with promises. This was more or less what Henry Beaumont, Earl of Warwick, had told him repeatedly for two days—promise Robert anything, but do not give him the crown and do not come to battle.

At that moment, a squire appeared in the doorway.

'My Lord King, a messenger has arrived from the enemy camp.'

Henry raised his eyebrows in surprise as it was getting late. He glanced over at Fitz Hamon to see if he knew anything of this, but the noble just gave a slight shrug.

'This could be the call to battle, the time and place tomorrow,' the King murmured.

'Show him in,' ordered Fitz Hamon.

A slightly plump man of average height, carrying a leather pouch, appeared before him. To Henry's surprise, it had his own insignia stamped on it—it was one of his. The messenger threw back his hood, and the King frowned at the smooth, bland features he vaguely recognised.

Fitz Hamon sat forward as he *did* recognise the miscreant. 'You were De Clare's steward, were you not?'

Bernard nodded. 'Only temporarily, my lord. I was also a cupbearer for King William Rufus, may God rest his soul. However, when my real master returned to England, I was summoned to his side.'

'Please share with us who that may be?' asked Henry in a cold, thin voice.

'Ranulf Flambard, who was Prince Bishop of Durham.'

Fitz Hamon shot to his feet and drew his blade.

'Shall I cut his throat now, Henry?' he shouted.

Bernard did not move. He had expected this. Flambard had taken a risk by sending him into King Henry's camp again, but he knew how good Bernard could be, and he was forced to do something to try to get ahead of Belleme and Mortain, who were pushing for war.

'If you do that, my Lord Fitz Hamon, then the King will not receive the information I carry—information which will be highly advantageous to him. You see, my master was not betraying you when he went to Normandy; he was working for you, hoping to gain the ear of Duke Robert. He has always despised the Duke, and Normandy would never have been returned to Robert if William Rufus had not been murdered. Now, my master is in a position to help you negotiate.'

So saying, he drew a letter from the pouch and, kneeling, handed it to the King, who scanned its contents before handing it to Fitz Hamon. He sheathed his sword as Bernard continued.

'You will see Flambard tells you that the Duke is wavering despite the size of his force. That is true. I have seen it with my own eyes. Robert de Belleme and Count William de Mortain want this war. They want to see you crushed, Sire. Neither of them has any love for you, and both have past grievances against you.'

Henry nodded as he knew this to be true. He took the letter back and read it again.

'He suggests that I meet my brother, one to one, just the two of us. But will the others allow that to happen?'

'Flambard will ensure it does, but it is imperative that you discuss this with Anselm and have him there with you at the negotiations. Flambard does not understand why our Archbishop of Canterbury has not raised the crucial point he highlights in his final paragraph. You are an anointed king; if anyone tries to usurp an anointed king, it can lead to excommunication by the Pope. Duke Robert is a pious crusader—that threat will be significant to him.'

Henry's eyes widened as he read it again. Flambard was right. They hadn't considered or discussed *that* argument.

'Tell Flambard I agree. Tell him to set up negotiations, and we will send intermediaries tomorrow who can arrange a meeting with Robert,' he said, as Fitz Hamon agreed to be one of them.

Suddenly, Henry narrowed his eyes at Bernard and raised a hand to stop him from leaving. 'Wait! What exactly does Ranulf Flambard expect from me for this assistance?' he demanded.

'Very little, my Lord King. Although he wants to keep your favour, he does not expect nor want a position at court. He only wishes to return to his diocese and his position as Bishop of Durham to finish building the cathedral. He intends to embrace a religious life, but of course, at the same time, he will guard your interests in the north. He has considerable influence in the wild borderlands, even amongst the Scots.'

'I will think on it,' announced Henry, and dismissed him.

Bernard left the King's pavilion very pleased with the results. He had bribed and brought two of Mortain's large bodyguards with him.

'I think we may have prevented a battle tomorrow. Flambard will be pleased, and perhaps he will reward all of us for getting the message in and out whilst staying alive, although it was a close call. Now, let us leave this camp and return to the horses without being recognised.'

He pulled up his hood and they headed southwest, wending through the campfires to the outskirts of the encampment. They made for the large copse of trees on a slight hill, where Henry had recently ridden to view his brother's camp; they had left their horses tied on the far side. The moon was high, and as they entered the copse, Bernard heard voices which he presumed were a patrol, so he raised a hand to stop his men, and they listened. Someone was ahead of them, but they could hear a woman's voice; she seemed to be pleading. They moved further into the trees. There was a clearing on their right, and he could see the dark shapes of the two figures who were turned away from him. One was tall and broad, the other smaller—a woman wearing a cloak. The man turned into the moonlight, and Bernard recognised him. It was Malvais, and he was without the famed crossed swords on his back.

Bernard stood, holding his men back as they watched, and then he turned and whispered, 'That man—I want him badly hurt but not killed; Flambard wants him alive. You cannot use swords—the noise of clashing blades would bring them running from the camp. Look for something else to use.'

The larger of the two men picked up a thick, sturdy branch, and Bernard nodded before turning to the other man. 'Grab the woman and stop her from screaming.'

All three men moved stealthily forward towards Malvais, who had Rohese in his arms and was kissing her. A strong breeze rustled the trees around them, and he didn't hear the attackers approach until the last second. He was turning at a sound when the blow descended, knocking him to the ground. The big man brought the heavy bough down again, with considerable force, across Conn's shoulders to keep him on the ground. Then he moved in front and stood over Conn's head to deliver another blow that would knock him out.

Conn was dazed, his face pressed into the wet leaves, his fingers curled into the moss and mud to get a grip and push himself up. Although reeling from the blows to his head and

CHAPTER TWENTY-FOUR

shoulders, he could hear Rohese's muted screams, and he knew he had to move to help her. Conn's hand frantically reached down for his dagger. He saw the man's foot move to beside his head and sensed that the next blow was about to be delivered. Conn slammed the long dagger, with as much force as he could muster, through his enemy's booted foot, and twisted it. The man let out a cry of pain and fell backwards, dropping the bough, which glanced off Conn's back, as he struggled to his knees, dizzy and lightheaded from the heavy blow to his temple. The other man held a struggling Rohese, who elbowed him sharply in the ribs and clamped her teeth down on the fingers over her mouth. He swore, swung her away and hit her hard, which laid her out on the ground.

Back in the camp, Richard de Clare had met Robert Fitz Hamon coming from the King's pavilion, who told him of Bernard's arrival in the camp and the message he delivered. De Clare was astonished at the brazen effrontery of the man, a traitor and a spy, to come back. At that moment, Robert de Courcy came striding up to them.

'Has anyone seen my wife?' he demanded. They shook their heads, and he turned away. Then he returned, moving his face close to De Clare's.

'He is *your* friend. If she's with him again, I swear they will pay for it!' he shouted.

De Clare held his hands up and shrugged to show he knew nothing. However, as soon as De Courcy disappeared between the tents, De Clare ran to Conn's pavilion to warn the erstwhile lovers, but it was empty. He pounced on Darius, who sat by the fire.

'Where are they? Her husband is coming, probably with his men,' he shouted.

Darius shot to his feet and pointed to the copse of trees in the distance, and both of them set off at a run.

Conn had thrown himself on the man he had pinned to the ground. The man had drawn his own dagger now, and although light-headed, Conn was wrestling him for possession of it. Rohese was out cold behind them. The second man, dagger drawn, gave a shout and began to run at Conn to help his friend.

Bernard, watching, quickly stepped back into the trees, horrified at how the situation was now out of his control. Fear filled him as he saw De Clare and Darius, swords drawn, running into the clearing. They initially thought it was De Courcy and his men they were facing until Darius saw the white, shocked face of Bernard in the moonlight and cried out to De Clare in warning.

Conn had finally wrenched the dagger from the big man's hand and, hearing the shout, had rolled sideways onto his back to face the second attacker when, to his surprise, the man's body arched and fell sideways, run through from behind by De Clare. This was enough for Bernard, who turned and ran as if the hounds of hell were on his heels. Seeing this, Darius screamed his name in rage, and Richard de Clare, followed by Conn, set off in pursuit.

'Stay and see to Rohese,' Conn shouted over his shoulder to Darius. Through the trees, sweeping and snapping branches from his path, he raced after De Clare, whose dark shape he could just see and hear, crashing ahead of him on the left.

Flambard's spy, Bernard, was running for his life. He reached their horses and hauled himself into the saddle of the nearest just as the two men burst from the trees. De Clare leapt for the reins and just caught them, jerking them

CHAPTER TWENTY-FOUR

downwards and clinging on as Bernard frantically kicked the horse onwards. The horse, alarmed, shook its head, swung its hindquarters round into De Clare, who hung on. Finally, unable to free itself from its attacker, the horse reared, toppling Bernard backwards to hit the ground but leaving it free to gallop riderless back to camp.

Bernard lay winded on the ground as De Clare and Conn stood over him. They pulled him to his feet, and De Clare dragged him back to the clearing. A dazed Rohese sat on the ground, her head in her hands. A large bruised swelling was appearing on the side of her face as Darius hovered over her. Conn turned quickly to where he had pinned the other man to the ground, but his attacker was gone. Conn's long, blood-stained dagger lay on the leaves.

De Clare threw Bernard to the ground and kicked him several times before grabbing him by the throat of his cloak and pulling him to his knees.

'Now, Bernard, tell us what Flambard is up to, having you creep around the King's camp, or I swear I will take both of your eyes out,' said De Clare, dropping to his haunches in front of the frightened man and drawing his dagger.

In minutes, they knew everything; Bernard was a coward and would do anything to save his skin. He hoped Malvais would let him go. Conn, however, had other plans.

'Give him your sword, De Clare,' he ordered as Bernard's eyes opened wide in terror, and he began to babble.

'I cannot fight you, Malvais; I am not a swordsman like you. It would be unfair, and I believe you to be a man of honour.'

'I do not intend to fight you, Bernard. I would not sully my hands or reputation with you, but you're a spy, and you must pay for what you have done. You employed Black Brynn to track my men, and he killed one of them, a young Greek boy, his name was Andreas. His friend, another Greek boy, will now take his revenge.'

He waved Darius forward while De Clare pulled Bernard to his feet, handing him a sword.

Bernard continued to protest. 'The Welshman was not ordered to do that; he was only meant to follow your men. We intended no harm, my lord. Do you not realise I even got rid of the Welsh mercenaries for you? I took my life in my hands again at the Hindhead Gap to sneak into King Henry's camp and pay them to go so that you would be troubled by them no longer. I had your interests at heart.'

Conn was no longer listening to his pleas, but De Clare was.

'Wait, you paid nearly fifty mercenaries to desert the King? You deserve to die twice over for that alone. I should take you to Henry, who would have you hung and drawn for that,' he shouted.

Conn, who had turned away to go to Rohese, turned back to stare at Bernard, and a cold shiver went through him. Georgio and Gracchus could face up to most things, but not a group of mercenaries of that size.

Darius had also been listening. 'But that means they left the same morning as Georgio and Gracchus, and now they are missing, gone, because of you,' he said, running at Bernard with a strangled cry.

It was over in no time. Now a competent swordsman, Darius, beat the hapless Bernard back, raining blows down on him until he dropped to his knees, begging for clemency. But Darius was in no mood for mercy. He could only think of Andreas, Georgio and Gracchus, and he finished him off far too quickly for De Clare, who, nonetheless, slapped the

CHAPTER TWENTY-FOUR

young squire on the shoulder in approval.

Chapter Twenty-Five

31st July 1101 – Alton

Flambard found he could not speak. He was consumed with rage as he regarded the injured man before him. He had been woken in the middle of the night as two others had helped Bernard's henchman to a chair in his tent. Once there, he had bled through the bandage onto the hessian floor of his tent and related his sorry tale. At one point, Flambard found that he had to turn away and clench his fists to get any control over his features before he turned back to the bruised and bleeding man.

'Let us try again, but I want you to truly wrack your brain for any more details of what happened at the King's pavilion—anything Bernard said to you.'

The man sighed. This was the third time of telling. He was exhausted, in pain, and had not been paid, so he tried to embellish, even more, the account of what happened.

'Bernard was allowed in, taken to the King, and we had to wait outside. We heard shouting at first, then the hum of conversation but not what was being said. He was in there with the King and my Lord Fitz Hamon for some time. When he came out, he only said you would be pleased with how things had gone. We moved swiftly through the camp and were almost at the horses when he suddenly saw a Horse Warrior he had some grudge with and told us to attack him in revenge.'

Flambard flung his arms into the air in frustration at this. 'Was he mad? Had he lost all use of his senses at that point? Why would he even think of doing such a thing when he knew I needed him back here? He would have needed ten men to attack and best a man like Malvais.'

'We did not know who we were attacking or would not even have considered it. We know his reputation, but it was dark; we only saw two shapes.'

Flambard gave a roar of rage that alarmed the man until he calmed and dropped into the chair opposite, his chin on his chest.

'Is there any chance he could be alive and only wounded? Are you sure that Bernard is dead?' he asked hopefully.

'There is no doubt, Sire. I could not run, so I hid myself in the trees under leaves until they had gone. I limped back to check on them—they were dead, and one of the men had run Bernard through the heart.'

Flambard shook his head at the hopelessness of it all, and, throwing a small purse at the man, he dismissed him and thought of what to do next. His problem lay in the fact that Belleme and the Count of Mortain kept him away from Robert under the pretext of inner circle only. It was no good, he had to find the courage to force his way into Robert's presence tomorrow. King Henry had obviously agreed to negotiate, but he had to get Robert to agree, or his dreams of returning to Durham were over.

He stood and paced while cursing Malvais and Chatillon, for he blamed them both, but he would take his revenge. When this was over, he would find a way to bring the Horse Warrior's parentage to light. Malvais was a danger to the two brothers as neither had a legitimate heir yet. A bastard child would not have been a problem for them, but a grown man with a reputation as an unbeatable warrior who had respect and admiration was—*he* could easily become a figurehead for discontented rebels.

In Henry's camp, Darius was ministering to Conn, holding a cold, wet compress to the swelling on his temple, and then he rubbed in an ointment from a small stone pot.

'In God's name, Darius, what *is* that?' he demanded.

'The Jew's wife in London gave it to me; it's a herb called arnica, which is said to prevent bruising. She said it would be useful in our profession,' he announced, with some satisfaction while replacing the lid.

Conn managed a smile despite his pounding head and bruised, aching shoulders.

'Are you turning into an apothecary? If so, I cannot wait to take you to Chatillon's estate outside Paris. Ahmed, the greatest physician and apothecary in Europe, lives there. Once in his workshop, you will find that you cannot stay away. He is also the foremost expert on poisons—along with Isabella, Chatillon's wife.'

'Is that the one that Georgio is in love with?' Darius asked

CHAPTER TWENTY-FIVE

innocently.

Conn turned and looked at his squire, perplexed, as he was unaware that Georgio was in love with anyone at Chatillon's home. Isabella was a famous beauty and, of course, much younger than Chatillon. He smiled at the thought of Georgio being in love with Piers De Chatillon's wife. Georgio certainly liked to live dangerously, but then he remembered De Clare's words: *You are playing with fire.* Was he not doing the same with Rohese?

'I was not aware of that, but Georgio has always been a romantic. She is stunning, and any young man would fall in love with her,' he answered.

'Do you think they are still alive after what Bernard told us?' asked Darius, staring at Conn's face intensely in the candlelight to see how much hope was there.

'We are talking of two exceptional Horse Warriors, and De Clare's men are going out to search today. Now, let us grab what sleep we can for the remaining few hours. It will likely come to battle tomorrow.'

However, when he lay on his camp bed, the sudden memory of Bernard's voice shouting, "Do not kill him, Flambard needs him!" came to him. It was a worrying thought that he was to play any part in Flambard's plans.

For all his reassurance to Darius, Owen's grinning face came to him. Was this why his men were missing? Could the two Horse Warriors have been chased and gone too far to find a way back easily? He couldn't imagine his life without Georgio. He closed his eyes in frustration and berated himself, for he knew it was pointless mourning them until they knew the truth.

At the centre of the camp, near the King's pavilion, De Clare had guided Rohese to her husband's tent. De Courcy had angrily leapt to his feet at the sight of them, but a glare from De Clare, and a raised hand, had stopped him.

'Your groundless suspicions and wild accusations against your wife were wrong. She was attacked by one of the thugs who escorted an enemy messenger into our camp. She recognised the spy, my previous lying, treacherous manservant, Bernard, and challenged him. For that, she was beaten and knocked out cold. Perhaps if you spent more time loving and caring for your wife instead of your career, you would see how blameless she is,' he said, coldly, before turning and leaving.

Shamed but stinging from his insults, De Courcy came forward and took Rohese by her hands. Lifting her hair, he saw the extent of the bruising to her face.

'I will kill them!' he said, pulling her into his arms.

'De Clare and his men already have,' she whispered, careful not to mention Malvais and Darius. Suddenly, as the images came back of what had happened, she began to shake. She initially thought her husband had hired them until she recognised Bernard. She had been convinced they were going to kill Conn, and at that point, she had realised she was in love with him.

Seeing the tears streaming down her cheeks, De Courcy called for her maid and handed her over, ordering the woman to take his wife into the other room and help her. He poured himself a goblet of wine and sat back in his chair. He had seen the messenger arrive late that night and had heard it was to negotiate—he was not ashamed of the relief he felt at that news. He was no coward but saw little point in dying needlessly, especially against heavy odds. He silently prayed that the negotiations worked.

Rohese only drank half of the sleeping draft her maid had prepared. She needed to slip out the next morning to send a message to Chatillon. He needed to know all of this urgently.

Early the next morning, King Henry summoned the Archbishop of Canterbury and his nobles to hear of the letter's contents. There were gasps of shock and grumbles at the mention of Flambard's name, but then there was silence for a while as they thought through the implications of this visit in the night. However, Henry had seen the flicker of hope on several faces. None of them wanted to engage in a battle where they could be maimed, killed or defeated, or lose their lands and wealth—not if another way could be found.

Malvais stepped forward and asked the same question Henry had thrown at Bernard.

'Flambard, wearing the cloak of the peacemaker? Does that ring true, for I find that difficult to believe? We all know him as a master manipulator. So what does he want for this new role?'

Henry smiled. Malvais was astute and had dared to ask the question, but Henry knew what the reaction of the Archbishop of Canterbury would be to his answer, for he hated and despised Flambard.

'Not as much as I imagined, not a place at court, just the return of the Bishopric of Durham, which I took away from him.'

Anselm almost choked on his breakfast ale. 'No!' he thundered, rising to his feet. 'Not while I have breath left in my body. He has stolen from the Church and the Holy See for years, filling his coffers and those of William Rufus. He needs to be brought to account for his crimes. He *must* stand in the ecclesiastical courts and be defrocked!'

Henry laid a hand on Anselm's shoulder and pressed him gently back into his seat to calm him before he spoke.

'Everyone here understands your well-deserved, past prejudices against him, Archbishop, but he tells me he has Robert's ear. He says he can bring my brother to the table to negotiate, avoiding a battle that could become a bloody slaughter for us. If he can indeed do this, then I can forgive him much. I hope to find that same forgiveness in you for his past transgressions, especially if we avoid the death of England's young men on the summer meadows out there.'

The Archbishop's mouth was clamped shut in disapproval as the King turned to Henry Beaumont and Robert Fitz Hamon. 'You will take my standard and ride to Robert's camp this afternoon, under a flag of truce. We will first ask for negotiations with intermediaries, but then I would like a face to face meeting with my brother.'

Henry then dismissed everyone except the Archbishop and told him of the last paragraph in the letter from Flambard.

'I did not want to raise it before them until I checked its veracity with you, Anselm. Does Flambard have the right of it? If so, this could be a major ploy for us.'

Anselm wrinkled his brow and considered Flambard's suggestion for several minutes.

'I hate to admit it, but he's right. Trying to usurp an anointed king from his throne is a treasonable act—one that the Pope would look on with disfavour and deliver an order of excommunication from the Church for those attempting it, thereby putting their souls in mortal danger. I reluctantly see both the wisdom and the leverage of such an argument against crusaders who have set foot in Jerusalem.'

CHAPTER TWENTY-FIVE

'I need you at my side during these talks, Anselm, as I know my brother will listen to you. You are right; I hear that the crusades have changed him, and he is far more pious. I need to work out what I'm prepared to give him in order to keep my crown,' he murmured, turning away.

'Money! I would imagine a lot of money, as I hear his wife's fortune has run through his fingers like water. I remember he was always somewhat profligate, and this invasion fleet must have cost the Duke a fortune,' said Anselm.

Henry smiled, for money was something he had in abundance.

Flambard was still awake at dawn as sleep had eluded him. He gave up and swung his legs out of bed, suddenly remembering that Robert often liked to ride out early in the morning, something that Belleme rarely did. He pulled on his boots and called for his horse. At a time like this, he missed Bernard, for his servant would have told him which direction the Duke usually rode on a morning.

He took a guess and trotted west, heading towards the river. At first, he thought he had misjudged as he saw no one but men setting eel traps. Then, through the trees, he saw four mounted horses in the distance. He prayed as he had never prayed before that the fiery, warlike Count of Mortain was not one of the riders, otherwise, his mission was doomed before he had uttered a word. However, he was lucky, as Count Henry of Eu and two guards were with the Duke.

He cantered towards them, gave a welcome smile, bowed, and reined in closer to the Duke.

'Sire, this is fortunate. I have come by some information early this morning from my source in your brother's camp. Henry is seeking to negotiate and may even send forth his intermediaries to discuss this today. He wants to avoid the bloodshed and death of England and Normandy's young men,' he said in a low, breathless voice.

Robert, with a wary eye, had watched Flambard's arrival as he emerged from the trees, and had even turned and grimaced in dismay at Henry of Eu, who had laughed. They both knew Flambard rarely took to horseback without a reason. He was a creature of the dark corridors of power, not of the hunting field. He had also grown quite stout and avoided any exertion where possible.

Now, however, Robert's interest was roused. 'This informer of yours, is he in my brother's inner circle, that he should know Henry's thoughts so well?' he asked with a wry smile.

'I have it on good authority, Sire, that he spoke to the King himself.'

Robert looked impressed, but he had never really trusted Flambard.

'And you swear that you now tell it true. My brother wishes to negotiate?'

'I do, my Lord Duke, as I have been assured that is the case. Others were present to hear this, and we will certainly know it is true if one of the Beaumont brothers, probably Fitz Hamon, arrives today.'

Duke Robert turned to the Count at his side for his opinion. Henry of Eu nodded in agreement. 'All attempts should be made to resolve this before a drop of blood is shed, Sire.'

CHAPTER TWENTY-FIVE

Robert gave a curt nod, shortened his reins and, raising a hand in farewell, cantered off back to camp, with Flambard frantically kicking his horse on to try and catch up. Having finally managed to get the Duke's ear, he needed to stay as close as possible and was determined to ride into camp at his side for all to see.

As usual, Belleme and Mortain sat outside the Duke's large striped pavilion. The weather had held fair, the fields were full of golden corn, and the morning sun was pleasant. Belleme shaded his eyes as he heard horses approaching, and then he let out a string of foul epithets about Flambard's parentage as he saw him riding in with a smug smile.

'I fear that our slippery friend has stolen a march on us this morning, Mortain. Let us hear what he has been dripping into Robert's ear,' he said, limping into the pavilion after the Duke.

Belleme heard Flambard's news with scepticism.

'An informer that close to the King, do you believe a word that comes out of this known liar's mouth, Sire? Can he produce this informer? Or is he purely trying to reline his empty nest by appearing useful and important?' he asked with his laughing trademark sneer.

Flambard's face was suffused with anger as he turned on Belleme.

'Always the doubting cynic, my Earl of Shrewsbury, but the answer is no, I cannot produce him because he was my steward, my man Bernard, who was then murdered by your friends, De Clare and Malvais, on his way back to us. Fortunately, one of the surviving men brought me the information,' declared Flambard.

There was silence in the tent, as little could be said to that, not even by Robert de Belleme.

He tried, however. 'You are in a position of great strength, Sire, and we know that Henry is full of fear, as are those around him. They have seen the size of your army. What could Henry possibly negotiate with? All you want from him is the English crown, which is rightfully yours, and once you have that, it gives you everything—the land and the Treasury.'

However, Flambard was not done either. His whole future depended on these negotiations going ahead.

'We would likely have to do battle to gain that crown. What if both claimants are killed during that battle, without any legitimate heirs? Then absolute chaos will ensue, with family fighting family, to clamber up the steps to that throne. We are talking about a civil war that could last for years, purely because we did not negotiate,' pleaded Flambard, who was nothing if not passionate and elegant when it came to speeches.

Robert looked from one face to another and sighed.

'Let us wait and see if any representatives arrive. If so, that will prove the veracity of Flambard's words;. If they do not, then we line up for battle tomorrow.'

It was an hour after noon when the horns blew to announce the arrival of a delegation from Henry's camp, much to Ranulf Flambard's immense relief. As he had also foretold, Henry Beaumont, the Earl of Warwick, Lord Fitz Hamon, Sir Richard Redvers, and their escort, brought the King's standard to the Duke's pavilion and asked for the rules of parley to be observed. They hadn't seen Duke Robert for many years and were taken aback. He was not only older, his skin was still tanned and weathered by the hot sun of the Levant, but it was far more than that. He seemed taller, had filled out, and looked what he was—the triumphant hero of Jerusalem. He seemed to have gained stature in more ways than one, and as they bowed to him and his nobles, and entered his pavilion, Redvers guiltily wondered if they had perhaps backed the wrong man.

'Your brother sends you greetings, Sire. He was pleased to receive the news that you were willing to negotiate and hopes we can agree to avoid bloodshed, which will satisfy both parties. He would particularly like a meeting with you alone, face to face, brother to brother, to try and resolve your differences. However, if agreement cannot be reached, we are prepared to fight if you decline his offer of reconciliation,' declared Henry Beaumont.

There was utmost silence in the pavilion as all eyes went to Duke Robert's face. He turned to look at Belleme, who shook his head in disbelief, not only at the words Beaumont used, but at the realisation that Flambard had sent that message asking for negotiations. Mortain, who was stony-faced, glared at Flambard. Belleme broke the shocked silence.

'You are the wronged party here, Sire, and yet in that last sentence, they try to transfer blame to you for not preventing this battle—an underhand trick. Henry Beauclerc is the guilty one. He is the Oathbreaker, so it is up to him to bring any offers to you. Only then, when they are on the table, should you consider his overtures,' proclaimed Robert de Belleme.

Duke Robert turned back to Beaumont. 'Who will be at the first meeting of intermediaries?' he asked.

'The three of us, Sire, then, William Warelwast, the King's advisor and chaplain and, of course, his Grace, Anselm, the Archbishop of Canterbury.'

Duke Robert raised his eyebrows at that news, for no one

had dared to mention that Anselm had not only agreed to support Henry, but was here on the battlefield at his side.

'You may leave in peace, gentlemen. We need to discuss this, and then my chosen intermediaries will be in touch to arrange a time and place—if I agree to negotiate.'

No sooner were they out of the door than Robert turned on his advisors.

'Anselm is there with him?'

Belleme answered. 'Yes, Sire, but I believe it is with some reluctance, for he did not crown him and had difficulty accepting it as a fait accompli. If Henry insists on him being there, we must fight fire with fire and insist that the Papal Envoy is also there. It is time for Pope Paschal to get off the fence. I suggest we send for Chatillon immediately. He can observe and ensure there are no underhand dealings,' he said, glaring at Flambard.

Flambard began to protest loudly, but Mortain stepped before him, his face almost touching his, as he hissed at him, 'I do not understand why you are here in the Duke's pavilion, Flambard. You are a devious minion who sent a message to the Oathbreaker without the Duke's permission, and you certainly have no right to comment on anything we discuss. I would have you flogged for your impertinence.'

Flambard made a hasty exit while Duke Robert, unsettled by the news of Archbishop Anselm's presence, took little notice of the altercation but instead turned to Belleme.

'Send for Chatillon. I need him here at my side,' he ordered.

CHAPTER TWENTY-FIVE

Bishop's Waltham

Chatillon was aware of recent developments, due to Rohese's quick actions, who let him know of Bernard's visit and death. He knew exactly what Flambard was trying to do, but of more concern to him were the words at the bottom of her message. "Conn needs help; Georgio and another Horse Warrior have been missing for days."

As usual, he talked various options over with Edvard until he came to a conclusion.

'Go to Malvais, find out what is afoot, and wear the cloak and insignia of a papal messenger—that way, you will not be challenged in Henry's camp.'

Edvard had barely reached the door when a messenger from Belleme came through it.

> You are needed immediately. We all need your advice, but your role must be as a papal advocate and observer to ensure that any agreement reached or treaty signed is valid, witnessed and sworn.
> I have them erecting a pavilion for you.

Edvard hesitated at the doorway.

'Surely you need me to oversee our move to Alton and, of course, to be by your side.'

'No, Edvard. Go to Malvais first—his need is greater. He is not free to leave Henry's side on the eve of a possible battle, and you can discover the truth of the matter. I hope that young Georgio is not dead, and I pray that Robert agrees to nothing foolish before I arrive. This is the one chance for him to take the crown that, as the eldest son of King William, should be rightfully his!' he exclaimed, waving his friend on his way.

Chapter Twenty-six

July 31st 1101 – Churt

Serjeant Fox was a Kent man who had been in the service of the De Clare family all his life, as had his father before him. However, his mother's family came from the Sussex Wolds, and he knew this area well. It took them a few hours, but they managed to find where Georgio and Gracchus had camped, and the signs on the ground told their own tale. Fortunately, it had rained heavily the night before the Horse Warriors had left, but it had not rained since, so the tracks were imprinted in the ground.

Lord De Clare had mentioned that the Welsh mercenaries had left, a group of men Serjeant Fox had little liking for, and it seemed as if his lordship was right. The numerous hoof prints within the trees surrounding the remains of the campfire showed that dozens of horses had been kept standing there. However, if the Horse Warriors were attacked, there were no bodies. Serjeant Fox could only assume that they had been captured or that their bodies had been dumped in a river or stream close by. Being thorough, he sent his men to search the woods around just in case, and before long, one of his grizzled veterans, a good, reliable man, came back to report.

'There was another camp, Sir, to the north, but it looks as if the occupants left in a hurry as the fire was kicked and stamped out. There are also many animal tracks—pigs, by the look of it, so probably drovers, and a family of them, by the footprints.'

Serjeant Fox thanked him and ordered his men to lead their horses up the hill and back onto the track above. As he mounted, he thought it all through—a drover family, who may have seen or heard the attack and had either hidden or fled, may be useful witnesses if he could find them. He followed the drover trail along the ridge. He could see the tracks of both groups until they dropped down to the stream, where many horses had completely churned the muddy banks. However, after walking around the area, he saw that the tracks diverged; the large group went north, while the drover and his family, who now appeared to have two large horses with them, went west.

He decided to follow the drover's tracks first, which led, after an hour or so, to the small hamlet of Churt. Once there, they were directed through the trees to the clearing of the drover's house. He saw the smoke rising above the trees, and after following a wide, well-worn track, he came on the long, low, sturdy house as the drover's dogs raced out barking. A young boy of eight or nine feeding the chickens and ducks stood staring open-mouthed at them before running for the cottage just as his father emerged, alerted by the dogs. Ned, the drover, was reassured by what he saw; these men were from the King's camp and wore their lord's livery.

'I was hoping someone would come looking for them soon,'

CHAPTER TWENTY-SIX

he said as his wife emerged behind him with the two boys.

The men dismounted, and the drover waved the serjeant to follow him into the cottage. Gracchus, bare-chested on the bed, was not a prepossessing sight. His ribs were bound up, his forearm was in a splint, and his body was still a mass of yellow and fading purple bruises. Serjeant Fox nodded in greeting but then quickly scanned the cottage for the other one, but there was no sign. Gracchus's face had lit up at the sight of him as he recognised both the man and the De Clare livery.

'Thank God, I thought you would never come,' he exclaimed.

Fox recognised the big Greek Horse Warrior immediately; he had watched him fight with Malvais several times at the training ground and was in awe of his skill and ferocity.

'It was the Welsh mercenaries. They attacked you, didn't they? But I imagine you took a few of them with you,' he said, indicating his bruised and battered body.

Gracchus nodded and told him what happened, but then reached up and clutched the sergeant's wrist.

'Georgio is gone. The drover found no trace of him at the camp, but he believes they had him roped behind a horse. They have taken him north, but that was days ago, so now I have no idea if he is dead or alive.'

Serjeant Fox saw the tears in the big man's eyes and patted him on the shoulder.

'I am sure you did your best. You took a truly bad beating for it but were outnumbered—you could not have done any more. You are a courageous man, Gracchus, but now we need to get you back to the camp, as you can imagine how worried they are there. Malvais could not leave as we are probably on the eve of battle, but he will be delighted we have found you, and he will look for Georgio as soon as he is able. The drover says he has your horses hidden at the back, and thinks you could manage to ride back if we take it easy and no jumping hedges.'

Gracchus smiled, the relief clear to see on his face that he was being taken back to Malvais.

The drover's wife produced warm bread, goat's cheese and jugs of beer for the men, which were gratefully received. Then, the horses were brought, and Gracchus, with a few groans, managed to mount. He bade farewell to the family and threw Ned the purse at his belt, in thanks for their care. He knew they had stayed at home to keep watch over him at their busiest time of the year. The boys, in particular, were sad to see him go as each night he had told them adventurous tales and stories about places in the East that they would probably never see. The drover took the serjeant to one side and drew a much shorter route back to Alton in the sand for them, which was only three or four leagues away.

Serjeant Fox hoped to reach the camp before dark, but as they rode, he wondered what they would find when they reached it. Was it war? He hoped not, as he had a wife and three children to support at home in Tonbridge, and no matter how good you were, the heat of battle could prove unpredictable.

July 31st 1101 - Alton

As the party was leaving the drover's cottage, Edvard was riding into Henry's camp. All was bustle and preparation as they expected to have to fight shortly if the talks failed. Lines of men queued with their weapons at the whetstone wheel, and sparks and noise filled the air as swords and daggers were sharpened. Everyone was so preoccupied that hardly a glance was thrown at him—he was just another messenger with a badge on his cloak.

Conn, De Clare and their men were returning from the training ground when Edvard rode up and dismounted. Conn suddenly felt an unusual wave of emotion as he clasped arms with his old friend; everything about Edvard was solid reassurance, and in no time, he felt his recent fears dissipate. They moved to sit inside Conn's pavilion, away from curious glances or listening ears, while Darius brought refreshments. He gave Edvard a wary glance, remembering his last run-in with the big man in Rouen.

'What news from Robert's camp?' asked De Clare, an old comrade of Edvard's from the days when he rode at the side of Morvan de Malvais.

'Flambard, as expected, is weaving his web and catching the unwary while trying to recreate a wealthier future for himself. Robert is undecided about what to do with his brother, but as you know, he's agreed to negotiate and has summoned Chatillon to be at his side to observe the talks. They will meet today. I don't have much time to spend with you, just an hour or two. So tell me what you know!'

Conn related the incidents with Owen and his men, the trailing of them in London, the role of Bernard, and the death of Andreas in Rye. Then, he moved to the current problem.

'Georgio and Gracchus rode out on what should have been a straightforward reconnaissance patrol. They should have returned two days ago. As you know, we killed Bernard, but before he died, he told us he had paid Owen and his men to desert Henry and return to Wales. These Welsh mercenaries then took the same route as Georgio and Gracchus. We have heard nothing since.'

'I sent some of my best men out at dawn to ride the route. If they are injured or dead, they will find them. Serjeant Fox is an expert tracker, a loyal man who saved my life in the last rebellion when Sir Hugh wanted to hang me,' explained De Clare.

'So, we can do nothing until this search party returns, and none of us can leave here until Henry and Robert come to an agreement and resolve their differences without resorting to war,' said Conn.

De Clare left them as he had to be with the King, while Edvard and Conn sat and talked of other things for a while. Edvard was concerned by the worry he saw in Conn's face—he had suffered enough loss recently.

'I have a feeling in here,' he said, slapping his chest, 'that he is alive, probably in trouble and cursing us for not finding him yet.'

Conn smiled. 'I miss his humour and even his godforsaken eternal optimism. He and Darius here spark off each other a lot.'

Edvard smiled. 'As you know, I spent several months with him at the chateau while you and Piers were jaunting around England last summer. He combines everything you would find in an honourable knight: bravery, loyalty, and courage, but he is stubborn as a mule at times. You should have seen the arguments he and Dion had over archery training. I thought she was going to hit him at one point when he shot a horse.'

This made Conn laugh and reminded him not only of his gruelling archery training with Dion, but also of what Darius

CHAPTER TWENTY-SIX

had said. 'I believe he developed a crush on Isabella while there,' he suggested.

Edvard laughed. 'No. That would be like putting your head in a lion's mouth if Chatillon found out, and honestly, Isabella would have eaten him alive. No, Georgio fell head over heels in love with Dion. Watching him follow her around like a puppy was interesting, yet they fought like cat and dog. But Georgio knew that it was a hopeless, unrequited love. Dion was married to one of the greatest Irish swordsmen in Europe, Finian Ui Neil, and was carrying their third child. Even a handsome young Horse Warrior could not live up to half of Finian's reputation, and Dion adored the ground he walked on. It was as if a light went out inside of her when news of his death arrived, and I wonder if she will ever recover from it.'

Conn had to turn away for a while; he knew what that felt like. Still, he was surprised that Georgio had never mentioned his love for Dion.

'Now to business. Chatillon wants you to stay at Henry's side, no matter the outcome of today's meetings. If Robert takes the crown, he cannot imagine Henry going quietly. He will lick his wounds and rise again. He has established a friendship and alliance with Louis, the Dauphin, and Piers can see him rallying rebels in the Vexin to ride with French troops against Robert and Normandy. Prince Louis has his own agenda—his father, King Philip, is fat and old, so he has taken control of the French forces. We believe he will try to take the Norman half of the Vexin, but his eyes are on the bigger prize—he wants Normandy absorbed into France. So Henry's defeat over here could play right into his hands,' explained Edvard.

'And if Henry should possibly win?' asked Conn.

'Then Robert will return to Normandy with whatever spoils that Henry offers. But, none of us believes that Henry will be content with that; he is too like his father and will have his eyes on Normandy in the future. This is why Chatillon needs you in the English court.'

Darius, wine sack in hand, stood transfixed, listening to all this. He shook his head.

'So, no matter what happens, no matter what is decided today, it is all war in the future.'

Edvard laughed. 'Welcome to Western Europe, Darius of Constantinople, but surely you would expect this here—there is constant war in your homeland. Men are tribal, and land is everything.'

Darius nodded in resignation. 'It seems as if I'll be employed for many years and will return to visit my mother a rich man.'

They both laughed at this, lightening the mood, and Edvard rose to go. Unusually, he pulled Conn into a bear hug.

'Do not worry too much, Conn Fitz Malvais; if they have him, I swear we will get him back! We got you both back once before, from far cleverer and more ferocious adversaries.'

With that, he was gone, leaving Conn reassured but, like the rest of the camp, still tense, waiting and watching for the result of the talks.

Chatillon arrived at Robert's pavilion an hour before noon and found Robert kneeling in prayer at his prie deux. He sank into a camp chair and waited until Robert crossed himself and then came to greet him. He could see the uncertainty and concern on his friend's face, so he took the blunt approach before the others were admitted to his presence.

'You have spent nine months preparing for this venture, and poured a fortune into the forces you have brought. Henry is afraid of you and will offer you anything apart from the crown, so tell me your biggest fear at the moment, Robert,' he said softly.

'That is exactly the problem, Piers—if I have to fight for the crown, I have no doubt I can take it, but at what cost to the men of both sides and even ourselves? I watched tens of thousands of our men and pilgrims die on the crusades to achieve our objective, and I find I am somewhat tired of death. I expected, and was told repeatedly, that he would give up the crown when he saw the might we have brought to bear, but it seems, despite the odds, that he is prepared to fight for it. That leaves me with little choice but to kill or imprison him.'

Chatillon understood. 'As the youngest, Henry has always felt badly done to, and both you and William Rufus did not help that in the way you treated him—there was little brotherly love from either of you. It would be best to decide what you want, Robert, but do nothing foolish, for you deserve this crown. Your intermediaries will meet in an hour or so, and you need to share your demands. Where are they to meet?'

'We could use Mortain's pavilion.'

Chatillon shook his head. 'No. That will not do. It may produce intimidation, but is that what you want? I seem to remember that the Church of Saint Lawrence has extensive grounds. Your father sold it to the Benedictines in exchange for land to build his palace in Winchester. Erect a pavilion there. Neutral ground, Robert.'

The stewards were summoned, and it was erected just as Henry's contingent rode into the camp. Robert Belleme and the Count of Mortain led them to the church. Belleme thought the Canterbury Archbishop was about to have an apoplexy when he told them that the Papal Envoy would sit in as observer. Anselm resented any interference in England by the Pope. He considered England *his* domain. In particular, he hated Piers De Chatillon, who had far more influence in the Lateran Palace in Rome than most of the senior cardinals had.

As the most senior and important Earl in England and Normandy, Belleme began the proceedings. It didn't begin well, as Belleme pointed out the betrayal and crimes of the 'Oathbreaker' against his brother, Robert, the rightful heir. He even recalled Henry's dash from the forest to Winchester to seize the Treasury while William Rufus' body was still warm on the ground. He lambasted the indecent haste of Henry's coronation when a council of senior nobles should have been allowed to establish a regency to await Robert's return from Jerusalem.

'A crusade that Pope Urban and the Holy See had sent him on with the promise that his belongings would be protected. Yet despite these crimes and broken oaths, we now have Anselm here on the Oathbreaker's behalf. How does that sit well with your Christian beliefs, my Lord Archbishop?' he demanded, jabbing a finger at Anselm.

As much as he was enjoying Belleme's vitriolic but accurate speech, Chatillon knew it was getting them nowhere, so he held up a hand.

'For the sake of clarity on both sides, my Lord Earl, I believe we should hear Henry Beauclerc's reasons for claiming the throne and, just as importantly, what he now offers in reparations or restitution for this blatant theft of the crown that should have been Duke Robert's by right.'

Robert Fitz Hamon inclined his head in thanks and respect to Chatillon and put forward the claim of porphyrogeniture.

'Henry Beauclerc is the only child of King William to be born in the purple. Both of his parents were reigning monarchs of England, and therefore, Henry's claim to the throne had more legitimacy. His Grace, Maurice, the Bishop of London, and the previous King's Chancellor recognised this stronger claim and therefore crowned Henry Beauclerc as King.'

This was too much for the Count of Mortain, who stood up.

'How does Henry Beauclerc sleep at night, Fitz Hamon? You were with us when he laid his hands on the holy relics and swore an oath to be loyal to Robert as the heir to William Rufus? Does he now sit there waiting for the devil to come and take his blackened soul?'

Flambard had been standing at the side, inconspicuously, among a few other nobles. Chatillon was, of course, immediately aware of his presence and his inability to meet the Papal Envoy's eyes.

Chatillon noticed that Flambard stepped forward and made certain signals to Anselm. He could not know that, earlier, Flambard had played a masterstroke. Finding Anselm in the church, he had debased himself, full length on the ground in front of the Archbishop, to beg his forgiveness. He then asked for his blessing and absolution of his previous mistakes while promising to protect and support the Holy See in England under Henry's reign. More importantly, he promised to pay a large tithe to the Diocese of Canterbury from Durham in restitution for the previous funds he had appropriated.

Anselm had reluctantly agreed, with other conditions and significant penance. Flambard had then reminded him about the clause he had included in the letter.

Anselm now stood and faced an angry Mortain, forcing him back into his seat and quietening everyone in the pavilion.

'It is a waste of time and breath trading insults. What's done is done, and yes, I now support the crowning of Henry Beauclerc. This is because he is a king who has been anointed with the blessed holy oils, and in Church law, an anointed king cannot be usurped. Any man or woman who tries to do so will be excommunicated from the Holy Church.'

There was a stunned silence at this announcement as shock reverberated through the assembled nobles. This was the direst sanction that could be pronounced on a man in the Christian world. It meant he could not be married in a church, receive Holy Unction at his death, or be buried in the sanctified ground of a churchyard. Yet Anselm threatened Duke Robert and his nobles with this extreme penalty if they tried to take the crown from Henry.

Belleme turned wide, questioning eyes on Chatillon, who shook his head and softly murmured, 'Clever. Very clever, Flambard,' before turning to Anselm.

'To say this is an extreme threat to the man who is the wronged party here, Anselm, is an understatement. I will relay your threats to Pope Paschal, for he is the only one who could decide to issue such a sanction, and I seem to remember that you are certainly not high in his favour at the moment. I suggest we all break for some air and refreshments while we relay your undeserved threats to the Duke, the man who saved Jerusalem and the Holy Sepulcher for you. We will reassemble in two hours, that is, if an angry Duke Robert has not decided by then that war is the better option. After all, Anselm, a false king like Henry, cannot be usurped if he lies dead on the field of battle.'

Chapter Twenty-Seven

July 31st 1101 –Alton, King Henry's camp

Malvais, De Clare, Robert Beaumont and several others were with the King when Henry Beaumont, Fitz Hamon and the others came galloping back in. Fitz Hamon relayed the gist of the meeting, including the insults, which made Henry smile— he could take any amount of name-calling if it meant he kept his crown. However, Archbishop Anselm refused to return for further negotiations that afternoon.

'I have played my part for you, Henry. There is no doubt that Mortain and Belleme will have my head on a spike beside yours if they decide to attack. We have given them food for thought. I am told that your brother has become very pious— let us hope so. I will leave for Winchester to be with the Queen; it is up to you now, Henry. If you truly want a face to face meeting, I suggest you go and talk to Robert privately. Offer him anything you can to try and prevent bloodshed.'

With that, he was gone, leaving Henry rooted to the spot. After several moments, he turned to his advisors. 'Arrange it, Fitz Hamon; I will speak to my brother first if he will agree to meet.'

CHAPTER TWENTY-SEVEN

A few hours later, Henry rode into Robert's camp. He was nervous—his hands were sweating on the reins—but he tried not to show it. Robert was standing outside the pavilion waiting for him, and Henry found he, also, was taken aback at the sight of his brother after so many years. He looked the hero he was—older and statesmanlike. Henry dismounted and, walking up to him, bowed his head in respect. Robert's lined face gave nothing away as he indicated his younger brother should enter the pavilion before him. Now was the moment, thought Henry, whilst out of sight of his entourage and guards; a swordsman placed in here could take off his head in a thrice. The sweat was beading on his brow as he preceded his brother into the tent.

Chatillon had ensured he was not anywhere in sight when Henry arrived. He was waiting in Robert's pavilion for developments when Edvard strode in to ask what had happened.

'I have no great hope of Robert taking back the crown he truly deserves. I saw the Duke's face when Mortain told him of the threat of excommunication—the fear that was instilled, the thought that he would imperil his own soul and that of others by attacking his brother. So now they speak alone, and we will see what happens when they emerge. After that, it will be up to the intermediaries to flesh out the details and fulfil Robert's demands.'

Edvard shook his head in frustration at the time, effort, and years they had spent trying to get Robert on the throne.

'How did things go with you?' Chatillon asked, waving for refreshments to be brought.

Edvard sipped the wine and gathered his thoughts. Piers waited. He never pushed for an answer because he knew that Edvard would be sorting the wheat from the chaff and telling him only what he needed to know, and he valued that skill in his friend.

'I cannot put my finger on why, but I do not like this disappearance of Georgio and Gracchus. I feel there is more to it, as if we are missing something. Yes, no love was lost between the two groups, but Owen is putting his neck on the line by his actions. He deserts King Henry at a crucial moment and, by doing so, makes an enemy of Robert Beaumont, who hired him—not a man to forget a grudge or to trifle with. Then he either kills or captures two Horse Warriors, who he knows have powerful affiliations to the King, to the Papal Envoy and to the dangerous Malvais family. It is almost as if he is daring them to come after him and hunt him down—as if his life is worth nothing.'

'Maybe that is exactly what he wants, Edvard; he wants the war to be brought to the north of Wales. Remember, we have conveniently removed Sir Hugh, the Earl of Chester, for them. We did this to weaken Henry, which it did, and it has created a large void in control of the North, which we knew it would. This was to keep Henry occupied elsewhere and away from Normandy if by any chance he kept the crown.'

Edvard sighed. 'We can do nothing until we hear what De Clare's men have found, if anything. Then, I can give a month or two to helping Malvais if we find that they have been captured. Mishna says our child is due in November, and I must be back there at the chateau by then, Piers.'

'Of course. I would expect nothing less, and I hope to be with you, but are we not ahead of ourselves? If Owen was only out for revenge, then they are likely both dead,' said Chatillon with a chilling finality.

'I truly hope not. There is a hardness about Conn since

the death of Marietta. I think the death of Georgio would exacerbate that and may turn him into something that neither of us would like, nor want, for him.'

There was little more to be said, and at that moment, Henry of Eu came running into the pavilion, sent by a disgusted Robert de Belleme.

'They have reached an accord! They are standing together with a hand on each other's shoulders. Belleme and Mortain are furious, of course, but there is to be no war!' he exclaimed, before turning and running out again.

Chatillon met Edward's eyes and shrugged. 'I find that I do not want to go and look into Robert's face. I will see immediately that he knows he has given the crown away. Now, the hard work truly begins in thrashing out the terms of the treaty, and I must, unfortunately, be there while I try to keep my hands away from the throat of Flambard.'

Edvard began to speak, but Chatillon raised a hand to stop him.

'I know, I know, you have said it often enough, and I admit you are right. We should have slit his throat when he first arrived in Rouen.'

The two sides were entering the pavilion in Saint Lawrence's grounds to discuss the generous terms and promises that Henry had made to prevent war, when Sergeant Fox rode into Henry's camp on the far side of Alton.

Darius saw them first and ran to find Malvais and De Clare, who were in the paddock looking at an injured hock on De Clare's big chestnut gelding.

'Your men are back, Sire, and they have Gracchus with them. He is alive, Malvais! He is alive!'

Conn, straightening up, rubbed his hands on the cloth the

groom handed him.

'Poultice that immediately as it will draw out any infection lurking in the wound,' he said.

Darius hovered, impatiently waiting for them to follow, but Conn's stomach had clenched at his squire's words because there was no mention of Georgio. If Gracchus was alive, did that mean that his friend was not, or surely they would have brought him back as well?

Sergeant Fox's column was still mounted, and Conn's eyes immediately scanned for a pack horse with a body on it. To his relief, there was none to be seen. He strode into the camp and took Gracchus gently by the shoulders; he could see how badly injured his man was.

'Welcome back, my friend. I never gave up on you returning, for who could take out the great Gracchus? Now, come and sit before you fall over. Darius, run to fetch one of the camp physicians. Tell him we will need salves, new bandages and theriac.'

De Clare was talking to his sergeant and thanking him. Conn also nodded in his direction and promised he would come and find him later.

'Do you feel up to telling us what happened?' he asked.

Gracchus closed his eyes against the throbbing pain in his head and body while gathering his thoughts. 'We were attacked late at night by Owen and his mercenaries. We were foolish, lord, in not keeping watch, but honestly, even if we had, we would not have escaped. There were forty or fifty of them.'

Conn nodded in understanding to put him at ease.

'Do not fear; there is no blame or recrimination for this, as I believe you were targeted on purpose.'

CHAPTER TWENTY-SEVEN

Gracchus went on to relate the story of the attack, what the drover said had happened while he was unconscious, and how the family rescued him.

'I am afraid I gave them the purse you gave us, my lord, to thank them,' he said guiltily.

Conn smiled at that. This was the type of man he was; despite the dreadful beating, he could be concerned about a detail such as that.

The physician arrived and tutted over Gracchus as Conn answered the big man.

'I would have given them much more, for if they had not found you, you would no doubt be lying dead in that glade,' he said, and led De Clare inside the pavilion, where they could talk.

'We know who took Georgio, and he took him for a reason, but we are not sure what that was. Thanks to the drover who followed their tracks, we know he was alive when they took him north,' reasoned Conn, sharing his thoughts with his friend.

'My serjeant tells me it was not money they were after; the purse still on his belt, the tack, the expensive horses, all left behind except the swords they took. This was not a robbery, Conn. However, we do not know if it was planned or whether Owen decided to take Georgio on a whim—he knew he was your captain and friend. They do have a history of kidnap and ransom up there in the wild borderlands. It is seen as a lucrative business.'

'I hope so, De Clare. In fact, I will pray so, for it means that he sees Georgio as valuable and may well keep him alive.'

Chapter Twenty-Eight

August 2nd 1101 – Winchester

The good news had been sent on ahead, and as he and his senior nobles rode into the castle bailey, King Henry received a rapturous reception and welcome from his Queen, knights and troops at Winchester . Despite being nearly four months pregnant, Matilda ran down the steps and into his arms when he dismounted.

'I thank God that you are safe, my Lord King. I prayed for hours each day that no matter the outcome, you would emerge unscathed.'

'It is the outcome that we wished for, my love, albeit expensive, as I had to promise him much to keep my crown. Robert and his men are only an hour or two behind us, so you must notify the stewards; beds and rooms must be found for many nobles here and in the town. It is an historic day, for we will ratify the Treaty of Alton here at Winchester this afternoon, and afterwards, a mass of thanksgiving will be held in the cathedral. I believe Anselm is here—he must officiate with the Bishop of Winchester. Then, we will all return for a feast in the Great Hall. However, do not exhaust yourself,

CHAPTER TWENTY-EIGHT

my love, in your condition, for De Courcy will see to the arrangements for the feast, and Rohese, your favourite lady-in-waiting, returns with us to be at your side once more to help.'

'Come to the solar, my lord, where we can be private, and tell us more. Anselm impatiently awaits you there.'

On entering the solar, Henry went to the Archbishop of Canterbury and humbly dropped to a knee to receive his blessing.

'Your Grace, with your wisdom and intervention, you have ensured that I keep my crown. I am told your pronouncement, that conspiracy against an anointed king would result in excommunication, persuaded my brother to abandon his military, advantage to seek a compromise between us. As you recommended, I made lavish promises to him that will cost me dear for several years, but as you asked, bloodshed has been avoided.'

Anselm, who suddenly looked and felt every one of his sixty-eight years, gave a weak smile. The months of discomfort, living with his men in the field, combined with the recent weeks of tension and fear, all for Henry, had taken its toll.

'I hate to admit it, Sire and I will never repeat it outside of this room, but Flambard brought this law to our notice and even reminded me of it during the negotiations.'

They both smiled at this admission as Henry dropped into a chair beside the Archbishop.

'I suppose we will return Durham to him as he requested, but I will direct his every move as Prince Bishop up there on those borders, and I will watch him like a hawk.'

'That is if Pope Paschal and his assassin allow him to live, of course,' added Anselm, which resulted in both men laughing.

Matilda watched them with dismay, for she felt grateful to Ranulf Flambard. A man of God and an anointed king discussing a man's death as if it meant nothing to them. She placed her hand on her stomach.

'What kind of world am I bringing you into, little one,' she whispered to herself.

An hour later, on the steps, dressed in her best green silk gown threaded with gold and with a thin gold circlet on her brow, she was at her husband's side to greet her godfather, Duke Robert, and his nobles.

Riding into Winchester, Conn was bemused at how quickly everything was moving, but De Clare, at his side, was not.

'Henry will want everything written down, sworn and witnessed, in case Robert changes his mind, hence the signing and oaths this afternoon. The Duke may stay at Winchester for a few weeks to rebuild his relationship with his brother and Matilda, but I know he is not sending his army home. Unlike Henry, who has already dismissed the fyrd to return to their fields ready to gather the harvest. The Duke's forces are dismantling his camp at Alton over the next few days and are marching back to Porchester. Ostensibly, this is to wait for the ships, which could take a few weeks. However, it is only a short march from there to Winchester, and they could have us surrounded and under siege in days!' he exclaimed.

'That would certainly please Belleme and Mortain. Do you realise the last time we were here together at Winchester was with the body of William Rufus,' he reminded De Clare as they rode into the bailey, whilst shouting to Darius to find accommodation for the men and stabling for the horses in the town.

'Something I am never likely to forget, Malvais, as I stood

CHAPTER TWENTY-EIGHT

vigil over his body on my own all night.'

Conn's face clouded as he suddenly remembered that it was here that they received the message that Sheik Ishmael was still alive and in Genoa; only weeks later, Marietta and Finian were dead at that man's hands. Now, he was here again, and he had the news that Georgio was missing and in danger, probably beaten and chained in a cell in some Welsh stronghold. With that thought, he frowned and nudged De Clare's arm.

'I need to find and speak to Robert Beaumont. Come with me when I do, for you know him much better than I do.'

De Clare assumed a resigned expression. 'Yes, but I do not like him. He is a hothead and a boor—even his own brother is not keen on him, I hear,' he replied to Conn, who laughed while trying to persuade Diablo into a strange stable block in the bailey.

They found Robert Beaumont with his men in the Great Hall, already celebrating and toasting with several jugs of wine and ale. He greeted them amiably, and was prepared to listen, before joining the other nobles to sign and swear an oath on the clauses agreed. Malvais explained what had been happening with Owen and his men over the past weeks, without giving too much away about London and Rye.

Beaumont's face darkened in anger. 'He killed one of our Horse Warriors, a man brought here into the King's service? How is it that I did not hear of this?' he demanded.

'We dealt with it, killing Black Brynn, the man he sent to do it. But as you know, Owen ran before the battle. We have since discovered that Bernard, Flambard's servant, paid him to abandon Henry.'

'Flambard! That treasonous rat! I told Henry not to trust a

word of his,' he yelled.

'There is more, and just as serious.'

They certainly had his attention now. He leaned forward as De Clare had purposefully lowered his voice.

'You may remember that King Henry sent two Horse Warriors out to scout the Wolds and ridges of the north when we reached the Hindhead Gap. Owen and his men followed and attacked them. The big Greek warrior, Gracchus, was badly beaten but survived only because a drover's family rescued him. However, Owen kidnapped Georgio di Milan, Conn's captain. They have taken him north, possibly to kill, probably to ransom. As you know, the King is preoccupied with the treaty, but as commander of Henry's forces, we want your permission to take a cohort of men to ride north and try to rescue him.'

Robert Beaumont could hardly believe what he heard: Owen had dared to attack the King's men and take a prisoner. His face was red with fury as he thumped a fist on the trestle table, which made every goblet jump and spill its contents.

'You will leave it with me, De Clare. This insults the King, so I must speak to Henry. I will do so first thing tomorrow and have an answer by then, but I assure you it will be positive. We will make Owen pay for this and his desertion.'

They stood and bowed, leaving a still glowering Beaumont to his wine, but Conn was pleased with how it had gone. He wanted to start the search for Georgio tomorrow, but he needed more men, and Beaumont could provide those.

'We can do no more at present, Malvais; let us go and join the celebrations. The treaty will be signed in a few hours, and hopefully, this crisis will pass.'

They joined several other knights around a long trestle

table. Spirits were high; they had come at the call of their patrons and liege lords but, ultimately, had not been called on to fight. Most were relieved, but some were disappointed, especially the younger ones who were excited about their first battle. Watching them and listening, Conn remembered when he and Georgio were like that—only sixteen years old, full of enthusiasm and excitement as they left their family in Morlaix to go and fight in the Reconquista wars in Spain. Now in his mid-twenties, he felt like a veteran, with many battles, skirmishes, blood, gore, and death under his belt.

He stood up. He was in no mood to celebrate; he needed air. He decided to find Darius to see if he had found rooms or if they would have to erect their pavilion, as many others were already doing, in the bailey. He ran down the steps just in time to see Chatillon and Edvard arrive and dismount. He had not seen the Papal Envoy since Rouen, but he was pleased to see him.

'Malvais, good to see you. Let us walk towards the cathedral. I believe we are all assembling just beyond it in the old Bishop's Hall to sign the treaty.'

They walked for a while until they were clear of the crowds, still gathered, hoping to glimpse King Henry, or Duke Robert as he rode in.

'I imagine this is not the outcome you would have liked, Chatillon.'

'No, but it does not surprise me. It is the most foolish decision that Robert has ever made in a long career of folly. I now wonder, in truth, if he ever really wanted the crown, especially the weight of responsibility and power that would go with it. I think he liked the idea, but since he became the well-deserved hero of Jerusalem, people tend to forget that Robert has always been a lazy man who hates making decisions. He usually surrounds himself with people who make decisions for him. Your father, Morvan, was a classic example, who won several battles for him.'

'So you were there, Piers. Are you at least pleased with what was finally agreed?'

'The treaty is a lengthy and complicated document designed to protect both parties, as they have promised to be each other's heirs until a legitimate male child is born. Robert has renounced his claim to the throne of England, and Henry has done the same for his lands in Normandy. The most surprising is the three thousand silver marks Henry is to pay Robert annually, similar to the Danegeld, designed to keep the peace and prevent future invasions.'

Conn gave a low whistle. 'That's a fortune! Can King Henry or England afford that?'

'It must be a tenth of his revenue, but he was ready to pay more to keep his crown. It will be interesting to see for how many years it is paid. I am not optimistic.'

'What about our devious friend, Flambard? Did he get what he wanted?' asked Conn.

'He will have his bishopric restored, and other nobles who have lost lands will also have them returned—those who truly deserve them, such as Eustace of Boulogne.'

Conn could feel his anger building. 'So, Flambard's manipulation and cunning, which resulted in the deaths, beating and kidnapping of my men, have paid off for him. Having ensured Henry's triumph, he will no doubt return to his lavish Bishop's Palace in Durham.'

To his surprise, Chatillon shrugged. 'Sometimes, Conn, some people are not worth the anger and hatred you pour into

CHAPTER TWENTY-EIGHT

them. I learned many years ago to become an opportunist—I wait for an opportunity to get my revenge rather than waste time trying to create it. Besides, others are ahead of us in this particular threat—having spoken to Belleme today, if he does not kill Flambard in the next few days, it will be a miracle,' he said. Then, both he and Edvard laughed as if at a private joke.

'Now, Malvais, I will not be staying; as soon as this treaty is signed, I will be gone. However, I am leaving Edvard with you for a few months. He must leave before the end of October for the birth of his child, so use him well while he is at your side. Keep your reports coming—if not through Rohese, then Edvard will find a way; we have informers throughout England who will send a message for you. He also has another large purse for you, as I imagine you will need it for bribes. I wish you godspeed on your quest to find Georgio, which I am sure you will.'

With that, they clasped arms in farewell, and he was gone with a swirl of his papal cloak.

The Great Hall was packed that evening with hundreds of nobles, knights and their retinues and a scattering of bishops, priests and clerics. The atmosphere, on the whole, was one of relief, for a major battle was rare but terrifying when it happened. Now, it had been avoided, and many were getting rousingly drunk. But underneath, especially among the senior nobles, the tension was still there, along with their anger and frustration at the outcome.

The crown had been there for the taking, and many believed it should have been taken by force. Also, for all Henry's smiling face as he raised toast after toast to his brother, many of Robert's senior nobles did not trust him. They did not believe he would keep his promises, or forget those who had ranged against him. Henry had proved before that he was not the forgiving type, as his father's blood truly ran in his veins; he had a ruthless streak. Some of them remembered watching him fling Conan, the rebel merchant, out of the window in the tower at Rouen.

Conn slipped into the space De Clare had saved him on a bench close to the dais. De Clare filled Conn's goblet with the special Rhenish wine and raised his goblet.

'To finding Georgio, and if the King does not need me now, I will ride at your side if you will have me. I am not quite in my dotage yet.'

Conn laughed. He knew that Richard de Clare was one of the youngest cadet sons who had ridden with his father at Duke Robert's side at the battle of Gerberoi. He was several years younger than Morvan, so he must only be coming to his late thirties now. He knew him to be a brave and tireless fighter with a wicked sense of humour.

'I would be honoured, De Clare,' he said, raising his goblet in return, but his eyes were scanning the other tables for Rohese.

She was there with her husband, who, as usual, was up and down to check that things were being served and done in the right way for the King and his guests. He found he could not keep his eyes off her as the music and entertainment surrounded them. He called over a serving maid, who smiled at the handsome knight and would have slipped into his lap if he had asked, but instead, he whispered a message and gave her a coin.

He watched her as she made her way over to Rohese, and on the pretext of filling her cup, whispered, 'Go to the garden for some air.'

Rohese raised her eyes immediately to Malvais. She had felt

CHAPTER TWENTY-EIGHT

his gaze on her all night, but her husband watched her like a hawk. She gave an imperceptible nod and slipped out of her seat when De Courcy was engaged with the King. Conn waited several minutes before following and asked De Clare to move along the bench and fill his space. His friend shook his head in resignation, for he knew where he was going. 'Playing with fire,' he murmured again, but did as he was asked.

Conn slipped into the long, narrow corridor that led to the back of the castle and pulled open the heavy door into the small garden that the first Queen Matilda had ordered planted. Rohese was waiting for him, and he pulled her into his arms and kissed her deeply. Her body moulded into his, and her arms wrapped around his waist, pulling him even closer.

'Is there anywhere we can go? You know this castle,' he murmured.

'We cannot stay here as he will notice we have gone, so come this way,' she whispered as she led him back along the corridor towards the Great Hall, her heart in her mouth that her husband would appear before they reached the narrow stairs.

He followed her to where the servants and children slept. Her son's nurse was not there tonight, as her mother was ill, so she took him to the servant's room. It was a bare, basic room with a palliasse on the floor, a stool and a bucket—but they didn't care. In minutes, they had pulled off each other's clothes, he had lain her down, and was deep inside her. She clung to him as her body moved to meet his, but her eyes filled with tears, as she knew he was leaving. It was a bittersweet moment, and he was equally moved as he kissed her salt tears away. He knew he was falling in love with Rohese de Courcy, and he could see and feel that she felt the same.

But she was married to the King's Royal Steward. He stilled in his lovemaking for a moment.

'I will return, I promise you, Rohese,' he whispered.

She took his face in her hands. 'Let us not make promises that may prove impossible to keep. And even if you did, we would be constantly looking over our shoulders. We must use this moment to say goodbye.'

He began to move again, and she moaned in pleasure as his mouth dropped to her breasts. It was over for both of them, far too soon, and for a while, she lay in his arms, then she kissed him, stroked the dark hair from his eyes and quickly dressed. She had only just made it into her son's room and lit the small lamp when she heard her husband shout her name, and he flung open the door just as she placed the wide velvet hair band back on her head.

She put her finger to her lips to silence him. 'Do not wake him again; his nurse is away, so I had to check on him,' she said, seeing the suspicion drop from his face and relief replace it.

He stood and regarded her. He did not love his wife—she was too headstrong and proud—it was a marriage he had been persuaded into. But her family were of good, Norman, noble stock, and he was Baron of Stoke Courcy, a good catch, so he made the best of it by having several mistresses in the town. They had one son, but he was now ten years old. There had been a few miscarriages, but she had not brought another child to term. He wondered if she was barren and if that was enough reason to set her aside. However, he also knew how attractive other men found her—he saw their eyes on her, especially that damned Horse Warrior, and he feared being cuckolded.

CHAPTER TWENTY-EIGHT

She watched the emotions play across his face and knew he was small-minded enough to go to the Church and demand she be punished if he discovered them together, so she smiled at him and thanked him for showing concern for their son. She listened to him making his way back along the corridor and down the stairs and breathed again.

Moments later, Conn appeared. He pulled her close, kissed her, and left. She lay on William's bed while silent tears ran down her face as she remembered and savoured every last moment of their lovemaking. Then, a thought occurred to her: this time, they had not moved apart, which meant she could be carrying his child. She smiled and prayed it could be so.

Chapter Twenty-Nine

2nd August 1101 – Winchester

It was dusk and the sun was almost down. In the late summer evening air, Chatillon trotted along the road with Edvard at his side, away from Winchester and back to Bishop's Waltham. He had witnessed the Treaty of Alton on behalf of Pope Paschal—King Henry had been delighted to see him, having been led to believe that the Papal Envoy had a hand in persuading Robert not to fight.

If only he knew the truth, thought Chatillon as he pushed his horse into a canter, looking forward to the comfortable bed and good food which lay ahead in the Bishop's Palace. Edvard had arranged a ship back to Rouen for him on the morrow, and from there, he would ride back to his beautiful wife, Isabella and their two sons. He intended to sit and enjoy his family and friends through the autumn and winter months, busying himself only with estate business until the spring. That was when he knew King Henry would begin to take his revenge, perhaps in small steps at first, and Chatillon was sure that the likes of Robert de Belleme and William, Count of Mortain, would be the first to feel the validated King's iron glove.

Belleme, at that moment, was following Flambard quietly to his room. The reinstated Prince Bishop of Durham, flushed with his success and triumph, had imbibed far more than usual since noon, and he now swayed along the corridor. It took several attempts to locate and open the heavy door-latch to his room. Just as he turned to use both hands to steady himself and close the door at the same time, Robert de Belleme kicked it violently open.

Flambard flew backwards into the room, his head connecting with a chair. He lay groaning on the ground. Within seconds, Belleme was on him, punching, kicking and then beating him repeatedly with the heavy stick he carried when his limp was painful.

Flambard cried out for mercy, over and over, making so much noise that Belleme knew someone would come, so he sat on his chest and put a hand over his bleeding mouth and nose while lowering his sneering face close to his.

'This beating, you lying treacherous worm, is a message. Mortain, Chatillon and I intend to ensure you spend the rest of your life looking over your shoulder. I will be watching your every move in Durham, and if you ever come to Normandy and go anywhere near deluded Duke Robert, whom you cheated out of his throne, I swear, Flambard, as God is my witness, I will kill you. That is if Chatillon does not arrange it first.'

His servant found him several hours later and managed to clean him up and get him into his bed, where he lay for the next day without moving. The physician assured him nothing was broken, he was just badly bruised with minor cuts and abrasions. On Sunday morning, he made his way, with some difficulty, to the early morning service in the cathedral.

He knew King Henry would be there and stepped out from behind a pillar as the King turned to leave.

'A word, Sire, if I may? Something of great import,' he said in a low voice so that the King's entourage would not hear.

Henry stepped back in alarm. 'God's blood, man, what happened to you?' asked the King, looking at the battered and bruised swollen face.

'An accident with my horse, Sire. I fell badly into the stall, and it trampled on me,' he glibly lied.

The King drew him to one side, and Flambard took his revenge on Chatillon and Belleme as he told King Henry what he knew of the parentage of Conn Fitz Malvais. Henry's eyes widened as Flambard continued.

'This man could be a great danger to you, Sire. He is your nephew, but to others, he is the grandson of your late father, King William. Many heard the comments and discontent of many of Robert's nobles at this treaty—they believed that Robert gave in too easily when the crown was his. Any group of rebels could use Malvais as a figurehead to overthrow you or your brother, for this Horse Warrior is respected and admired. People are in awe of his skill on the battlefield as they are of his father and uncle. Only a few know who his parents are, but Robert de Belleme is one of them. Think how the wealthy and powerful Earl of Shrewsbury could use this young man. After what you have done for me, I thought it only right that you should know this,' he said in the same low whisper.

Henry's mind was in a whirl as he paced in the aisle behind the pillars of the great cathedral. He could see his entourage of the usual nobles and courtiers waiting for him and looking askance at Flambard. He took a deep breath, for he still did not

CHAPTER TWENTY-NINE

trust Flambard, and this revelation needed thinking through.

'If you repeat this information or share your suspicions with anyone else, I will have your head,' he growled.

Flambard bowed and scurried away to order his horses to ride for Durham. He had planted the seed; now, he would watch it grow and flourish.

Henry stood for a moment longer and then waved Robert Beaumont over.

'When does Malvais leave for Wales?' he asked.

'He left with De Clare and twenty of my men just after dawn this morning, Sire.'

'I believe we should keep him up there, Beaumont. We will miss Sir Hugh in that dangerous area, and Malvais can cut his teeth on the Welsh for a year or two. But keep a close eye on him.'

Beaumont left, and Henry, waving his entourage away, returned to the altar to stare at the cross and tapestries without seeing them, for he was bringing to mind the face of Malvais. He suddenly remembered first meeting him in Paris, at Chatillon's house, close by the river. He had turned to Chatillon and asked if he had met him before because he looked so familiar. He now wondered if that was because he was looking into the large blue eyes of his sister, Constance.

'Dear God, is it true?' he muttered.

Did Conn Fitz Malvais know who his parents were? He seemed to think that Luc De Malvais was his father. Had they kept it from him on purpose? He had so many questions, but he was certain of one thing: Piers De Chatillon knew, and *there* was a man who knew all of their secrets. He was not a man you could threaten, for he had no fear.

If it was true, and even that was not certain, Henry felt

a certain sadness, for he truly liked the Horse Warrior and thought of him as a friend. But a king could not always have the luxury of friends, especially not ones who could endanger him.

'Wales. I will keep him in Wales while I look into this. As many have before him, he will likely die up there fighting the wild Welsh. Even Belleme's older brother, Hugh, was killed there,' he murmured.

That brought him to his second problem—he needed to deal with Belleme, and soon.

Oblivious to the furore that had been created in the mind of the King, Conn rode north. Edvard was on one side and De Clare on the other, while his and Beaumont's men, led by the skillful Serjeant Fox, galloped behind them. They were heading to Churt, the drover's cottage, to talk to him and pick up the trail. A group of mercenaries that size in their distinctive stained black leather doublets would have been noticed, and that trail hopefully would lead them straight to Georgio.

If his friend was still alive...

The End

Author Note

I have followed the interesting and highly frustrating career of Robert Curthose with interest since I wrote 'Betrayal,' the third book in the Breton Horse Warrior series, which detailed his rebellion against his father, King William. At times, like many historians, I found it difficult to fathom his somewhat complex character. His desperate desire for recognition from his father as the eldest son, and his demand for Normandy before his father's death, dominated and drove him for several years—to such an extent that he went to war with his father and defeated him at Gerberoi, which sent shock waves through Europe.

However, a few years later, knowing his father was dying, he did not go to his deathbed, unlike his quick-thinking brother, William Rufus, who had a horse ready to take him to England to claim the throne as soon as his father breathed his last. Meanwhile, Robert Curthose sulked in France, refusing to go to Rouen, and was then outraged that William Rufus had stolen the crown.

In 1088, Robert launched an invasion to take back the crown from William Rufus, but even though his armies, led by Bishop Odo, were in England, he did not care to get on a ship to support them, and as we know from Book Two of the Papal

Assassin series, that did not end well for those who risked their lives in England supporting him. The crusades, however, transformed him into a European hero. It was well deserved, and he revelled in that acclamation as he travelled slowly back to Normandy to take his dukedom back from his brother William Rufus. It was fortunate for Robert that William was killed, as he was unlikely to have handed it back to Robert.

Then, Henry seizes his crown before he reaches Normandy, the English throne is lost again, and Robert prepares an invasion, the size of which his father would have been proud. Yet, once assembled and facing his brother's much smaller rag-tag army in England, Robert seems to roll over and give up the opportunity to take the crown. Once again, he puts his supporters' lives and lands at risk by doing so.

The famous historian and national biographer, Henry W.C. Davis, describes Robert's decision very succinctly.

'This was the most ill-considered step in the whole of Robert's long career of folly.'

After the Treaty of Alton was signed, Robert stayed in his Brother Henry's court in England until Michaelmas, hunting and enjoying himself before he returned to Normandy. The annual three thousand silver marks agreed upon by Henry at the Treaty of Alton were never paid, and Henry planned for revenge.

Sir Hugh, Earl of Chester, died very suddenly, leaving a huge power vacuum in Wales. Agnes de Ribemont did die mysteriously before her birthday. Unfortunately, she made plans for her supporters in Normandy to keep slowly poisoning the Duchess Sibylla, which did not end well for her.

Being a historian, I love the research entailed in a new book, spending weeks poring over books, journals and sources from the period to find those all-important threads. Some of you have asked for the details of some of the research books I use for each series. This would fill several pages, so I will include a few recommendations instead. If you are interested in Robert Curthose, then William M. Aird - *Robert Curthose Duke of Normandy,* is excellent, as is the lighter volume by Katherine Lack - *Conqueror's Son.* For anyone interested in Henry I, then, Warren Hollister's - *Henry I is* superb.

Thank you for reading *The Oathbreaker,* and I hope you enjoyed this book. I hope to launch book three at the end of April 2024. If you are on my newsletter list, you will get an advance warning.

If you have not signed up for the newsletter, you can do so here:- Moonstorm Books

S.J. Martin

March 2024

List of Characters

Fictional characters in *italics*

Rouen
Robert, Duke of Normandy
Sibylla of Conversano, Duchess of Normandy
William, Count of Mortain and Earl of Cornwall
Robert de Belleme, Earl of Shrewsbury
Agnes de Ribemont, Countess of Buckingham
Henry, Count of Eu
Ranulf Flambard
Piers De Chatillon, Papal Envoy
Edvard of Silesia, Chatillon's vavasseur and friend
Conn Fitz Malvais
Georgio di Milan
Darius, the squire
Gracchus, serjeant of the Horse Warriors
Andreas, Horse Warrior
John Mason, the pilot
Jean Baptiste, pedlar and spy

London & Winchester
King Henry I

Matilda of Scotland (Queen)
Robert de Beaumont, Earl of Leicester
Henry de Beaumont, Earl of Warwick
Robert Fitz Hamon, Baron of Gloucester
Anselm, Archbishop of Canterbury
Gilbert Fitz Richard (Richard de Clare,) Baron de Clare
Robert de Courcy
Rohese de Courcy
Jacob, the apothecary

Alton
Philip de Braose, Lord of Bramber and Powys
Richard de Redvers, Lord of Devon
Ansfride Anskil, Henry's mistress
Edith Forne, Henry's mistress
Serjeant Fox
Owen from Gwynedd
Black Brynn
Rhys, Owen's serjeant

Oxford
Sir Hugh d'Avranches, Earl of Chester
Nigel D'Oyley, castellan of Oxford
Adeline D'Ivry, elder sister of Rohese
Abbot Columbanus of Eynsham
Bernard, servant of De Clare and spy for Flambard

Glossary

Anchorite – A religious recluse who has withdrawn to lead a prayer-orientated life, usually in a cell attached to a church.

Bailey - A ward or courtyard in a castle, some outer baileys could be huge, encompassing grazing land.

Braies - A type of trouser often used as an undergarment to mid-calf and made of light or heavier linen. Usually covered by chausses.

Castellan – Responsible for the administration and defence of a castle.

Chausses – Attached by laces to the waist of the braies, these were tighter-fitting coverings for the legs.

Dais – A raised platform in a hall for a throne or tables, often for nobles.

Destrier – A knight's large warhorse, often trained to fight, bite and strike out.

Doublet – A close-fitting jacket or jerkin often made from leather, with or without sleeves. Laced at the front and worn either under or over, a chain mail hauberk.

Fyrd – An army raised from a lord's manor, freemen and villeins pledged to fight for their lord.

Gee-gaw – A showy trifle, a bauble, or a trinket.

Give no quarter – to give no mercy or compassion for the vanquished.

Hauberk – A tunic of chain mail, often reaching to mid-thigh.

Holy See – The jurisdiction of the Bishop of Rome – the Pope.

Holy Sepulchre – The burial chamber where Christ's body lay between burial and resurrection. A sacred, holy place in Jerusalem.

League – A league is equivalent to approx. 3 miles, in modern terms.

Liege lord – A feudal lord, such as a count or baron, entitled to allegiance and service from his knights.

Marcher Lords – Nobles entrusted to guard the border between England and Wales. King William I created three new earldoms to do so: Hereford, Shrewsbury and Chester. (March is an Anglo-Saxon term for a border.)

Pallet Bed – A bed made of straw or hay. Close to the ground, generally covered by a linen sheet and also known as a **palliasse.**

Patron – An individual who gives financial, political, or social patronage to others. Often through wealth or influence in return for loyalty and homage.

Pell – A stout wooden post for sword practice.

Porphyrogeniture – The right to rule because they are born in the purple; both parents were crowned king or queen.

Pottage – A staple of the medieval diet, a thick soup made by boiling grains and vegetables and, if available, meat or fish.

Prelate – A high-ranking member of the clergy.

Retainer – A dependent or follower often rewarded or paid for their services.

Serjeant – The soldier serjeant was a man who often came from a higher class; most experienced medieval mercenaries fell into this class; they were deemed 'half of the value of a knight' in military terms.

Topoteretes – A senior military commander.

Vavasseur – A right-hand man, more than a servant.

Vedette - An outrider or scout used by cavalry.

Vellum - Finest scraped and treated calfskin, used for writing messages.

Weald – An uncultivated upland region. Often covered in scrub forest.

Wolds- Upland areas and softer, low-rolling hills, often previously covered in forest.

Maps

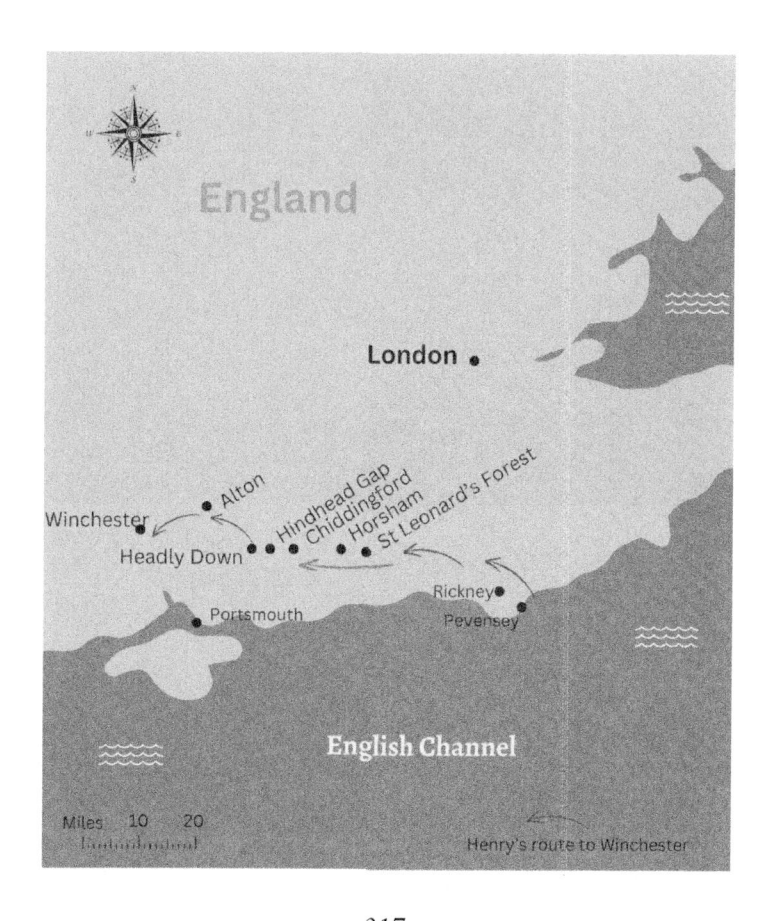

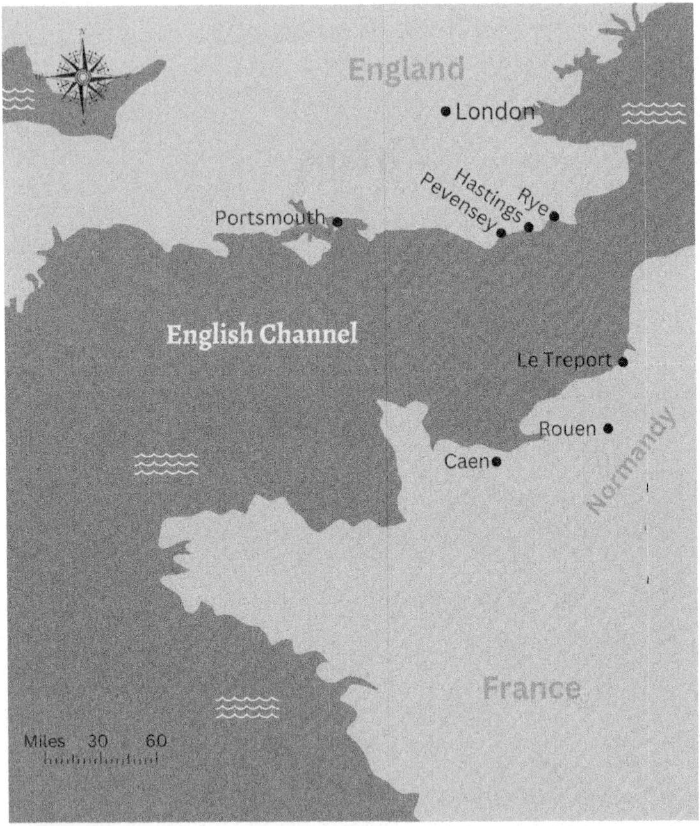
England
London
Hastings
Rye
Pevensey
Portsmouth
English Channel
Le Treport
Rouen
Caen
Normandy
France
Miles 30 60

MAPS

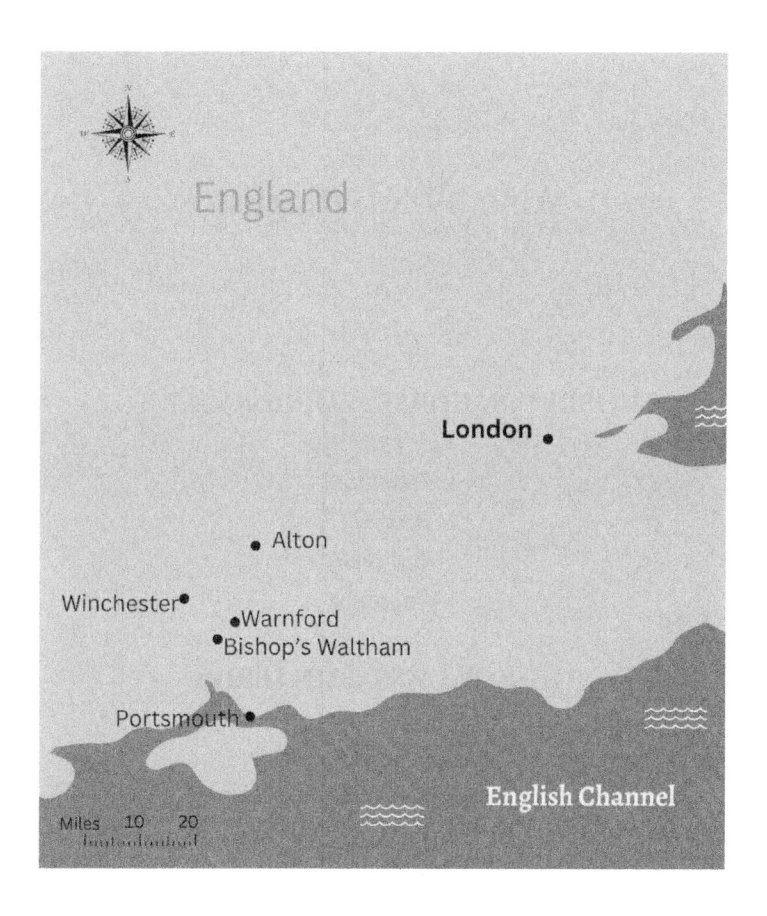

Also by S.J. Martin

THE BRETON HORSE WARRIORS SERIES
Ravensworth
Rebellion
Betrayal
Banished
Vengeance

THE PAPAL ASSASSIN SERIES
The Papal Assassin
The Papal Assassin's Wife
The Papal Assassin's Curse
The Papal Assassin's Wrath
The Papal Assassin's Nemesis

THE TATTOOED WARRIOR SERIES
Byzantium
The Oathbreaker

SHORT STORIES
The Girl, the Duke and the Ermine

About the author

From an early age, I loved and was fascinated by all aspects of history, but I find the lawlessness, intrigue, and danger of medieval times fascinating. This interest in history influenced my choices at university and my career. I spent several years with my trowel in the interesting world of archaeology before becoming a storyteller as a history teacher. I wanted to encourage young people to find that same interest in history that had enlivened my life.

I always read historical novels from an early age and wanted to write historical fiction. The opportunity came when I left education; I then gleefully re-entered the world of engaging and fascinating research into the background of some of my favourite historical periods.

There are so many stories out there still waiting to be told, and my first series of books, 'The Breton Horse Warriors' proved to be one of them. The Breton lords, such as my fictional Luc De Malvais, played a significant role in the Battle of Hastings and helped to give William the Conqueror a decisive win. They were one of the most feared and exciting troops of cavalry and swordmasters in Western Europe, fighting for William the Conqueror and then for his son, Duke Robert.

My second series of novels is based on a captivating character from the first series. My readers clamoured for the ruthless Papal Envoy, Piers De Chatillon, to have his own series, and so the Papal Assassin Series was born. It is amazing how an immoral, murdering, manipulative diplomat and assassin can seize the imagination as he cuts a swathe through Europe. Undoubtedly, he is an enthralling and mesmerising character; I will be sad to let him finally go.

I hope you enjoy reading my books as much as I have enjoyed writing them.

You can follow me on social media channels
Facebook, Instagram and X

Printed in Great Britain
by Amazon